Ecstasy Claimed

SETTA JAY

Titles by Setta Jay:

The Guardians of the Realms Series:

0.5) Hidden Ecstasy

1) Ecstasy Unbound

2) Ecstasy Claimed

3) Denying Ecstasy

4) Tempting Ecstasy

5) Piercing Ecstasy

6) Binding Ecstasy

7) Searing Ecstasy

8) Divine Ecstasy

9) Storm of Ecstasy

10) Eternal Ecstasy

Ecstasy Claimed

Setta Jay

A Guardians of the Realms Novel

Copyright:

Disclaimer:

This book is a work of fiction. Any resemblance to any person living or dead is purely coincidental. The characters are products of the author's imagination and used fictitiously.

Warning – This book is intended for an adult audience. It contains explicit sex; a dirty talking, possessive alpha male; scenes of sexual exhibition; an instance of f/f; spankings and more.

Contributors:

Editor: BookBlinders

Proofreader: Pauline Nolet

Back cover blurb: BookBlinders

Acknowledgements:

First and foremost, thank you to all the readers for your support of the series.

A big thank you to Lindy, the best friend a girl could have. Without your encouragement, support, girl days, and brutally honest editing, my writing, and this book would not be all that it could be. You help me to be a better writer and keep me sane while doing it. I would be lost without you!

Thank you to my sexy husband, for your constant love, support and willingness to sacrifice your body in the name of research. Without your dedication I might never know if certain things would line up accurately.

Thank you for the support of my new friends Lisa Sproat and Kaylee Hurt. Love you gals! You always push me in the right direction.

Thank you to my beta readers Laura R. and Rebekah N. for your love and encouragement.

Thank you to all the bloggers who were so helpful and supportive during the release of my first book, Ecstasy Unbound. You've been a great group of women that have guided me through all the craziness of being a new author. I'm listing you in alphabetical order and cringing at the thought of missing anyone. I valued each and every critique and I hope that you see your mark on this book. Thank you!

BookBlinders Reviews

Lana at Dirty Girl Romance Bookblog

Marie at Marie's Tempting Reads

SETTA JAY

Storm at Paranormal Romance Junkies

Donna and Cori at Reading in Pajamas

Mistresses L & M and Eagle at S&M's Book Obsessions

Nina, Neda & Rachel at The SubClub Books

Tracey at Tracey's Vampy and Racey's Bookblog

Edict Set Forth by the Creators Millennia Ago:

"We deem you twelve the Guardians of this world. It is now *your* duty to ensure the fragile seeds of humanity evolve free from slavery to Immortal beings. Above all else, you will watch over the slumbering Gods, for they will one day be needed on Earth..."

SETTA JAY

Chapter 1

Los Angeles, Earth Realm

Gregoire lifted the short glass of whiskey to his lips and savored the burn in the back of his throat. It had been a long-assed day, week. More like two and a half fucking decades.

Heavy music beat in the background of the dark bar and the scent of stale booze and peanuts filled the air. The nuts were piled in the metal bucket in the center of the wood table and shells littered the concrete floor. They crunched beneath his boots as he shifted back in the chair, denim pulling tight over his thighs. Shouts of laughter coming from the mostly tattooed bikers drew his attention for a minute before he tuned out the humans.

"Are you good, man?" Conn asked as he leaned back, watching him with intent amber eyes. The wolf wore a black tee under his green and black flannel, his tattoos showing beneath the rolled sleeves. Brown shaggy hair looked as wild as his beast half, and three small black rings lifted as the male cocked his pierced brow.

Gregoire nodded as he absently rotated his tumbler glass on the table. "Yeah."

"It only took Uri's ass getting mated for you to hang with the rest of us." Conn smirked as he said the words. The wolf was right; he and Uri used to frequent a far different kind of bar. One that catered to fucking and sharing women. That had been his norm until his friend found Alexandra.

It was obvious the wolf was wondering how he was dealing with the change.

He pointed out, "You could have come out with us any fucking time," before taking another drink, his dark tee shirt stretching tight over his shoulders.

Conn smirked, "Yeah, I could've." What the wolf wasn't saying was that he was picky as hell. A lot of that had to do with his beast half. Perfumes and shit turned the Lykos off more than anything, which meant he'd take any female he chose somewhere private instead of fucking her in a crowded club or bar.

The amber-eyed male winked playfully at the waitress as she dropped off another dark ale in front of him, making sure she leaned over far enough to give his brother Guardian a good look at the big tits barely contained in the leather vest she wore.

After she left, Conn murmured, "I still can't believe Uri's mated. It's been a fucking week, but it still blows my mind. I never thought one of us would find a mate, much less a Guardian mating a powerful Demi-Goddess." When a normal Immortal found their rare-as-hell mate, the two became more powerful, sharing abilities. Conn was bringing up what all of his brethren were likely thinking. Guardians were already the strongest of all the Immortal races. They were nearly as powerful as the Gods themselves without the enhanced power of mating the child of a Goddess and warrior-class Immortal, which was exactly what Alex was.

He only grunted in Conn's direction, because his brother had no idea that Uri wasn't the first of them to find a mate.

Gregoire was.

Twenty-five long-assed years ago and he was finally days from claiming her. It was a fact that not even Drake, their dragon leader, knew. Gregoire's warhorse half twitched at the thought of anyone learning about Alyssa's existence. Keeping her secret was an ingrained protective instinct he'd never once questioned.

He might have known of her since her birth, but it had always been complicated as hell.

He still remembered the day he'd gone to his friend Adras' home to congratulate the male on his new young. The electric charge that had surged straight to his heart as he'd been infused with the jarring knowledge that the tiny infant would be his, was his. The connection so electric, so strong, the small babe nearly brought all seven feet of him to his knees. When she'd looked up at him with innocent pale green eyes, his entire existence had shifted.

All that mattered from that moment on was Alyssa's safety and security. He'd gotten reports about her over the years, but five fucking years ago she'd reached twenty years, an Immortal's majority or full maturity, and he'd watched her from a distance ever since. She'd still been too damned young for a male born fully formed by the Creators millennia ago. At twenty-five he hoped to hell he'd given her enough time, because he couldn't wait much longer.

Not after seeing and feeling the bond between Uri and Alex as he'd watched over their ceremonies. Witnessing their connection had unhinged something inside Gregoire. Immortals were sexual beings, needing release like they needed to feed from the world's energies, and Guardians weren't exempt from that twist of fate. If anything, they required more of the energies created from a *mutual* fucking release. Jacking off was practically useless though it had never stopped him from trying.

He'd suffered having other females wrapped around his cock for two and a half decades just to stay strong, but now the thought of his dick touching any other female made his skin fucking crawl.

It was something that had become painfully clear during Uri and Alex's bonding. Matings between Immortals were different from a human marriage. During the consummation, some males allowed others to help them bring their female's fantasies to life. For that one night it was all about giving their female every pleasure she could dream of. It was an honor Uri had even invited him to join them in something so sacred... but, thank fuck, Alex had called off his participation before he'd had to do it himself. His mind and body had already started rebelling at the thought of anyone else's touch.

A sign that his nightmare was almost over.

It had been over a week since he'd last dealt with his needs and he felt the lack of energy dragging him down. Which meant his innocent Alyssa had only a few more days before he came for her. That was all the time he could allow her before it would start affecting his duties.

There was no denying that once he claimed her, her entire life would be forever changed. Not only was he a Guardian, he was dominant and possessive as hell where his tiny female was concerned. He would be demanding of her and couldn't fucking wait to have her under him where she belonged.

He noticed Dorian and Bastian in the crowd, making their way to the back of the bar where he and Conn sat. Dorian's blond hair with blue spiked tips and the bright orange tee shirt were like a damned spotlight in a sea of dark colors and leather. That mixed with the fact that both the Nereid and Bastian were a few inches under seven feet tall made their heads visible above those in the crowd.

He watched as half-dressed females prowled closer, like tiny moths. Dorian grinned down, but the smile was only half friendly despite his beaconlike appearance.

A couple of women waylaid Bastian, the Kairos' race was that of calm teleporters, but his dark brother was still a warrior like the rest of them. His tanned features were relaxed as he disentangled questing hands from his black-clad body, a match to his goatee and long, tied-back hair. He leaned in and whispered something into a brunette's ear and Gregoire could see her tanned skin flush as she grinned and nodded up at him.

A guess said that his brother Guardian had ensured his entertainment for later. She twirled a long lock of hair as her hungry eyes ate up the view of Bastian's back as the male trailed behind Dorian to where Gregoire and Conn sat.

Nearly the second they slid into the other chairs, the waitress sauntered up with a seductive smile. "What can I get ya?"

Gregoire took another drink as his brothers ordered. Dorian rolled his neck as the female was leaving. "I need a drink and then a fuck."

Conn asked, "I'm guessing this means you came up empty on Cyril's location?"

"We haven't found dick in the rubble of the bastard's hiding place," Dorian growled. Cyril was enemy number one in the Immortal Realm. The son of Apollo, he was just as twisted and liked to experiment on people like his fucking father had.

That particular God had caused mass suffering to nearly all the Immortals in the fucking world. Gregoire included. He had vivid memories of being enslaved by the God and forced to breed like a damned animal. Apollo and Hermes had been determined to create a perfect army of Immortals, infusing them all with beast blood to

15

make them stronger or more powerful. Some shifted like he, Conn and Dorian, while others like Bastian only gained a beast's instincts.

After a minute of tuning out the specifics in Dorian and Bastian's fruitless search, the waitress came and set down his brothers' drinks. The clank of glasses barely registered in his mind.

When the Creators had freed all Immortals from Apollo and Hermes' slavery, it was only to confine them in Tetartos Realm. Only Guardians could teleport out of the place, but the space was massive and Cyril had a knack for hiding. The damned Realm was a general geographic match to Earth, yet only hosted a tiny fraction of the population. The land was raw and wild in comparison. Not overrun with skyscrapers and freeways. That made it a pain in the ass for him and his brethren to find the bastard. Immortals didn't need food and could easily live in a cavern with spells hiding their location. They'd been damned close to catching the asshole a couple of weeks ago, yet he'd slipped through their fingers.

Cyril's near downfall had come from the fact that he'd found a way to acquire Mageia, magic-wielding mortals, to experiment on. The bastard had apparently been attempting to circumvent the fucking fact that Immortal matings were destined, hoping to find a way to force that bond with a female of his choosing in order to gain her power. The Guardians wouldn't have even known what he'd been up to if not for Uri's mate, Alex, and her brothers, Vane and Erik.

As the daughter of Athena, Alex held a unique power that had been sending her into the bodies of Cyril's victims. Only his last victim had turned out to be her brother Erik's fated mate, Sam. Because of that, Erik had been able to track Sam in a way that defied reason.

"Any news about Erik?" Bastian asked Conn. The tension at the table kicked up a notch at the topic. They'd rescued Sam, but Sirena, their healer, had been forced to put Erik into a deep spelled sleep to give Sam time to adjust to everything that had happened to her. If they hadn't, Erik would be going slowly insane with the need to physically claim his female.

Conn shook his head. "No. Sirena's keeping him knocked out as long as she can." Since Sam was a mortal, the effects would be slower to hit her, at least that was what Sirena hoped. They didn't have a damned precedent for this shit. They were lucky to see a few matings in an entire century, and none had happened like this. Not that he'd ever known.

Gregoire couldn't even imagine what Erik was going to go through when he woke. He'd be in a frenzy of lust, yet his female had just been through fucking hell at the hands of Cyril. Uri might have used his power over the mind to dull Sam's trauma for her, but he doubted it would be easy for either of them being faced with the mating's ruthless physical demands and all that had happened to her all at once.

"Well, fuck." Dorian said it all in those two words.

"Were you able to find anything out on a location for Cynthia?" How could the damned Earth-based Mageia have been so fucked up to abduct females and send them to Cyril in the Immortal Realm. They still had no idea how or why the female would do that shit. Why sell out her own kind? Yet when the Guardians had come for her, she'd had a fucking arsenal and was far more prepared than any Mageia should be in how to escape them.

Gregoire noticed females on the edge of the dance floor sending seductive looks to their darkened corner. He had a feeling his "stay the fuck back" vibe was the only thing keeping them from approaching at the moment. That meant he was effectively cock-blocking his brothers without intending to.

17

He barely heard Conn's ground-out answer about Cynthia. "I'll find her. Unfortunately she's smart and has money, so hiding on Earth is easier for her than most. So far she hasn't used credit cards. Vane and I went through the files from her place and found dick on locations she could be hiding. Other than that, I have feelers out in the Mageia covens and alerts set on all her known shit. We'll find her." Now that Alex was part of the Guardian fold, her brother Vane was also making himself useful with all the tech crap Conn usually handled.

A crash sounded as a drunk human knocked into a waitress's tray.

The sound of shattering was enough distraction that his thoughts moved away from work and centered back on his tiny mate.

He and the others sat for long moments before he saw Bastian nod to the brunette he'd talked to when he'd walked in. She and a few friends had been dancing seductively at the edge of the dance floor, apparently waiting for that signal. The female and her friends stopped mid-dance and eagerly set a course toward the table.

That was Gregoire's cue to leave.

"Hey," the brunette practically purred to Bastian before climbing into his lap, her short skirt riding up. She was giggling as she trailed her hands over his brother Guardian's chest as if transfixed by the size of him. Two of her friends moved to Conn and Dorian as Gregoire stood.

He shook his head at a dark-haired female who'd been smiling and moving in his direction. Her lips fell a little at his rejection, but Dorian easily pulled her in with the redhead he was already talking to.

"You leaving, G?" Conn asked with a frown.

18

He nodded. "Yeah. I've got other plans."

You sure you're good, man? the wolf asked through the telepathic link all Guardians shared. Gregoire could already smell the arousal building around him and wasn't interested in the least.

Gregoire's Immortal hearing picked up sultry propositions whispered by one of the females to Dorian, "Do you think you can handle both of us, handsome? If you're really good, maybe we'll take turns licking the beast of a cock I feel against my ass."

He saw the Nereid slide his hand under her short skirt before speaking. "Is that what you want? To suck my dick?" His hand kept moving under her skirt until she moaned. "Where else do you want my cock?" Gregoire could smell arousal all around him now, because Dorian's other hand was already riding up the other female's skirt as they crowded his brother's lap.

He turned his attention back to the wolf. *Yeah, I'm good.*

Mouths and hands were already roaming as he fished some cash from his pocket and set it with his glass before heading to the door.

Gregoire needed to get out of there. Things were getting more intense as pussies slicked and got wetter by the second. Little moans lifted around him, his brothers focused on fucking.

His cock didn't even twitch.

Chapter 2

Outside The City Of Lofodes, Tetartos Realm

Alyssa darted through the soft grass of the meadow as quickly as her legs could move. She wanted to rage at someone. Tears threatened, but she beat them back as she made her way through the lush green expanse up the rise. It felt like even the birds were mocking her, because their happy songs did nothing to improve her mood.

She passed moss-covered trees. The scents usually relaxed her, but nothing so simple could take away the pain and betrayal.

Or the harsh bite of rejection.

How could her parents have kept her in the dark about something as important as the fact that she had a damned *mate*? Why force the issue of her going through Emfanisi after Emfanisi, being displayed like a prized ox ready for breeding every year since she'd hit her majority? The whole point of the event was to find a *mate*.

The only enjoyable part of those yearly, week-long celebrations was that she got to wear the beautiful dresses she made as part of her business. The rest of it was nerve-racking and uncomfortable. She was introduced to male after male.

She understood birthrates were notoriously low in their world. Immortal children like her were few and far between. That left the mortal Mageias who'd made the one-way trip from Earth to Tetartos Realm as the only other beings compatible as a potential Immortal mate. Even with those numbers, only a few Immortals would likely find a destined match in this damned century alone.

It was all anyone dreamed about in this whole place. Her own mother had been a Mageia who'd long ago chosen to come to this Realm to live, knowing that the Creators had cast a confinement spell over Tetartos, meaning she'd never be able to return to Earth.

In fact, her mother was the last Mageia Alyssa had heard of mating an Immortal, and that had been many decades ago.

Mageia were a large part of their Realm now. Over the centuries the cities of Tetartos had grown with generations of mortals born and protected here. One being Alyssa's childhood friend Rain.

She planned to talk to her friend, but not until she calmed down. Rain was everything Alyssa was not, adventurous and bold to Alyssa's staid and quiet.

Maybe all of that needed to change. Maybe it was time Alyssa stopped being so damned agreeable.

Alyssa dug her fingers in her long brown hair, wishing for a tie. How could she have a mate that she'd never met? How were her parents so sure the Guardian was hers? Had her blood been tested against his at some point?

It didn't matter. According to what she'd just overheard, he'd known about her for the last five years and hadn't come for her. That knowledge hurt and didn't make sense. Why had her parents made her suffer through the yearly events if she hadn't needed to find a mate? Why hadn't they told her anything about this? It was her life.

Had they been hoping to spare her feelings? That made the

most sense, but didn't ease the betrayal.

The infamous Gregoire had to have some reason for not coming to her for the five years since she'd hit her majority. She rubbed at the ache in the pit of her stomach as her ever-present insecurities swamped her. Males of her own race had never shown any interest in her, with or without her father's protectiveness coming into the mix. She didn't care about their interest, but she hated that they'd always seen and treated her as weak. It had been in their eyes her entire life. Did the Guardian think she was too weak to be his mate?

Screw all of it. If he didn't want her, fine. She'd never met him, but she'd seen pictures... everyone had.

She blew out a breath and ran her fingers through her hair. If she was honest with herself, she'd admit that he was the most gorgeous male she'd ever seen, which was why she'd had plenty of fantasies featuring him in her bed that seemed humiliating now. She pathetically knew all his features by heart, from the hint of red tinting his brown hair to every dip of muscle hinted at beneath his fighting leathers. His short beard was even lickable looking.

Damn him. Damn it all.

It was beyond time she found out who *she* truly was instead of living by other people's expectations. This was her own fault for never demanding more independence. Yes, her parents were overprotective, but she had never done anything to dissuade their tendencies, especially her father's.

Her mind wouldn't stop conjuring images of what might have been if the Guardian had actually wanted her. Would he have held her to his big body and whispered seductive words in her ear? Maybe he would have lifted her up and carried her away to do dirty things to her because he just couldn't wait to touch her. She forced those thoughts away, shaking her head.

The problem was that she'd grown up being told that mated males coveted and cherished the rare gift of finding their other half. A soul bond was supposed to be unimaginably beautiful.

Her mother hadn't helped by sharing all the human tales of princes and happily ever afters. The damned stories had fostered ridiculous notions. Add those to the soul-bond stories and she'd been convinced that someday a male would come along, take one look at her, and fall deeply in love. Of course there would be the wild instant lust that came with the mating frenzy, but it would all lead to an unimaginable bond that connected them for all eternity.

Apparently that didn't interest her destined mate. He, no doubt, enjoyed himself with whomever he wanted anywhere he went; females of Tetartos or Earth no doubt flocked to him. With all the freedom afforded a Guardian, maybe he didn't want or need a mate.

It wasn't as if she could confront him. The second they came into contact, there'd be no going back; fate would take all semblance of choice from them. That was how matings worked. She could write him a letter, but what would she even say? All her options where he was concerned felt needy and pathetic.

Suddenly, she found herself regretting not having made an effort to live a little more. She could have accepted some of the more lascivious offers of experienced Immortals she'd met at the Emfanisis. Her father's presence curbed most advances, but she could have found a way to experience some dirty trysts if she'd cared to make an effort.

Rain had partaken in some of the more wicked propositions and had shared every erotic detail with her. Why hadn't she done anything like that? She had zero experience with the opposite sex.

How would it feel to have warm hands and lips on her skin? There'd never been a male who'd interested her much, but why hadn't she at least played?

A beautiful green expanse surrounded her as she crossed over the border and out of the territory surrounding Lofodes. Her mother and father were the mated pair charged with the safety of the population inside the borders. Stepping mere feet out of her parents' domain had always felt freeing. She was finally getting her breathing under control as she slowed to walk over the top rise.

It was a sunny day, and the peaceful meadow shone with morning dew as she breathed deeply of the crisp air. According to Rain, this particular section of the Realm would be considered a wilder version of Earth's Scotland. Rain collected anything she could find about the Realm of humanity to sell at her shop and to appease her own obsession with all things related to Earth.

It'd been her friend's collecting that had resulted in Alyssa's infatuation with clothing. Fashion magazines from the other Realm had started Alyssa's fascination. Her mother and father had happily acquired fabrics and sewing equipment for her, feeding her excitement for creating. She wondered if they'd been only too happy just to keep her at home because they'd been incredibly supportive of her business.

It didn't matter. Her designs and work had provided a sense of worth that she had so greatly needed through the years.

She rolled the tension from her shoulders as she gazed at her destination. The sparkling lake was just outside the border and far from the city. Its restfulness called to her often. She needed to think and plan her next course of action. At least some luck was on her side; she didn't see any of her father's warriors. She was in no mood to deal with them.

As she walked to the bank, she called to the air currents and allowed them to lift her body into a tree, where she settled astride its sturdy limb. She didn't care how scratchy it was or that her green cargo shorts and white tank top were getting dirty.

She was busy trying to stave off the myriad of emotions beating at her, but they settled inside her bones without permission. Leaning her head against the rough bark, she looked out over the smooth, dark water. The lake usually soothed her when she felt like she was suffocating from her family's protectiveness.

As a child she'd learned how to block the telepathic link to her mother and father so they couldn't constantly track her location. She supposed she'd needed a sense of freedom even then. All Immortal families shared those mental connections and it was an effective way to communicate at a distance. Even though she'd set those privacy barriers, her parents could still reach her as if knocking on a door.

The morning light filtered through billowing clouds, and the air was cool on her skin. One of the benefits of being Hippeus was that her temperature was higher. Rain wouldn't have been caught dead in shorts right now. It would be too chilly for her mortal friend.

She heard birds flutter from the trees further down the shore. A lake serpent lurched out of the water, catching a bird that had flown too low and taking it below the frigid depths. The rippling waters mesmerized her, the smooth and glassy expanse replaced with rolling waves. It perfectly matched her mood.

For a long while she just sat and welcomed the peacefulness of the place around her.

She was so lost in thought that the crackling branches and leaves below was the first signal that she wasn't alone. Her entire body stiffened.

Looking down, she saw not just one, but three Akanthodis. Her mother and father were warriors and had trained her well through the years, so dispatching the evil creatures wouldn't be difficult. The infuriating beasts and those like them were cast into Tetartos by powerful and demented beings imprisoned in Hell Realm. Immortal warriors patrolled the area and dispatched them before they ever made it to the cities. Their poison could kill any mortal Mageia who lived there.

As far as hell beasts went, these were the weakest of the bunch. She watched to see if there were more, but detected only the three. They stank of tainted blood, which she would have noticed sooner if they hadn't been downwind. Double sets of crimson eyes looked around the bank as they sniffed snubbed noses along the ground. Sharp, poisonous spindles fanned from their backs. They were close to her height of five foot three.

Suddenly wild red eyes lifted to her, and the beast let out a piercing screech, no doubt to alert the others. She called to the earth, an ability gifted from her father's side. Roots lifted and lashed out, wrapping around the beasts' legs. They shrieked and fought, breaking some limbs before spewing fire in her direction. She darted to another limb while snuffing the flames with a thought. She took the air from the flames as well as the beasts' lungs, pulling hard, a gift from her mother. It was taxing on her energy stores to use those particular abilities, but they were her best alternative at the moment.

The animals gasped and writhed, unable to get air for long minutes before finally collapsing in ground-shaking heaps. She kept using the power, hopping back to the original limb, watching to be sure they were dead.

Her breathing was ragged by the end and she kept taking in more oxygen, waiting for it to even out. If they weren't so evil, she would have felt bad for killing the creatures.

When her heartbeat finally relaxed, she turned to face the trunk of the tree. Closing her eyes, she touched a palm to the rough bark, releasing power to soothe and repair the damage she'd wrought. When she opened her eyes again, she saw it. A massive fur-covered spider crawling not an inch from her hand. Shrieking nearly as loud as the downed hell beasts, she lost her position and flailed toward the ground. She called to the winds in order to catch her just before landing hard on the poisonous spines of a dead Akanthodis. She lay on the cushion of air, using the currents only to push her away from the beast as she gulped lungfuls of air. Her heart was racing, not from the spider, though she loathed them, but from nearly being impaled on the venomous spines known for their paralyzing effects on Immortals.

"Alyssa! What are you doing outside the border?"

Damn, it just kept getting better. She knew that deep hearty bellow. She closed her eyes a second and listened to hooves clopping in her direction. Looking up, she saw she was, indeed, correct. The rich, chocolate-colored flank of her father's half-warhorse form suddenly stood beside her. All Hippeus chose partial horse form while patrolling and her father was no different. It was convenient for added height while allowing for the use of a sword. His was sheathed at his back at the moment. The long waves of his brown hair fell over his shoulders as he gazed down at her with worried hazel eyes.

Seeing the concern in his eyes made her stomach clench. She shook her head, irritated that she still felt bad for worrying him. He and her mother had been keeping a huge secret from her.

She clenched her teeth and stood, feeling anger and frustration rising up inside her. She needed to get out of there before she said something she'd regret.

"Sweeting, are you all right?"

At his soft tone, she pasted what she hoped looked like a smile to her lips. It felt brittle, but she didn't want to discuss anything with him until she had some time to figure out exactly what she was going to do.

"I'm fine, Father. Just lost my footing in the tree. I went for a run and ended up here," she said as she brushed off the back of her shorts. No way was she mentioning the spider. She noticed, to her complete mortification, that it wasn't only her father that had come running, likely drawn to the screeches of the now dead hell beasts.

Standing behind him were his two favorite warriors, Curran and Duncan. She had been distracted and hadn't even heard their approach, and she'd truly been trained better than that. She felt her face heat in embarrassment as she swiftly used power to stand up. Curran's eyes scanned the area for additional threats. His shoulder-length light hair was back in a band. He turned and gave her a look of amusement. Laughing at her, not with her.

Duncan, her father's second in command, nudged the downed hell beasts with a hoof. "Dead. We should take their heads and burn them." He didn't even give her a glance as he said the words. He had dark hair and brilliant green eyes. The behemoth was sought after by all the females in the surrounding areas, and he hadn't spared a single glance in her direction.

The asses could have at least given her credit on having minor skills in killing hell beasts.

"I'm going into the city to see Rain. Bye, Father," she said, lifting one hand in a wave, not bothering to look behind her.

She needed to get the hell away from there before she snapped.

She rushed through the trees and meadows toward the iridescent blue of the spelled dome protecting the city, her heightened emotion giving her legs flight.

Once she arrived through the gate to the cobbled streets, she felt her tight muscles relax a bit. They eased even more the second she stepped in front of Rain's small shop of bright white.

The bell jingled overhead as she entered and she spotted her friend unboxing some books and setting them on the shelves for sale. She was wearing a lavender sweater and dark jeans. It was a good look with her shoulder-length blond hair with purple dyed at the ends.

Her beautiful face lit up when she saw Alyssa, aqua eyes shining. "Hey, what's up? I didn't expect to see you until tomorrow night. Tell me we're moving girls' night to tonight. It's been the restocking week from hell, and cocktails and a movie sound amazing." She groaned playfully and paused, narrowing her eyes. "What's wrong?"

Alyssa blurted out everything that had happened as Rain dusted off her hands on her jeans before moving to sit behind the counter with her. She even included the spider in the narration of her horrible morning. To Rain's credit she didn't laugh, just coughed out a chuckle.

Thankfully, it was still early for customers, having a breakdown in front of witnesses would have been humiliating. She rubbed the bridge of her nose. "I need to get out of here for a while. I should have moved out of my parents' house well before now, but the sad look on my father's face always ended the conversation. If I go there now to talk to them, I'll just end up saying things I'll regret."

She blew out a frustrated breath. "I'm completely aware that I did this to myself, but it ends now." She rolled her shoulders. "I don't have any pieces that are urgent." She had set aside the next few weeks for creating new designs. She couldn't have asked for a more perfect time to get away. Work could wait, or she could draft some sketches wherever they went. She had plenty of coin set aside from her years of running her small business. It would be easy enough to set herself up in a place of her own and indulge in a nice trip. She'd never done anything like that, and it was well past time to start living.

"Is there any way you can get someone to watch the shop and go with me? Take a vacation?"

Rain's eyes lit with understanding and excitement. She started rummaging around in drawers. "You've needed to move out on your own for a while now." Drawers opened and closed. "I'm sorry about your folks. I'd be angry as hell too, and the Guardian is a fucking idiot. He has to be some big ass on a power trip if he hasn't claimed you as a mate." She paused in her search. "Just let me think for a second. How long do you want to be gone?"

Alyssa had already been thinking about that. "Can you get out of here for a couple of weeks?"

Rain bit the top of her pen, contemplating, then started writing on the stationery she'd pulled out of a drawer. "Where do you want to go?" They sat talking and planning for a while. Her friend sputtered out a million different options, but one struck her as so completely perfect that she couldn't resist.

"If you'll take this note to Mrs. Lewis, I'll get instructions ready for her. She doesn't usually have much to do now that her kids are grown, and she really likes it here. I'm sure she'd be excited to keep the store open for me, and she usually spends everything I pay her in the store. It's a win-win for me." Rain grinned. "If she can't do it, I'll figure something out. I should be able to get everything in order so

30

we can get out of here fairly quickly." Rain began running around the shop as she spoke.

Rain rambled off more plans and Alyssa felt her tension and pain subside a little with each and every word.

A second later she ran over and spoke to Mrs. Lewis, who conveniently lived less than a block away. Rain had been correct, the older Mageia was thrilled to watch the shop. The female was in her sixties, with rosy cheeks and a smile that said she knew everything and found it all quite amusing. Alyssa had found herself grinning from Mrs. Lewis' exuberance by the time she made it back to the shop.

"She said to give her an hour and she'll be here to take over." It was all happening fast and Alyssa couldn't be more grateful for that.

"I can be ready after I get her settled and get packed," Rain assured her. Her friend's living quarters were in the back of the shop, so packing would be easy.

That would give Alyssa time to run home and pack a bag. She did a quick telepathic check and found her mother and father were currently together at the border. Good, she didn't want to talk to them at the moment.

Chapter 3

Guardian Manor, Tetartos Realm

Gregoire and Uri reformed with his brother's hellhound, Havoc, onto the balcony of the manor after patrolling Earth Realm.

It was up to the Guardians to watch over all four Realms of the world, each with their own issues. Heaven, Hell and Tetartos, known as the Realm of Immortals and Beasts, were one thing, but Earth was the damned human Realm and the mortals had no idea Immortals existed.

He and Uri didn't make a move into the media room of the massive manor-style compound; both seemed more content to breathe in some fresh fucking night air. It smelled a hell of a lot better than the human refuse from the dank alley they'd just left in New York.

The hound wiggled his massive black body between them, all wired up after hunting demon souls with them. He looked vaguely like a Doberman, only two or three times the size and his coat was a slick-looking black. The bright red eyes were another dead giveaway he wasn't a damned dog. Uri, an Aletheia, those Immortals who spawned vampire myth, had the ability to ensure no mortal remembered seeing a hellhound.

Uri shook his dark head, his sensitive silver eyes swirling with amusement as he opened the French doors for his pup. "As if we

32

didn't have enough to deal with searching for Cyril and Cynthia, the Tria won't fucking let up on sending shit out of Hell Realm. Over half a dozen demon-possessed in that last fucking alley alone?" Ares and Artemis' twisted offspring, the Tria, had been imprisoned in the bowels of Hell Realm millennia ago. The pure evil triplets might not be able to get free, but they'd long ago learned to send shit out to make the Guardians' jobs fucking harder. At least they couldn't send anything solid into Earth, only demon souls.

No one could figure out why the Creators had left the assholes in their hole instead of sending them to sleep like they'd done with all the other Gods.

Havoc bounded through the open doors, leaving him and Uri alone. They absently watched the couple-hundred-pound beast launch onto one of the big couches.

"Havoc does make this shit easier," he admitted, looking at the happy animal staring at them. The pup was like a damned magnet for demon-possessed and was able to feed off their evil energies, leaving the human demon free. That darkness was food for the pup just as the world's energies were fuel for Immortals.

"Yeah, he does," his brother agreed. The pup was actually the first advantage they'd ever had over the possessed problem. After all the hell the Gods put humanity through, the Creators demanded the mortals be allowed to evolve free of more powerful beings. That went for him and his brethren as well, even though they were the twelve chosen warriors bound to watch over the Realms.

As a safeguard for the damned mortals, the Great Beings cursed the Guardians with ten times the pain they inflicted on a human.

It wasn't until the Tria started sending out demon souls to possess evil mortals that it became a problem. The tainted souls destroyed their host eventually, but not before the fiends caused all kinds of trouble with their added power and strength.

Uri ran his hand under the back of his dark hair. "You good, G? I need to head to Alex. She's over checking on her brother and Sam; she's worried."

"I'm good." He planned to seek Drake that evening and tell their leader that he'd found his female. "Is Erik awake now?" Last he'd heard, Uri's new brother-in-law was still in a spelled sleep.

"Sirena thinks he'll wake up soon. Sam refused to allow Sirena to extend his sleep again. She said she can handle it."

"She understands he'll be working completely on instinct when he sees her?" Gregoire asked. Erik was the Demi-God son of Athena and his father was an Ailouros, half lion. Neither animal nor male would ever fucking harm their mate, but they'd never dealt with this kind of situation either. His instincts would be to protect, but the mating frenzy would drive him to fuck and claim her.

"Yeah, and she still refused to leave his side. Sam knows he saved her life, and watching over him seems to be helping her heal. She's fucking strong and determined."

The pup bounded back to Uri's side, this time bumping his brother's hand until Uri subconsciously scratched behind Havoc's ears.

He nodded thoughtfully. "Good luck."

Uri grunted before they both stepped inside. Before entering the hall, his brother stilled for a split second.

When the male turned his head in Gregoire's direction, he saw his brother's silver eyes swirling and knew Uri had been telepathically communicating with someone. Aletheia were the only race with extensive telepathic range, and the manor was far from any city in the Immortal Realm and they didn't have phones in Tetartos.

"The Lofodes Aletheia said that Adras needs to see you right away, G. He wouldn't say why. What's that all about?" Gregoire noted his brother's confused look, but his heart had started pounding a heavy beat as he turned back to the balcony.

"It's nothing. I have to go." Gregoire didn't like the worry that pitted in his gut as he teleported away. His little mate's father would never contact him unless there was a problem.

Minutes later he was standing in Adras' home. The home he hadn't been in for over twenty-five years. He looked up the stairs toward the bedroom where he'd first seen Alyssa as a tiny babe. It had been cozy and warm with a fire burning in the hearth. As one of Adras' closest friends, he'd been ushered up to offer his congratulations and view the child. Gregoire's shocked expression had obviously divulged his knowledge of what Alyssa was to him because within seconds of his stunning discovery he'd found himself outside.

Adras had been completely enraged at the idea of Gregoire as his tiny infant's mate. Gregoire had never been an angel and Adras knew that he and Uri shared females. Not that he'd ever fucking share his damned mate, but Adras hadn't been seeing clearly.

He'd allowed his old friend to hit him over and over, knowing he would have likely felt the same in his old friend's position. Hippeus were known to be some of the most possessive of the Immortal races and the male had only just welcomed his first child.

He shook off the memory. Her scent was in the room, and it was affecting him on a base level that made him grit his damned teeth.

His body was reacting, and he forced himself to somehow dial it back. It smelled so fucking good and sweet, the scent of a mature and perfect female. He mentally pulled it together, trying to focus on his mate's mother.

"What did you say?" Gregoire's voice sounded dangerously low in the comfortable living room. He couldn't have heard her correctly. He looked over at Alyssa's father, and Adras narrowed his eyes in warning. Ava had been pacing in front of them, her movements jerky and agitated.

"She's gone. Adras spoke to her while on his morning patrol, and he said she was acting odd. By the time we both got home, she was gone."

Gregoire looked at his friend. The male stood, muscles tight, jaw twitching as he watched Ava pace. It had not been an easy couple of decades, knowing that he would mate his friend's daughter. Both had been uncomfortable, especially when she was a child; it hadn't mattered that his feelings weren't fucking sexual back then.

"You can't track her through the familial link?"

Adras' muscles pulled tight as he glared at Gregoire. "If I could do that, I would not need you."

Gregoire gritted out, "What happened?" He tugged at his short hair. Why would she leave and not tell her parents where she'd gone? She'd left for a damned reason and he glared at her father, demanding to know what the hell had upset her.

"She left this note. She must have heard us talking." Ava's beautiful green eyes welled up as she handed him the paper. After Gregoire relieved her of it, Adras caught his mate into his chest and kissed her forehead as he gently rubbed her back, quietly comforting her.

36

His mind already on the paper, Gregoire attempted to gain an understanding as to what the fuck was going on. His brow furrowed as he looked down at the words in front of him.

Dear Mother and Father,

I am going on vacation with Rain. I need to get away, see some of the world, and sort out my life. I know I have a mate who isn't inclined to claim me. That makes my first decision really simple. I will not be attending any more Emfanisis.

Don't expect me for a couple of weeks. I'll let you know what I've decided to do when I return. I love you both.

Alyssa

Son of a bitch. "You were discussing her being my mate?" he thundered.

"Yes," Adras bit back. "Not that I've been looking forward to your claiming her, but the next Emfanisi is mere months away, and she hates going. Damn, I hate going and fending off all the damned Aletheia that keep sniffing around her."

Gregoire gritted his teeth at the possessiveness that comment invoked.

Adras took a pained breath. "I went to see Rain's mother and father, and they are just as worried. Rain is a bit wild, but she has been Alyssa's one friend since they were young."

Gregoire unfolded the next note that was handed to him.

Mom and Dad,

I'm going on VACATION, bitches! Alyssa and I will be gone for two weeks. We'll be safe. Mrs. Lewis is watching my shop. Everything should be fine, but she knows to go to you if she needs anything.

Love ya,

Rain

"This is my mate's friend?" Gregoire gritted his teeth as he held out the letter. Irritation and worry churned inside his gut while he considered the potential amount of trouble two females, by themselves, could get into. Beasts and feral Immortals concerned him, but Cyril was also part of his worry now that the bastard had finally surfaced again after centuries of silence. Added to that was the fact that his mate seemed to have befriended someone from *Mageias Gone Wild*. He growled, knowing he needed to find them quickly.

"How did they leave?"

His mind was buzzing as he listened to Adras answer, "I checked all the patrols, and no one saw them. I'm sure they paid a Kairos to teleport them somewhere." Adras snarled the rest, "When I went to the Kairos office, it said that they were gone for the rest of the day, and I couldn't find them through any of the locals."

Adras nearly shook with frustration. There was nothing worse for a warrior than feeling out of control, and as powerful as the male was, he couldn't teleport. Only Gods, Guardians and Kairos could travel that way.

"One office in the city?"

Adras gave a tight nod.

Gregoire knew it was killing his friend to ask for help.

With his beast half itching at the idea of hunting her tight little ass, he warned Adras, "The next time you see her, she'll be mine."

Adras growled low in his throat as Ava put a small hand to his chest.

Gregoire clenched his teeth and spoke low, attempting to remember that he would likely feel the same in Adras' position. "You knew this time would come. You knew it when you called for me. I've waited five extra years, giving you time. Giving *her* time to have her youth. Do not act as though I haven't taken everything into consideration. You have no *idea* the sacrifice I've made in this."

"You better have a care with her. She is young and small." Adras' eyes glittered in warning. This was never going to be a comfortable situation. The whole issue was fucked up beyond anything else. Adras was fully aware of how demanding he'd be.

"You know better than to assume I would harm what's mine," Gregoire growled in warning. He didn't appreciate the insinuation that he would not care for his own mate.

He walked out the door without another word, exiting into the crisp night air, inhaling deep to clear his fogged mind. Her scent had been all over the home, and it had gotten inside him.

Chapter 4

Guardian Compound, Tetartos Realm

Erik's eyes slit open slowly. He lay on his side on top of soft bedding, not his own. His eyes opened wider to assess the change in location. Light filtered around dark curtains, but he was more interested in the soft female resting in his arms. She smelled like nothing he'd ever scented in his life and his beast half purred and clawed for more.

His cock was stiff between them as she lay against him. He became transfixed by the intoxicating fragrance and feel of her. Erik looked at the small slender female sleeping against him. Her shoulder-length, sun-streaked hair lay in sleepy disarray. The scent of her skin blanketed him as he leaned in to draw more of it into his lungs. He felt drugged as he rolled her to her back and leaned in, dipping his face into her hair... her throat. His breath caught at the soul-deep knowledge that she was his. He nipped at the sweet bit of skin he could see at her neck, completely intoxicated. It hadn't been sharp enough to sting, just enough that she moaned.

He growled his approval and kissed and sucked at her collarbone until she gasped his name. Looking up, he saw half-lidded leaf-green eyes pulling him in. A small tongue darted out to wet plump bowed lips as she said his name. He ached to nip and savor them until they were swollen from his attentions.

More beast than man, he groaned low before settling in to do just that. His heartbeat thrummed inside his head. He needed to devour, to take... claim. His cock pushed into her leg as he tucked her further beneath him and took her lips. This small female was his, and he forced himself to be careful, knowing from her scent that she was mortal, and easily half his size.

She writhed and moaned as he possessed her mouth, taking her tongue in a deep plundering. He lifted up the sweatshirt she wore, uncovering soft ripe mounds already peaked and swollen, begging for his touch. He plumped them high in his palms. They were perfect and soft in his hands. Not overly large but enough to play with. Mesmerized, he leaned down, his eyes closed as he suckled and bit at the dusky tips, loving the taste of her skin. Her tight athletic frame bowed beneath his bigger, stronger body. He heard his name echoed over and over inside his mind, and the sound of it pulled him deeper into the hazy thrall.

Lowering the soft pants she wore, he watched as every tanned inch of skin was uncovered. He ripped them free from her small feet and tossed them across the room. Looking his fill, he was drawn in by the thin line of softly shorn hair, knowing it would lead him straight to paradise. It guided his mouth, beckoned him lower. He salivated, his chest rising with heavy pants. There was no way he'd ever been so out of his mind with lust. His mind was buzzing with the need to be buried deep inside her, but the urge to taste her was stronger.

He wasn't even sure anything existed before that moment, couldn't think of anything but her. He was hit with the relentless desire to possess what he knew was his. He lifted and spread long, shapely thighs apart and looked his fill at her glistening folds, all slick and ready for him.

His thumbs caressed the skin behind her knees. He rubbed his rough cheek along the inside of her thigh, his animal wanting to mark her skin. Her breathing accelerated, and he smelled her heat. His head felt hazy; deep inside he was hit with an odd sense of uneasiness. He shook it off, his need for her overriding all other thought. Her body shook beneath his hands; she needed him. He forced his wide shoulders into the space he'd made between her thighs and buried his face in her soft wet pussy, licking and sucking every sweet inch of wet succulent flesh. He had to consume her, wanted her to come on his lips before he plunged his painfully hard cock inside her. He would take her so deep she wouldn't realize anything existed beyond his cock stretching her, owning her.

The buzzing unease and odd, feminine sounds in his mind were a soft background hum to his booming internal voice telling him to take... pleasure. A sense of sudden panic jerked him up. What the fuck was happening? He was so hot, so hungry he dove in again to plunder her slick lower lips, pushing his tongue as far into her pussy as he could get. He held her legs firmly, felt her channel pulsing around him. He moaned as her hips thrust against his face.

His eyes closed as he tasted her pleasure. Her body was new to him. He knew that he'd never tasted anything so damn good in his long existence. He hadn't claimed her... He knew that instinctually. The only sounds, outside the roaring in his brain, were his wet suckling and the moans that fell from her lips. It was hard to focus through his body's need to fill her, but he had to bring her higher until she exploded. He needed to taste it, wanted it all over his mouth.

He growled deep as he replaced his tongue with a thick finger, tunneling into her tight channel. He needed to know how much to prepare her for his fist-sized dick. Fuck, she was snug, he thought as he pumped while simultaneously squeezing his aching cock with his other hand. He swirled his tongue around her clit. Took the tiny bud into his mouth and sucked. Her hips pushed against his face, and he moaned his approval against her skin. She cried out, her climax pulsing around his finger as she worked to hold him deep.

He lifted up on arm muscles aching with tension. Need to be buried deep inside her tight, hot pussy clenched his gut and tightened his balls. Nothing would be right until he did. He pushed to his knees, holding tight to the base of his cock as he panted for breath. He refused to come until he was balls deep inside her. He wiped his mouth and held his cock to her opening, slicking it in her juices as he looked up to her eyes.

He stopped cold at the fear he saw reflected there an instant before she closed her lids against him. What the fuck was happening? Answers came; he just didn't understand them at first.

The litany in the background of his mind. That feminine voice. He listened to it for the first time. *"Sam, you are strong. Have to stop panicking. His mouth felt so damn good, focus on the pleasure. Stop feeling dirty. The need is strong. Focus on that. You can do this. He saved you. He's so damn perfect."* He reared back at the words, looking at her lying before him, beautifully nude and wet with the release he'd given her. His fucked-up cock still pounded in need. Her eyes crinkled at the corners with how tight she'd shut them. She was frightened. But if it was her mind he was hearing... What the hell was happening? Then the flashes of memory hit.

A human's apartment.

No. It belonged to one of the Elemental Mageias taken by Cyril to Tetartos. Sam. His sister told him her name before they went to investigate.

A soft pillow. The smell of heaven. Then anger and anguish so strong it nearly ripped his soul from his body.

Danger. Mate. She was his, and they had taken her. They were experimenting on and hurting her.

43

A link in his mind pulsed. Searching. Working to find her. She was too far to reach. He needed more energy. Earth's energies were fueling him, but he needed more. He had to complete the link. He settled inside his mind, his body, instinctually refusing to expend energies on anything not related to finding her. Saving her.

He saw Vane's blond hair, his twin's face contorted in concern as he yelled, "Shit, Erik, what the fuck's wrong?" Erik wanted to answer but, finding her, reaching her was more important.

Later... there was a constant funneling of energy into his body as he pushed the link to complete. Everything was blurry. His focus was in finding her. His mate. He would not fail her like he'd failed his sister.

He *had* failed her. He knew it. The memories stopped as he looked down at the beautiful form of the mortal Mageia lying suppliantly before him on the unfamiliar bed. He felt sweat beading on his chest.

The pain was too much. He had to make the words stop. He was having trouble catching his breath. On instinct, he gently pushed inside her mind, trying to find a way. He finally lifted a shield for her thoughts. They abruptly cut out of his head. Then, the full impact and painful realization nearly destroyed him.

He had to leave.

The things she'd revealed in his mind were too much for him to handle while arousal beat at his body. The burning need was so deep he knew he wouldn't be able to fight it for long.

He looked at her beautiful face and asked with a voice that sounded raspy and pained to his own ears, "Are you safe here?"

Sam, he knew his mate's name. Just as he knew without a doubt that she was his. Her soulful green eyes popped open, and he heard the soft cadence of confusion filling her voice as she answered, "Yes, we're safe here." He saw and felt the truth of her words as her delicate brow furrowed. He couldn't stay there a minute longer. Erik was off the bed and through the balcony doors within a second.

He hit a solid barrier when he tried to teleport away to his home. He was slammed back, reforming again on the balcony with a jolt. The horrible need to claim her nearly overwhelmed him. Made him close his eyes.

He transformed into his lion form and leapt two stories down and into the forest below. He left his mate, praying she was right, that she was safe. But she wouldn't be if he stayed. He would have taken her, claimed her. His instincts roared at him to do just that. She had already been forced and he refused to be another monster to her.

Erik bounded through trees and over forest shrubbery. It would have been a serene setting if he hadn't been bolting for fear of what he was capable of. The chilled mountain air did nothing to cool his overheated body. His cock was past the point of pain; he gritted his teeth against it, refusing to turn around. He had to get away from her before he did something he would regret. Something she would hate him for. Fuck, something he would hate himself for. Erik concentrated on the sound of his paws padding along the forest floor. He could still taste her on his tongue.

He shook his head. It wasn't smart to be so distracted when he still didn't know the terrain. His memories were slow and fuzzy, but the pounding he took trying to teleport home indicated he was in Tetartos Realm instead of Earth, where he, his twin and sister lived hidden among several billion humans.

He hadn't even tried to contact his sister and brother, not wanting them to see him like this. He needed to calm down and find those memories first.

A true mate?

From the mating spell cast by an abused Immortal within the hells of Apollo and Hermes' labs so many centuries ago. It was a way for Immortals to be free from breeding the Gods' armies as if they were livestock. It was said to have cost the Immortal Charybdis her life.

In the centuries living among humans on Earth Realm, Erik never thought to have one. How the hell was it possible that he'd somehow mated a *mortal*? What the fuck? What did that mean? That he would find her to only lose her in mere decades? He roared, the sound echoing into the trees. It felt like his intestines were being ripped from him. His animal's rage rang free, loosing feathered prey from their homes.

She'd said in her mind that he had saved her. That provided little solace when thoughts of her feeling dirty were there. Sam had been raped. He wanted to rip something, *anything*, limb from limb. His fury was banging inside the walls of his mind. He ached for a fight. Hoped the beasts of Tetartos were out there watching him. He called to them, needing blood to flow.

No more snippets of blurred memories came as he ran. His head pounded. He could at least remember his life before Sam. He forced himself to run through what he knew of his life to see if it would bring the memories he sought.

His mother was the Goddess Athena. His father, Niall, was Athena's powerful Immortal mate. His sister, Alex, had been born before their father had been abducted and experimented on by Apollo and Hermes. He and Vane, his brother, his twin... light to his dark, were born after their mother rescued their father from their

46

uncles' vile clutches. They'd gotten their lion form from their father. A form the labs had forced into him.

Erik growled. None of that mattered or helped jog any new memories.

He remembered being in the penthouse he shared with his brother and sister in New York. They'd avoided the Immortal exile from Earth because of his sister's abilities. They were there when this started... Alex, his raven-haired sister, had been taken into the mind of another of Cyril's victims. Was it the sixth female in a damned year? Alex's rare power of head-hopping, as they called it, was unpredictable. It sent her where it wanted, whenever it wanted.

He remembered her *hopping* to Sam before he understood Cyril's newest victim was his fucking mate. Vane had telepathically sent the information of the abduction to the Guardians of the Realms, making sure to stay far enough away not to get exiled to Tetartos. Their sister had always thought they were needed on Earth, so that was where they fucking stayed.

Erik growled as more memories came. He remembered he, Vane and Alex going to Sam's apartment, the heavenly scent, pain, blurry visuals of his siblings and the Guardians? Were the Guardians of the Realms there with them?

Shit, he needed to know more. The bastard, Cyril, lived on Tetartos and appeared to have been collecting Mageia for some kind of experimentation. When Alex went into a victim's mind, she suffered with them. Whatever horrors they were going through, she experienced and he always fucking hated it. His sister had been through enough pain from being violated by the bastard Tria centuries ago.

Now his female had been abused.

He clenched his jaw tight. He'd obviously come to this Realm to save his female. She'd said he had.

The question was how everything had gone down? Had he gotten his siblings exiled in the process?

When their mother and father were sent away to sleep with the other Gods, Erik, as firstborn male, took his father's place in caring for his siblings. It was a duty he took seriously. He hadn't been able to prevent Alex's rape those millennia ago, but he would do anything in his power to ensure she was safe. She and Vane both.

A niggling at the back of his neck alerted him that he wasn't alone.

He was relieved and concerned when he saw his twin. Vane's long sun-streaked hair lay against his shoulders, and blue eyes stared back at him, knowing. Alex stood next to him. His family.

Hey, man, good to see you back, his twin said inside Erik's mind.

Chapter 5

Paradeisos Island, Tetartos Realm

After a whirlwind of writing notes, packing and finally teleporting, which was never fun, Rain and Alyssa were finally situated on comfortable lounges at an island paradise.

"I'm getting more cocktails and paying for these waxing packages. I may not be getting the full training arrangement like you, but hell if I'm not going to blow some coin on this vacation," Rain announced with a cheeky little grin.

They had only been in Paradeisos for a few short hours, and Alyssa truly felt like she'd entered the paradise the island had been named for. It felt like a huge weight had been lifted from her. Neither of them had ever gone anywhere but the Emfanisis and she'd never truly realized how trapped she'd felt within her existence in Lofodes. Her nerves were no longer twisted. She still felt the pang of rejection in the pit of her stomach, but her new resolve made it less piercing. She refused to let herself wallow any more.

The first thing they'd done after arriving was drop their bags in the huge two-room suite she'd splurged on. They'd set their stuff in the opulent rooms and then checked out the view of the gorgeous sparkling sea visible from their balcony. The salty breeze had called to them, so they'd slipped into tiny bikinis and headed to the beach.

She lay back on the cushioned lounge and relaxed with the sound of the waves hitting soft sand in front of them. It was a truly magical place, so different from their home.

This was a turning point in her life. A new Alyssa would emerge from this trip, and she had plenty of coin saved to let loose while figuring out what that meant for her. The resort had the most decadent amenities, and she refused to skimp. Gaining true independence was cause to celebrate.

She sipped from the fruity drink Rain had ordered, enjoying the icy slide of it down her throat. The warm air was cooled by a salty breeze, lulling her in its caress. The seating areas were separated by trees and shrubbery, giving the illusion that they were the only guests there.

Two Nereid males stood in the water, patrolling the swim area for serpents. They were even more gorgeous than the sea surrounding them. She and Rain had spent the first twenty minutes completely entranced by their male beauty.

"I'm not kidding. I don't care if my whole savings gets spent. I plan to do this right. When will we ever leave our businesses again? Neither of us has gone on a real vacation before, and we work our asses off. Not to mention, you deserve some fun for all of your years buried in sketches and fabric, avoiding the idiots of the Hippeus clans." Rain barely took a breath between words. "I promise to make you enjoy yourself to the fullest and forget all the crap while you make plans for the new independent Alyssa," Rain said with feeling as she continued to read through the brochure she'd been absorbing since sitting down.

She grinned at her friend's exuberance. She was so glad Rain had made this happen.

The sun was high, and sparkles flickered along the beautiful turquoise waters. They were nothing like the deep cold navy of the sea by her home.

The condensation dripping from her glass felt nice against her heated skin. It was absolutely perfect in their shaded spot.

For a moment she considered relocating her business to the island and grinned to herself. She would be broke in no time if she attempted that. She'd done well through the years and spent very little, but the island was decadent and extravagant.

It was owned by some Aletheia male named Tynan. He was apparently something to be excited about, at least according to Rain, who had been reading every bit of literature they'd found in their room. There were pictures of the owner and the staff, and Alyssa agreed he was beautiful, with dark hair and silver eyes. All of the staff working on the island were gorgeous. Immortals tended to be attractive as a rule, so it really hadn't surprised her.

"Do you think they're on the menu after the swim area closes?" Rain asked with her eyes glued to the naked male torsos of the two Nereids patrolling the waters. Safe swimming and snorkeling were just a couple of the offerings on the beach, making it so that the guests could enjoy the warm water without dealing with sea creatures. Not that she needed to worry about sea beasts with Rain's affinity. Rain was a Water Mageia, and her abilities had an effect on creatures living within that element.

"Were they in the brochure?" Alyssa asked, amused. Still taking in the view of the two blond Immortals standing sentry and fighting off any sea beasts that swam too close. Their lean, tanned muscle stood out even from so far away. Their hair was slicked back, and she caught sight of their iridescent tails flipping out of the water when they dove. She'd never seen a Nereid in their other form, and she couldn't seem to turn her head from the beauty of it.

51

"Maybe. There are a few Nereids in here, but I can't see those guy's faces from this far away. Damn mortal eyesight. Mmm. I don't think you'll care when you see your options." She paused, scanning the pages. "Okay, I think we should focus on pampering and prep work first."

Rain's voice pulled her from her daze.

Her friend looked around and caught the attention of one of the resort's attendants. The female that came over had to be six foot tall, common for any Immortal that wasn't Alyssa. She had long blond hair and smiled pleasantly at them as Rain requested all kinds of treatments for both of them.

Alyssa sipped at the delicious fruity concoction, loving how cool it was, only half-listening to the two making arrangements. She had never been this carefree, not even on movie and Jell-O shot nights at Rain's place. Her creations had always been her outlet. She spent practically every free moment sewing or drawing new designs. She had brought her sketchbooks, but decided to leave them in the room for their first day here. She might leave them in there the entire time.

Her body's desires were something she fully intended to address while she was here. It was part of her "new and independent Alyssa" plan. She had fantasies that had never been fulfilled. She would find what pleased her, and she would make sure to take what she wanted.

Just because the almighty Gregoire along with her own kind weren't attracted to her didn't mean she needed to stay holed up like some damn human spinster.

Hell, she'd already purchased a guidance package in the art of pleasure. The island had been built with sex in mind.

She and Rain had garnered a lot of male attention on the way to the beach, but she wanted the instruction they offered.

She had little doubt that her father had scared off any male that came near her to keep her chaste and that wasn't continuing. It offended everything in her that she'd somehow been kept pure for a male that didn't even want her.

Rain continued reading as Alyssa looked out on the view. "You get to pick any of the following with your package. It says, 'Any combination of male and female instructors, not to exceed three.' They suggest that those new to the art of pleasure choose at least one in the same sex."

Alyssa's entire body heated in nervous anticipation.

"Oh, how I wish this was where I lost my virginity," Rain said on a sigh.

Alyssa laughed at her friend's breathlessness. "Why don't you sign up? Just because you're a dirty whore doesn't mean you couldn't still pick up some pointers." She grinned cheekily at her friend, who tossed a cardboard coaster at her head. It glided in the wrong direction and pinged off Alyssa's leg before landing in the sand.

"You give me too much credit," her friend said without heat, then seemed to ponder it. "Maybe I will... Well, damn, if I do it, I'm totally getting this upgrade."

Dare she ask? "What upgrade?"

"Aletheia venom. Oh, yeah, we both need to try it." Rain's face lit. "It's supposed to be amazing. An aphrodisiac that makes you wild."

Alyssa thought it sounded interesting, but she wasn't sure

getting that wild was a good idea. She shook her head. Screw it; why the hell wouldn't she try some? Her new motto was to experience everything life had to offer.

"Females, if you will follow me," the tall attendant said as she walked up to their lounges. She gave them both friendly smiles and led them through an outdoor pool area toward one of four long wings of the resort. Tall shrubs lined the walkway as if they were in a labyrinth. They passed all kinds of hidden alcoves that promised all kinds of wicked play, and the sight gave her a pang to the chest. She imagined couples sneaking away for trysts. She really needed to stop watching romantic human movies with Rain. It was not the same in this Realm and only made her want things that would never be. She was alone for one reason. She'd been rejected, likely on appearance alone, if he'd even bothered finding out what she looked like.

The doorway they entered opened up to a big circular entry of soft rose marble and glass. The ceiling was domed, and potted trees filled the space around a big counter, where another female sat smiling at them. The blonde ushered them into separate rooms to get their treatments. Alyssa shed her bathing suit and snuggled onto the narrow bed as she had been instructed before relaxing under a soft sheet.

She lay there contemplating where she would settle. She didn't like the idea of venturing to another city, but could she stay so close to home and still feel like she was truly living her life independently? Plus, Lofodes' outskirts were predominately Hippeus, and the city contained mostly Mageia. Would that provide her with any chance at having her physical desires unleashed? Something she'd denied herself for too long and had no intention of denying herself after they left. Immortals were known as sexual beings, yet she'd been raised more like a human.

She could easily get back and forth if she went to another city.

That was one advantage in having a Kairos as a friend. The Kairos race teleported people all over the Realm for a fee.

Their friend Astrid had taken them to the island for free. The dark-haired beauty had shaken her head and smirked at the two of them and fit them into her scheduled trips. Astrid owned the Kairos office in Lofodes and had been working with both her and Rain to sell their items to shops in the other cities for years.

Astrid's beauty was exotic with ancient eyes that appeared to see everything. She had seen potential with Alyssa's designs and made suggestions that proved quite popular with the females of Tetartos.

She was one of Alyssa's first repeat customers, and now Astrid made a profit selling to the other cities, just like she did with Rain's business. Alyssa smiled when she remembered the indulgent looks Astrid had given the two of them when she dropped them off. They'd invited her to come along, but she had said she was too busy to join them. The Kairos was not one for any big shows of emotion, but Alyssa had caught the slight lifting of her lips at their choice of destination.

Alyssa was jarred from her thoughts at a knock on the door. Thinking of Kairos seemed to make them appear... A big, gorgeous male with long black hair and exotically tanned skin walked in, grinning wickedly at her. Her mouth went dry, and she suddenly wished she had paid more attention to what Rain had booked, because if this was the waxing package, she was out of there.

He must have caught her moment of horror because he seemed to be suppressing a laugh. "I came in to let you know that Therina will be with you shortly. Would you like anything while you wait?"

She relaxed back and enjoyed the rest of her day, meeting Rain in between their treatments or doing them together, as was the case when getting their nails done.

They went back to the room relaxed, but then the nervousness set in. A note was delivered with a location for her first lesson. Rain attempted a pep talk, but it had been drowned out by the buzzing in Alyssa's ears. She dressed nervously and left before she could back out.

She hadn't known what to wear, so she'd settled on a light sundress with easy access to the bare skin beneath. Her face heated as she arrived at her destination. Things were about to change. For the entire walk down the halls, any time she thought about turning back, she focused on her end goal.

She wanted to feel empowered instead of just finding a quick end to her virginal status. If Gregoire ever came for her, it would be to find a female that had taken control of her needs and was able to judge him. Let him see how he enjoyed being on the receiving end.

She still had no idea what he'd even based his rejection on. Appearance? Size? Perceived weakness? She had plenty of insecurities that all clambered to the forefront of her mind, and she pushed them away. She was doing this for herself, taking her life and making it her own.

Her hand hovered at the door for a second before she knocked. The heavy wood swung open to reveal a tall beautiful redhead standing just inside; a seductive smile painted her bow lips. The female wore a pretty orange halter dress that flowed to her bare feet. "You must be Alyssa."

She cleared her suddenly dry throat before speaking. "Yes."

"Come in. This is Kerr and Calder, and I'm Morgan." The males she'd picked based on their pictures in the brochure gave her wicked grins, and Calder, the Nereid she'd chosen, winked at her. They were dark and light in coloring and had magnificent bodies mostly visible, as they were only wearing shorts; then she noticed the big bed blocked by a short wall that served to separate it from the rest of the room.

It was large enough to accommodate ten writhing bodies. Her skin heated, and her nipples peaked in anticipation of what would happen there later. She lifted her chin, ready for anything they had planned. Her fingers running over her own flesh beneath warm bath water had never been fulfilling, had only left her feeling mildly relaxed, yet still frustrated.

"How about we get a drink and chat for a bit so that you can get to know us and relax a little," Morgan suggested, already sauntering over to the small bar set up on the opposite side of the seating arrangement.

Alyssa took a good look at the males. Kerr was a Geraki, like Morgan. Those of their race were able to transform into large birds of prey or partially shift with massive wings on their human-looking backs. He was a little shorter than Calder, as Nereids seemed to be taller and leaner. They were both stunning in different ways. Calder had sea-colored eyes and sun-kissed hair, and Kerr had brown hair and eyes.

"That sounds great." A drink was just the thing she needed and she flushed slightly as the female offered her a wine known in their Realm for its relaxing and arousing qualities, without dulling the mind. She nodded as she rubbed her hands down the front of her short teal dress. The material hugged her breasts and waist before flaring almost to her knees. She hadn't worn lingerie, so the fabric was rasping at her sensitive skin.

Calder and Kerr stalked forward and something in their heated looks emboldened her. Calder grasped her hand in his and ushered her to sit between them on the couch and she forced her body to relax into the heat radiating from their larger bodies.

When Morgan came back and handed her a glass, she drank deeply, allowing the magic within to ease her nerves as they calmly explained how things worked.

They showed her toys, explaining their uses before sharing that they'd have her choose some for them to demonstrate the next evening. Morgan's soft voice soothed as she explained that nothing was taboo and that if she wanted anything, she needed only to ask. Alyssa was lulled into a comfortable yet aroused state.

"After we've let you explore and learn how to bring us pleasure, we'll lay you out on the bed and use our mouths and hands on your body to find the things that get you the most excited. Tonight is all about oral pleasure, Alyssa."

Her ears buzzed, and her pussy ached for them to do everything Morgan said.

"Mmm, you smell good." Kerr groaned next to her. His head bent so that he was nuzzling at her ear. Shivers ran over her skin.

"I agree. I can't wait to get my mouth on all that sweetness, but kissing is first," Calder said, and the blond Nereid lifted her to straddle his lap before taking her mouth gently. It was a slow tasting of her lips before his tongue eased over the seam. She opened, allowing him to explore.

She felt a pang in her chest that quickly disappeared when his hands stroked circles on her thighs. She moaned as his mouth tempted and seduced her.

"My turn." She was passed to straddle Kerr next. He was more aggressive in the way his tongue plundered her mouth until she was writhing against his erection, and his thumbs strummed against her nipples through the fabric of her dress.

"Very nice, you learn quickly," Kerr said when he broke the kiss.

She was flipped with her legs spread over his knees, her back to his chest, and Morgan kneeled in front of them. She pushed her lean frame between Alyssa's and Kerr's thighs and kissed her.

Morgan's lips were softer, her tongue a smooth caress as she tempted Alyssa with a palm against her flushed cheek. Delicate fingers tunneled in her hair as Morgan delved deeper. She heard the males groan and felt Kerr's hard cock twitching beneath her bottom, which made her more aroused.

Alyssa liked them watching and wanting. Years of being made to feel less by those of her kind had hurt, made her feel undesirable, and now she felt the opposite.

Morgan moaned, and Alyssa smelled all of their combined desires as Kerr held her in his big arms. He kept her thighs wide, and being splayed with Morgan between her legs made her ache for more. She enjoyed how hard Kerr was beneath her bottom, getting even thicker as the female kissed her.

Soon they were all naked, and her lips met Morgan's over Calder's long shaft. He groaned above them. "Fuck, yeah, Alyssa, massage my sac with one hand and try to take my cock as deep as you can down your throat. The more you take, the hotter I'll get." She liked how silky his cock felt in her mouth, enjoyed his sweet salty taste as she took him deep, but loved even more how strong and sexy she felt. Morgan had moved back to watch with heated eyes and her sultry voice instructed her, "When you get him to the back of your throat, swallow and breathe through your nose. You'll be able to take him deeper that way. Just keep swallowing until you take him all, Alyssa. He'll go wild if you do that. Keep massaging his sac and just behind and you'll own him."

Calder groaned and pumped his hips against her lips. The fact that she could put him in that uncontrolled state set her off. She moaned and sucked hard until he was shouting and filling her mouth with come.

"Swallow it all. Males get off on it," Morgan encouraged.

"Shit, for someone new to this, she did a damn good job of making him come faster than I've ever seen," Kerr said. "I can't wait to get those pouty lips all over my cock."

Her heart was thumping in her head, her nipples ached, and her pussy was clenching in excitement.

She took a deep breath before lifting her eyes to Kerr's.

She wasn't sure how she managed exploring and touching them all without becoming completely unglued. It was torture and sweet bliss wrapped up in one. She was proud as she made them beg for more while she listened to their heated instructions. They told her just where and how hard or soft to stroke. How deep and firm she needed to suck.

Morgan had smaller breasts that were beautifully pierced. Alyssa and Calder worked the hard plastic of the bars in her taut nipples, sucking and nipping until the Geraki's back bowed in pleasure. The scent of their combined desire filled the room, filling her mind with the sheer headiness.

She felt hot and empowered all at once. Kerr lifted his mouth from the female's body and groaned deep as he seemed to lose control, slipping his cock inside Morgan's pussy. Calder instructed

Alyssa to lick the female's clit as he held her arms over her head. Alyssa was wild, imagining the same being done to her. It had been hot and wicked. She sucked the tight clit and got lost in the eroticism of it while Kerr shafted uncontrollably against her cheek. Alyssa was panting by the time they'd finally come apart.

Calder flipped her over so that she was on her back, laid out for them. Her mind stopped functioning as they kissed, nipped and licked at her heated flesh until racking sensations rocked her body. "Shit, I know tonight isn't the time, but I want inside your pussy," Kerr said as he trailed a finger through her juices, licking and flicking at her clit with his tongue. Her hips lifted on their own, but she'd stiffened a little. In reality she didn't want him to touch her any deeper. At least not yet. "Don't worry, Alyssa. You just taste so damn good."

Morgan warned, "You know the order of things, Kerr." The female's voice was breathless as she licked around Alyssa's nipple, then nipped lightly, making her moan. Calder was on the other side, giving her other swollen breast just as much attention. She allowed herself to be lost in the moment, as they watched or asked her what felt best. Pangs kept beating against her chest, and she clenched her teeth and ignored the stupid guilt and concentrated completely on the hands and mouths caressing her. Alyssa's traitorous mind suddenly replaced Kerr's heated gaze with Gregoire's and she crested in an orgasm that bowed her back off the bed. She gasped and moaned in blessed relief that left her feeling shaky.

"Your tits are incredible. They're made for fucking," she thought she heard Calder say as he rubbed his rough cheeks against one, giving her a burn that only enhanced her sensitivity. "Alyssa, would you let me bind your arms over your head and fuck them?"

"Not tonight, Calder. You know how we do this; you've had yours. Now, it's all about Alyssa, so get down there and lick that

61

pussy. Kerr and I will hold her legs back while you work. I know you like space."

He moaned and changed positions with Kerr. He gave her a stunning grin and then winked at her before greedily delving between her thighs. His tongue roved back and circled her back entrance while his talented fingers circled her clit.

She loved that Morgan and Kerr just held her legs and pinched her nipples as they watched. It somehow made her hotter knowing they saw every lick as Calder drove her, but she couldn't seem to find relief. Not until she shut her eyes and imagined being bound by others as Gregoire shafted inside her did she find completion.

She was feeling out of sorts now, yet she forced her mind to stop tormenting her.

"Damn, I need to be fucked," Morgan said on a pained groan. The males flipped them around so that Morgan was on her back, ass at the end of the bed, with Alyssa straddling her mouth. The female sucked her clit and used her fingers to tease her openings. It was a softer assault to the senses. She turned her head, watching as Calder entered Morgan on a tight groan and then began thrusting hard. Morgan moved beneath her. Kerr got on his knees and held onto her as he kissed her, devouring her mouth, she tasted both she and Morgan on his lips and whimpered when the female sucked hard. His fingers pinched her nipples and grounded her down on Morgan's mouth.

The walk back to her room was exhausting. The fact that she imagined Gregoire each time she orgasmed wasn't right and she knew it. Morgan had said there was no shame in fantasies and desire. A motto for most all Immortals, but fantasizing about a male who didn't want her was pathetic.

Worse were the pangs of guilt. She wasn't doing anything wrong. Her mate had rejected her, a mate she didn't even know and had never met. Seeking her own pleasure was her right.

It all stemmed from those dumb fairy tales and human movies she loved. If only her mother hadn't said those sweet tales were nothing compared to the beauty of an Immortal mating bond.

She just needed to forget him, forget everything she'd been told and find a way to take care of herself without feeling guilty about it. The Guardian hadn't earned her loyalty.

After blowing out a breath, she unlocked the door to her suite and stepped inside. Rain was sitting on the couch with a book in her hand, and she wondered why her friend hadn't gone out and gotten a little action.

Rain perked up and put her book aside the minute the door clicked shut.

"Well? Tell me everything."

"I thought you were going out to the bar."

Her friend looked sheepish. "After all the spa treatments today, I was too relaxed to leave. The amazing bathtub in my room, which looks out on the sea, got together with the wine bottle and my book and demanded I loaf instead. Pathetic, I know. I fully intend to remedy that tomorrow night." Rain's dimples peeked out as she grinned. "Plus, I wanted to make sure I was here to get all the details when you got in."

"Okay, but I'm exhausted, so you're only getting the CliffsNotes version until I've showered and slept."

Chapter 6

Paradeisos Island, Tetartos Realm

Gregoire was furious as hell by the time his body reformed on the island. It had taken him all fucking night to find the Kairos who'd teleported his mate away from Lofodes, and convince her to divulge Alyssa's whereabouts.

He was enraged. What was his little mate doing at an island known for sexual excess? He breathed in the cool salty air. Knowing the answer to his own question wasn't making him any happier. She thought he hadn't wanted to claim her. Her note had indicated as much.

Fucking Adras and Ava.

He shook his head as a soft breeze slid over his skin. He entered the area he knew led to Tynan's suite. The owner of this particular location was an Aletheia he'd known for centuries. Tynan had claimed the island shortly after the Immortals were exiled to fucking Tetartos.

Gregoire banged his fist on the door inside the secluded circular courtyard.

It was thrust open by the irritated Aletheia. Tynan was clad in a pair of silk black pants, and his short dark hair was tousled. An evening's worth of stubble surrounded a deep scowl that quickly transformed into a welcoming grin, silver eyes shining. "Hello, old

64

friend. To what to I owe the pleasure?" he said as he opened the door wider in an invitation to enter.

Dark plum walls enclosed the room, wainscoted with pale marble. He didn't even pay attention to the artwork depicting all manner of sexual excess lining the room that led out to a private balcony. A glance through the open bedroom door showed a trio of females curled in sleep on the large bed. He let out a breath as he quickly assessed that none were his damn mate.

He hadn't smelled Alyssa's delectable scent and his old friend had no fucking idea how lucky he was that she wasn't in his bed. Gregoire could barely contain the roiling possessiveness inside him as the male led him through to the patio area and sprawled into a chair.

"Would you like a drink?" Tynan raised an eyebrow in question as he said the words. "Maybe a companion?" His mouth tilted wickedly. "It's been a while since we've shared in our enjoyments."

Gregoire shook his head. The Aletheia was a few inches shorter than Gregoire and much leaner, but they had once shared similar carnal appetites. There were many other vacation areas in the cities that would have been less erotically focused than Paradeisos and his entire being was offended and enraged that Alyssa had chosen the island.

His friend eyed him curiously but didn't fill the air while Gregoire stood, choosing his wording. The male was comfortable in his life in Tetartos, had made a profitable business and enjoyed the fruits of his labor. He tended to handpick any guest that piqued his interest for whatever pleasures he decided to partake in. The trio of females in his bed indicated that little had changed. Had he sampled Alyssa when she arrived? He clenched his jaw tight. If he didn't find her snuggled alone in her own bed, he would likely kill someone.

"I need the location of a specific female that arrived yesterday with a friend." At Tynan's raised brow, Gregoire continued, "Alyssa." He felt his muscles tighten. He needed to find her now.

"I've been busy for the last forty-eight hours, give or take," Tynan said, assessing him thoughtfully. He looked far away for a moment, speaking to one of his people telepathically.

The male's grin widened as his brows rose, intent silver eyes focused and interested. "An innocent, really?"

Gregoire's cock stood at attention with the confirmation that his mate remained pure. Both beast and man thrilled that she'd be only his. He hoped to hell she was old enough to deal with the animal inside him. Their coupling would be wild. Violent joinings were common in their race and the whole thing fucked with his head. He'd never in his life been possessive of any female and had always enjoyed sharing, but he'd never allow another to lay a finger on what was his.

"Where is she?" His voice came out dangerously low. His cock was full, demanding that he find her; he was slowly losing his mind and control. He wondered if he'd be able to restrain himself for their first time. She was so small everywhere but those fuckable breasts. He had thought of them every moment since she'd reached maturity. He pictured running his hands and mouth and cock all over them right fucking now.

His friend's hearty laugh echoed from the patio. "She's here attempting to rectify that particular situation. She started her training program last evening."

His vision hazed with red, and his next words came out as a growl. "What the hell are you talking about?"

Tynan lost his grin and eyed him speculatively. "I set up the course long ago. It's quite popular. Her beginning lessons would have started with oral skills."

Gregoire felt his skin heat, heard the menacing snarl that left his lips. The thought of her plump little lips surrounding another male's cock made him insane. His muscles twitched, and he nearly vibrated with the need to do damage. Tynan looked at him with suspicious concern, then understanding.

"Gregoire?" Tynan lowered his voice, looking into the living area before returning his attention back to Gregoire. The male sent the visuals into Gregoire's mind of a room overlooking the sea. He nodded. He needed to claim her before he lost his mind. He took a deep breath, knowing she needed care, but, fuck, he wanted to turn her over his knee for thinking to give away what belonged to him.

Get all your usses to Lofodes. They're under attack. City has been breached. Drake's voice practically roared in Gregoire's mind.

Son of a bitch! He slammed a fist into the table, smashing the glass, at the interruption.

"Fuck!" he snarled, scrubbing a hand over his jaw.

He forced back his beast's need to tell his brothers to fucking handle Lofodes themselves. He knew by Drake's tone that they were all called in. "I have to leave." Whoever had delayed him claiming his mate would not like what they'd unleashed. Gregoire gave Tynan a harsh look and demanded, "You will watch after her personally until I get back. No one touches her. Not you, not anyone and do *not* tell her I was here."

Tynan got up from his lounging position, tension in his body. "Is there something I should know?"

"Lofodes is under attack. No details, you may want to up your security just in case." He got in his friend's face. "No. One. Puts their hands on her. Do you understand me, Tynan? Don't let her out of your sight."

With that he was gone.

Chapter 7

Guardian Compound, Tetartos Realm

"**D**rug him? Woman, are you out of your damned mind?" Vane was obviously as shocked as Sam was at hearing Sirena's suggestion to drug Erik. It wasn't like when they'd kept him unconscious. Sirena was talking about an entirely different kind of drugging.

Vane's golden hair hung to the collar of his blue tee shirt, and he had his hands planted on his hips as he faced off against the Guardian healer. His mouth was set in a tight line as he stared down at the blonde woman in clear exasperation.

Sam's chest hurt as her eyes caught at his jawline and the other strong features that were so similar to Erik's. As twins, their build and height was just about identical. They only seemed to differ in hair color and eyes. Erik's hair was a dark brown, almost black, cut much shorter than Vane's, and his eyes were a light icy blue, where Vane's were more of a sapphire. Vane's matched more to their sister, Alex's.

"I know it sounds rash, but the circumstances are extreme. You and Alex haven't been able to change his mind. He refuses to come near Sam because he is afraid to hurt her. Uri borrowed Jax's guest house for him because he won't risk staying here. It's commendable that your brother is determined she have time to heal, no matter the pain he's in." Sirena took a frustrated breath before continuing. "Vane, the pain is only going to get worse. It will become debilitating, to the point that it'll affect his mind. Sam will go through it as well, but it should be easier for her since she is still mortal. The effects always seem to be worse for the Immortal."

Her heart clenched painfully. This was all her fault, he'd left after hearing her thoughts.

At Sam's initial confused look, Sirena had explained that Erik would have heard her inner turbulence. Sam couldn't even remember exactly what she had been thinking. There were thoughts of insecurity and feeling dirty, that much she remembered. Now that Sirena had explained, she understood what had happened, remembered the soft feel of him in her head. Her damned insecurities had caused the situation.

"But if you drug him, he might not be aware enough to temper his strength. Until they complete the mating ceremony and she becomes Immortal, she's still breakable. He would fucking hate us all if he harmed her. He's determined to fight this for as long as he can. I don't agree with him, but he's fucking stubborn as shit." Vane ran his hands through his hair while he argued with Sirena.

She was starting to get used to the new world and all of the information they'd given her, but at some point she really thought she might lose it. Immortality, evolved humans, shape-shifting Demi-Gods and mating for eternity between people who'd never met was a lot to accept.

Sirena and Vane both faced her, and she realized they wanted her opinion. "I don't like the idea of taking his choice from him, but if it's going to affect his mind, what do we do? It's been days since he left. I can feel sharp pains that Sirena told me are coming from Erik. What do we do to help him, Vane? He won't even *talk* to me so that I can tell him I can handle it."

70

The memory of the first time she'd seen him had been haunting her. He'd been nude and injured as he moved toward her in the hallway where he'd killed the guards who'd kept her imprisoned. He was a lion one moment, then a beautiful, bloodied God the next. He'd touched her cheek. His pained ice-blue eyes drew her in and made her want so much as he spoke the words, "You're safe now," right before he'd collapsed. She'd been so worried that he would die in her arms. But he hadn't. His body had warmed her inside and out even though he'd been hurt and unconscious. It hadn't made sense at the time. Nothing had. She would always remember that as the first time she'd felt safe after her nightmare.

She took a deep breath and tuned out Vane and Sirena's arguing. Her skin felt healed, and she ached for him to come to her.

"Is there anything I can get for you?" Sirena asked as she and Vane readied to leave without having come up with a resolution to the problem.

"Actually, do you mind sending someone for more clothes and my running shoes? Drake said he would have someone clear my apartment and bring all my personal items as soon as he could."

"I'll personally get you some things and make sure more food is brought up. I'm sorry, but I have to check on the other females, and then I'll come back after you've had time to think about all we went over." Sirena paused, eying her sympathetically. "Sam, this is your choice. It has to do with your body as much as it has to do with Erik's. That leaves you as the person who decides what we do next. I hate to put you in this position, but as his mate, the choice of what we do next is yours."

Sam heard Vane continue arguing with the healer as the door shut. She blew out a breath. Her skin felt tight, and her breasts were swollen. She'd love to go for a run, but she was told it wasn't safe.

71

They did have a gym though and it might help relax her mind, but she'd have to wait for her running shoes.

She sat on the nearest chair, shaking her head as she tried to think logically. How could she be responsible for this choice? Soon his pain would become worse and affect his mind. If she was feeling even a fraction of what he was going through, it was going to be very bad. Her desire, which even now pulsed at her, was starting to build. There was a discomfiting swirling of something running through her entire body, keeping her on the edge of arousal.

Sirena was right. They needed to finish this no matter how much her stomach churned that she might have trouble keeping her nightmares at bay while he touched her. At least Uri and Alex had mentally dulled the experience in her mind so it wasn't debilitating. It wasn't the memories that got to her when he'd woken. Not really. It was that she felt dirty. The shame caused from being aroused while Cyril's men raped her was a big issue. Sirena said that the rapists had most likely dosed her with an aphrodisiac to assuage their own guilt, but it was still causing her major issues.

Everything was so screwed up. She was somewhat calm now, but she felt like it was only a matter of time before she snapped. Too many major aspects of her life had changed along with her abduction and violation. She was somehow managing to keep all the new adjustments in different sections of her mind, but the boxes were getting past the full mark. She was losing space fast. Soon it would all be tumbling out around her in a big heap.

She took a deep breath. Right now she could only focus on one thing, and that was Erik. He was leaving the decision in her hands even though she really doubted he saw it quite the same. He'd saved her life, and he was hurting for no good reason. She appreciated that he had tried to save her from her own suffering, but she'd never felt safer and more at peace than when she'd watched over him while he'd slept. His soul had called to hers even then. There was no way she could explain the feeling.

She was human, a fairly boring IT person whose prior knowledge consisted of small cubicles and people's abilities to impatiently click their way into computer hell.

She wasn't even close to his league. He was the most magnificent man she'd ever seen. His eyes were a light icy blue that drew her in, and his jaw was hard and strong, making his face a thing of pure masculine beauty. His body was like nothing she'd ever seen in real life. He had to be close to seven feet tall with a sheer muscle mass that was nothing short of tanned, chiseled perfection, and when he touched and kissed her, she'd felt somehow cherished. If not for the supernatural stuff, she'd think she had a major white knight psychological issue.

Her heartbeat suddenly stuttered, and she was finding it harder to breathe. She rushed out onto the balcony, and the cool mountain air felt good on her heated skin. She sat on a cushioned chair, taking deep breaths to clear the spots that dotted her vision while she attempted to get her shit together.

What's wrong? The deep, pained voice in her mind warmed her chilled skin. Erik. The sound left a tingling sensation inside her head and body. Crazy, but, man, her body responded to him. No matter what had happened to her, everything about Erik called to her. Did she just think an answer at him? Well, hell, she'd try it. *I'm fine. Will you come back to the manor so we can talk?* She waited, unsure if it worked. She thought she felt something in her mind, the connection Sirena had spoken of. She wasn't sure how that was possible. Nothing in the last week should have been possible. Her life and world had changed.

No. Rest. Then, nothing. That was all he was going to say? His voice had sounded strained. He was in pain. She could feel it deep in her stomach at certain moments for the last couple of days.

Okay, will you talk to me like this? Nothing. It was like her message didn't go through. It hadn't even felt the same as before. Was he blocking her? Ignoring her? Her face heated in annoyance. That stupid caveman. Had he just ordered her to rest? Was he aware of what century they were in?

She sat there with her mouth open and her brows furrowed. Why the hell did any of that turn her on? It had to be those damn messed-up mating hormones. His words had shot deep to her core. She'd dated guys that worked in office buildings. She'd never even met a man like him. Probably because he was a fucking real live Demi-God not some suit-wearing guy in an office building. She tried for steady breaths again as she felt herself starting to panic.

She paced the living room. She'd stayed in Erik's suite since the moment he'd left her. Sleeping in his bed every night. She could have gone back to the room the Guardians had given her after she was rescued, but she felt safer in the space they'd given to Erik. His scent was on the bedding, and something about it soothed her.

She looked into the bedroom, to the big bed they'd shared. He'd woken after days of being unconscious and given her pleasure like she'd never known. Sirena had warned her that he'd wake up aroused and desperate for release. She'd been prepared for that. She hadn't been prepared for him to go down on her. She expected frenzied sex with no foreplay, but that hadn't been the case. The touch of his fingers and lips had made every nerve ending stand at attention. She had been getting his thoughts; his intense need had filtered into her mind, mingling with her own desire. He'd set his mouth to her, groaning and lapping at her arousal as if he would consume her whole. Erik had been gentle, even in the frenzy, sending her over the precipice into the hardest climax she'd ever

74

experienced.

She closed her eyes when she remembered the look of pained horror on his face as he'd heard her thoughts. Her fears and panic. He'd refused to hurt her. Even as he sat between her open thighs, stroking his swollen shaft, deep in his own need. His glistening chest had risen and fallen with arousal, but he'd held back, asking her if she was in a safe place before leaving her. There were no real men like that in her old world. She blinked back tears.

She clenched her teeth as another jolt of pain hit hard. Damn, she wished with everything she was that she could just get to him. She was nervous more of the unknown and wanted to get through whatever they needed to and move on. Time was only making everything worse.

Wrenching pain racked at her mind and body, so strong that she doubled over. Shit, she panicked. It was so much worse, so fast. Damn it, Erik. She felt helpless, and the need to go to him was stronger than anything she'd ever felt in her life.

An odd sensation came over her then; it was as if she were breaking apart. Flying in wild abandon, a part of the air, but not. She followed a shining string into a sucking funnel. All she could do was hold onto that light.

Chapter 8

Lofodes, Tetartos Realm

Gregoire detoured home for weapons before teleporting into a fucking mess. He heard the alarms sounding in the city, up on the grassy rise, and felt a vein throb in his forehead. There had to be hundreds of damned hell beasts of all forms swarming the hills, trying to get up and into the breach in the city's protection spell. He started slicing through the closest beasts while the stench of sulfur burned his nose.

Gregoire spun and cut down one hellhound, then another, that had been trying to make it through the wall of soil blocking the lower hill from the city above. He was sure Adras and Ava were responsible for the wall of earth.

Looking to the sky, he saw Drake in flight, picking off the much smaller black hell dragons. His leader was impressive to behold. Huge wings of iridescent greens expanded as he clawed the creatures from the sky and ripped their heads off with powerful jaws and piercing teeth. Gregoire could hear wings flapping, the death screams of beasts and the calls of warriors all around and on the rise above. He cut down another hound that charged forward; black blood covered his leather fighting gear.

The fighting started to relax his needy body. He'd been so close to finally claiming his mate. The creatures would pay for this delay. He slashed his sword again, decapitating a smaller beast that thought to catch him off guard. He was surprised at just how many there were on the hill. This was the biggest attack the Tria had ever made. They usually sent the beasts a pack or two at a time in this Realm.

He saw Adras, Ava and their warriors surrounding and slicing away at an ofioeidis. The massive serpent was one of the more difficult hell beasts to kill. Fortunately, he didn't see any others further in the fray. The Guardians who patrolled Hell Realm spent most of their shift killing the damn creatures before the Tria could send them to other Realms. They were huge fucking snakelike monstrosities as tall as a man with painfully poisonous venom. They were fast as shit and strong. Add that to their regeneration skills, which were too damn fast, and they were the biggest pain in the ass of the demon Tria's arsenal. It looked as if Adras, Ava and their warriors had that one covered. Hippeus in half-warhorse form fought and reared. Brown and black flanks glistened as they struck at the snapping and slithering creature.

Just as Gregoire was about to move toward the city, the beast struck dangerously close to Ava. He teleported in and quickly cut off its tail. The intended distraction worked well. When it shot in his direction, Adras sent the final slice through the beast's neck, severing its head. He nodded tightly to Gregoire.

Gregoire was able to telepath across the short distance, *"Alyssa is safe and protected."*

Adras' shoulders relaxed with another quick nod. Gregoire knew his friend worried for his daughter. Alyssa was their only child, and Adras adored her. He blew out a frustrated breath.

The long barrier of earth rising up behind the mated pair seemed to be slowing the flow of beasts toward the city. He needed to get up there. With little thought, he cut down another hellhound, its head joining the rest of the carnage littering the ground.

He looked around. The warriors were fighting beasts everywhere, but no one seemed to be outnumbered. He needed to get into the city and help make sure the inhabitants were safe. It consisted of a predominately Mageia population and he hoped they'd had the sense to get inside when the alarms sounded.

Teleporting up to the city's breach, he saw Sacha and Bastian porting in and around the horde that was attempting to enter the city. The two Kairos Guardians were taking heads gracefully with their curved blades. Gregoire dove in and killed an ophiotaurus, severing both its horned, bull head and serpent tail. He had dodged and ported until the beast joined Sacha and Bastian's kills.

Adrenaline surged inside him, and his muscles flexed as he fought. He saw Sander fighting close by, just a little below the two Guardians trying to clear the breached area. Flames shot from the beasts toward his brother. The crazy fucker's laughter boomed as he took the flames into himself and spewed his own dangerously scorching ability back, easily incinerating the beasts. Screeches of dying creatures filled the air.

Gregoire downed a couple more of the beasts to get through the hole in the city's shielding, which was a good eight feet in width. Easily big enough for the larger animals to navigate. His strength and sharp blade made it easy to cut down the threat.

His frustration was biting, joining the burning of his flesh from the tainted blood. He was happy for the violence he was unleashing. It settled his cock, some. He had been so close to claiming her. He needed to make quick work of his duty and get back to the damn island.

He felt rage burning inside as he imagined her lips surrounding another male's cock. Red edged his sight as he cut down beast after beast. He didn't care that he was covered in the creatures' blood. His mind kept picturing those pouty lips, her big breasts out as she knelt in front of a faceless male. He roared in outrage, cutting down every beast in sight. She'd known she was his, but instead of finding him, she had gone straight to lose her fucking virginity. Went to give another male her sweet body.

He issued a battle roar as he surged up and around another fucking ophiotaurus. Those lips were his. That fucking tongue was his. If another male had slid inside her pussy and taken her innocence, he'd likely find and kill him. Her pleasure belonged to him.

He swiped a hand over his face. What the fuck was happening to him? He'd never felt so out of control in his life. He took several deep breaths to calm his beast and stop the ringing in his ears. He looked into the cobbled streets and found Uri and Alex fighting side by side as they beheaded more creatures running amuck in the city streets. A big grin painted Alex's features. Her long dark hair was caught in a ponytail that swung as she moved through the beasts. She looked to be enjoying herself, and she made a damn good warrior. Her antics were obviously not as endearing to Uri, who was taking care of her leavings with a tense jaw and shaking head. Gregoire ported further into the town.

Mageias were trying to fight the creatures, but they were causing more damage instead. Using their limited elemental abilities only angered the creatures, making them lash out at the buildings that the Mageias were fighting from. He blew out an annoyed breath. He just wished they would stop, but, damn, he had to give them some credit for fighting for what was theirs. At least he didn't see any of the damn mortals on the streets. They seemed to have all gone indoors and were using upstairs windows to forge their fight. The blaring alarms had done their job.

Gregoire watched as P flew above, midnight wings extended and flapping as the Guardian glided in the air above the city. He wore leather fighting pants, but his upper torso was bare except for his weapons harness. There appeared to be little more than twenty feet between him and the faint blue of the domed spell still holding above the city. At least the breach was relatively small and at the ground. If the dome had failed, hell dragons would have swarmed into the breach and made a fucking huge mess.

He found Brianne further inside the city as he cut through more beasts. Her titian hair was held back in a braid. Her earthy-colored wings fanned out behind her. She made deep swoops between buildings, where he saw smoke billowing. She was likely using her ability with air, dousing flames that had been started by the invading creatures. He caught sight of her diving into an alley to his side. She gracefully dodged a snake tail and lopped off the horned head of an ophiotaurus before issuing a triumphant battle cry and flying in the opposite direction.

He dispatched a few more hellhounds on his way to the back of the city, but it seemed the horde was thinning.

How is the fight in the city? We are almost wrapped up out here, Drake sent into the Guardian link.

Still cleaning up. If the Mageias would stop "helping," that would be great, P announced.

No fucking kidding. I've had to tell countless mortals they need to stay inside. Conn's tone said it all.

Bastian and Sacha will go in and help clear the city while the warriors, Sander and I work on the breach.

Heading in now, Sacha sent.

Gregoire dodged a venomous bite from another ophiotaurus as

the beast hunched its head low and attempted to gore him. He ported away, just missing the horns as well as the bite of the snake that made up the creature's tail. He landed a clean slice to the tail. The animal roared, its front hooves just missing him as it leapt in pain and rage; bucking, it spewed flame onto the nearest dwelling. A Mageia sent a ball of flame into the beast from the second story of the building. The Mageia was an old male and whooped when his flame found the creature's flank. The animal reared up in fury, and Gregoire dodged before making a sharp cut to its head. It fell in a heap next to the creature's body. He heard the excited yells from the aging mortal as Gregoire continued down the road to another hound, which he quickly dispatched.

Brianne, can you come douse a flame? he asked, sending her a visual of the old Mageia's home.

On my way.

He worked his way through more beasts until he met Conn and Dorian fighting a couple of tsouximo. The scorpion-like creatures were huge pains in the ass, courtesy of the Tria. Their armor was fucking tough. It generally took more than a few swipes of a good sharp blade to get through, all the while avoiding the lightning-quick stinger and thick, snapping claws.

Dorian and Conn were making quick work of their opponents, porting in and around the creatures without getting in each other's way. It was a kind of dance that only warriors who'd fought together for centuries managed. They each landed lash after lash with their long swords, hitting in exactly the same spot with each swipe of their blades.

Dorian's blue-tipped blond hair was wet. He had likely come directly from the sea. He was in leather fighting pants that hung low, but he hadn't bothered with a shirt, just threw a harness on for his sword. In his wilder years Dorian had fought in the rings, battling other Immortals for sport almost nightly after patrolling.

Dorian had just made another swift cut through the creature's armor when a young male Mageia came barreling around the corner. He was no more than a decade old and held a blade in his small hands. A hellhound pack bounded around the corner right behind the child. Gregoire ported over and began dispatching the hounds at the child's back while Dorian lunged for the boy. The sharp, deadly point of the stinger came down with lightning-quick speed. Dorian grabbed the child no more than a second before it would have pierced the kid's skin, killing him instantly. A door to one of the townhomes opened, and Dorian practically tossed the boy inside. Gregoire heard the relieved shouts of the Mageias in their second-floor windows.

Dorian quickly jumped back in to finish off his prey before moving to take care of another ophiotaurus as it bounded around another corner to join the fray. Conn finished with his creature, and they all stood for a moment. The three of them were covered in nasty tainted hell beast blood. Conn was in his usual flannel and jeans. His brother Guardian hadn't even taken time to don leathers. His amber eyes were glowing with the rush of the fight. Dorian looked just as wild eyed, and Gregoire felt the same. Sulfur stench clung to the air, and his skin stung. It was an irritating effect of demon-tainted blood. Only mildly annoying to a Guardian, but that would not be the case for the mortals. For them it could be deadly.

Brianne was in flight over the three of them, searching the streets from her higher vantage point and then communicating through the link. *P, everything clear on your side? It looks like everything is okay over here.*

P answered, *Bastian called dibs on the last tsouximo. I'm taking one final sweep now. There will be a fucking mess to clean up, but no flames that I can see.*

The breach was a pain in the ass. We're cinching shit up now. I want to know how this happened. Uri, get with Adras' people. Drake's voice echoed his anger. There was power even in his mental voice. Heads would roll for this. *Sirena, how many casualties?*

Three that I've confirmed. A dozen are in bad shape, and I'm working with some of the locals to get them taken care of. She sounded beyond incensed.

Shouts from above indicated that the streets were cleared. There would be major cleanup to contend with before he could get to his damn mate.

Tynan had better be looking after her and keeping his damned hands to himself.

Chapter 9

Cyril's Compound, Tetartos Realm

Cyril paced the confines of his new suite, awaiting news. His servants had cleaned and arranged everything for him, but it would never feel the same. He'd had the other facility for decades. He fumed that his father's bed had been reduced to rubble because of the Guardians' attack. It had been his most prized possession. The fools had taken that along with his test subjects. Just the thought of it all made him seethe. His muscles twitched with the strength of his anger.

It was impossible to get close to the bastards. If he was able to, he would make them pay personally, but the Guardians kept their dealings in Tetartos with only a select group mentally checked personally by the Aletheia Guardian, Urian. They were too damn cautious.

It grated that they'd yet to let their guard down in the centuries since he had managed to capture Dorian. The unconscious Guardian had only been in his grasp for minutes before the others had come for him. Cyril had underestimated their skills in tracking. He had assumed that Dorian's drugged state would render their tracking abilities useless. It was an assumption that Cyril constantly castigated himself for.

Two of his facilities were now in rubble because of them.

He looked around. His new cave system had been developed by

just a select few of his trusted warriors, centuries ago. It had done little but sit since its creation, meant as a backup only. Cyril had always kept his warriors and labs close. The only location that functioned separately was his eastern facility. There were things done there that he kept the majority of his people unaware of.

He was fortunate the lab tech that Drake had taken in the attack the week before had no knowledge of his current location or the other facility. He continued to pace, looking with anger at the new space. The more he considered the attack, the more concerned it made him. Not only had the Guardians found his facility after centuries, but they'd learned of his contact on Earth and had gone after her. It reeked of a mole. His most trusted warriors maintained that everything was secure. They had taken the blood memories of all his current staff and uncovered no traitor among them.

He had angrily instructed Elizabeth to use her ability to connect mentally with Cynthia, the Mageia contact. He had the bitch inform Cynthia to go into hiding amongst the billions of humans on Earth until he was able to sort out how the Guardians had found them both. Elizabeth, the rabid Aletheia who had been put under the control of his second, was subdued of late. Her quiet made him wonder what she was up to, or was it that Kane really was keeping her under tight wraps? If he didn't need her ability to contact the other Realms, he would have just killed her, but that was not possible. She had contacted and made it clear to Cynthia that she needed to hide and not risk being taken by the Guardians.

Cynthia had never been privy to much information, but she did know that he wanted to acquire Subject Nine's family, and he would rather that information not get into the Guardians' hands. She had not acquired them before the attack, so their abduction and testing would have to wait.

He needed to get back to his lab. There was something he was missing. He ground his teeth against the anger caused by losing Subject Nine to those bastards. At least he had secured all of his samples before the compound had been destroyed. At some point the Guardians would have to release the females into the covens on Tetartos; he would get her back when that happened.

Where was his fucking second? He wanted answers before he went to the lab. He had that irritating itch on the back of his neck he'd gotten every time he prepared to leave his suite. Paranoia was an infuriating emotion. He needed to leave his damn room to get to the lab, but every time he walked the tunnels, he found himself scrutinizing everyone that passed. He refused to let his rage and suspicion eat away at his sanity.

He continued pacing, impatiently awaiting Kane's arrival.

His door slid open, and Kane entered.

"Hell beasts are storming the city."

The news lightened his mood.

Cyril's plan had been truly exceptional. Getting the spell to breach the city's protection spell had been time consuming, but well worth the effort. Tipping off the Tria about an impending breach had been the true brilliance. As trial runs went, he was pleased. It hadn't risked any of his ranks, which had already suffered great losses against the Guardians. The next step in his plan was already set into motion. There was nothing the Guardians would be able to do to stop it. They would be too busy cleaning up the mess in Lofodes and trying to figure out how the city was breached.

"Go on."

"The Guardians and Immortal warriors have quickly slayed the Tria's beasts." Kane's silver eyes looked hard as he continued, "I do have some unpleasant news." He waited a breath before adding, "It seems that the Guardian Urian was mated to the daughter of Athena. The news is spreading through the cities as we speak."

The news settled like a bomb inside Cyril's stomach.

Cyril felt his blood heating. "How was I unaware that Athena had a daughter?"

"It's been said that she was sheltered away by her Goddess mother. No one knew about her. She'd been on Earth this whole time, avoiding exile."

A Guardian, mated? His vision blurred a deep crimson. Damn them, they already held too much power and now a mated pair? Cyril paced the confines of the chambers, balling and relaxing his fists at his sides. The fates were mocking him. The Guardian had not only gotten mated, but to a child of the Gods. Like him. He imagined all the power Urian was even now acquiring, and his teeth clamped tight. "Do you know what her abilities are?" he bit out.

"Nothing yet."

He needed to know what to expect from the horrendous situation. Athena was high in the mental skill sets, and she was a warrior. "Find out." Cyril noticed that Kane's muscles were tense.

"There's more?" Cyril knew there was more. Felt it.

"It seems information has come that could be to our advantage. Elizabeth had word from a contact that the Guardian Gregoire was seen on Paradeisos. He seemed interested in a female there. One that arrived separately from him. Gregoire left abruptly but demanded the owner protect her, personally."

Another mate? No, matings were far more rare than that.

It was still interesting in a way that made the hair on the back of Cyril's neck rise.

"Get one of the Kairos, and go collect the female." They took something of his; he would return the favor. She would become his new pet. His cock twitched at the thought of all of the ways he would ruin her.

Chapter 10

Paradeisos Island, Tetartos Realm

Gregoire had asked Tynan to watch over her, not take Alyssa and her friend on a fucking trip. He'd arrived expecting to find his mate in the room Tynan had given him a mental image of. Her scent was there, but she wasn't.

When he'd gone to his friend's suite and found it empty, he'd let himself in and was greeted with an envelope. It had been lying on the ground with a big G scrawled on it. He'd ripped the paper to shreds in his annoyance to get to the contents. His muscles had tensed as he read.

Old Friend,

I have taken the females out on my boat for the day. They will be safe. My staff was kept unaware that they would be accompanying me. Only my personal assistant knows that I have taken the boat out. We will be back at dusk. Whiskey's out on the bar.

T

So he'd sat impatiently drinking his friend's whiskey and listening to the waves washing over the sand. His cock seemed in no better shape after imbibing the prized spirits. His damn muscles still twitched with tension, and he felt the uncomfortable feeling that something or someone was out there. He'd checked and seen nothing.

He'd gotten the same feeling at the Guardian meeting he'd been forced to endure before telling his brethren he needed to leave and claim his mate. They'd been shocked, but he hadn't stayed long enough to chat. The report said that three Mageia had died and several others were injured. Conn was trying to figure out the spell used to breach the city, and Alex and Uri were working with Adras and his people to figure out who was responsible and interrogate the suspects. It was a clusterfuck and not the best timing for him to be gone, but he didn't care. He wanted his mate, needed to claim her.

He heard the soft trill of feminine laughter and then a loud bellow of mirth and knew the sound came from Tynan. He shot out of his seat and watched as they walked along the path. They all wore bathing suits, and his mate's breasts were barely contained in their rose-colored prison.

His eyes narrowed at the small scrap of fabric, and he growled low. He couldn't wait to rip the material off to expose her to his eyes and mouth. He took a deep breath, detecting her citrus and cream scent mixed with a hint of salt water. The breeze shifted, and he caught the tightening of her muscles a second before her gaze darted to him. Even from twenty feet away he heard her gasp his name before something flashed in her eyes. Pain? Anger?

He frowned.

Before he could do anything, he caught shifting movement. A male Aletheia darted through a gap in the shrubbery and quickly tackled Tynan. The element of surprise was the only advantage against his old friend. Fury ripped through Gregoire as another came into view, appearing directly behind Alyssa. Kairos. Too fucking fast his mate darted into the fray to assist Tynan, unwittingly saving herself from the other male's grasp.

Fury riding him, Gregoire immediately ported to Alyssa, grabbing her from behind, ensuring the Kairos wouldn't be able to teleport her away unless he planned on taking Gregoire with them. That initial contact of her smooth skin against his palm was like an electrical charge and he knew she'd felt it too.

The touch and scent of her skin instantly drove his cock to new heights of painful need. He held her tight to his side, but she seemed focused on Tynan even though her breathing kicked up at his touch and he could already sense the rising heat from the frenzy that would soon control them. Off to the side, Rain kicked at the Kairos' knee, calling attention to herself, and if the little Mageia wasn't careful, she'd be taken.

He felt Alyssa pulling power and pushing it at his friend's attacker with a force of wind so strong the male's body was launched off Tynan and slammed hard against the wall of a bungalow.

There was a hard crunching sound as his skull impacted with the stucco. What the hell had happened on that damn boat to make her so damn protective of Tynan?

He narrowed his eyes, that familiar red tinge almost blinding him as he glared at his friend, who looked angry as hell. Tynan launched up and grabbed a furious Rain against him, ensuring the Kairos couldn't port the Mageia away without taking Tynan as well.

The teleporter only seemed interested in Gregoire's fucking female and glared in Alyssa's direction before porting to the fallen Aletheia, and then they were both gone.

"How the fuck did they know?" he growled, looking at Tynan furiously. Logic was gone.

91

His friend's jaw was also tight, eyes flashing and nearly as livid. Gregoire couldn't remember the last time he'd seen his friend that angry. "I don't know, but I have an idea. I have a couple of people to talk to."

Before the male could release Rain and leave to interrogate whoever the fuck he assumed was responsible, Gregoire stopped him, gritting out, "Not yet."

Gregoire still had a firm grip on Alyssa's trim waist, and his breathing was rough. Hers was ragged as well as he held her against his hard body. He couldn't help but turn her, pleased with her soft gasp as he lifted her against him. He wanted to bury his head in her neck, her pussy. Her scent was fucking intoxicating. He smelled her desire, and his cock swelled thicker than should be possible. Her new position crushed her beautiful tits against his chest and she wrapped her bare legs around his waist.

Fuck. He snarled deep as he felt her pussy settle against his rock-hard cock. Her pale green eyes were slightly wide, and she was fighting for breath as she narrowed her gaze defiantly at him. Something about that look set him off.

He grasped Rain's hand while holding his tiny mate's ass with the other. The Mageia was still attached to Tynan, so he ported them all away. His brothers needed to investigate what the fuck happened because he was in no position to think.

The group landed on the balcony of the manor, and he let go of Rain's hand before opening the door that was spelled to sound an alarm if opened by someone not magically keyed to it.

He barely heard Rain and Tynan groaning. "A little warning would have been nice," Rain grumbled under her breath. Most struggled with porting until they got used to it, and traveling with a

Guardian was even faster than teleporting with a Kairos.

Gregoire's entire focus was on his female and he was nearly feral by the time they entered the media room. He struggled to handle whatever the fuck had just happened. He'd never melded with anyone while he teleported, but it felt like that was exactly what had happened with his mate. He could still feel the sensation of her in his skin. He clasped both hands onto Alyssa's tight ass.

"Mine," he growled against her ear before burying his head in her neck, licking her sweet-tasting skin. He ground his erection into her core and heard a small gasp and low moan as she rubbed her barely covered tits against his chest. He looked down at the full mounds pressed tight against him. She was hot and aroused as his fingers caressed the soft, smooth skin of her ass; his palms spanned each firm cheek, she was so fucking tiny. He'd need to be fucking careful not to break her when he finally buried his cock deep.

Concentration on anything but his mate proved nearly impossible. She leaned up and bit his lower lip. "I don't belong to anyone." Her challenging words hit him hard. His grip on her ass tightened, and he rubbed her pussy up his shaft until she tilted her head and bit his neck before licking away the sting.

He needed to get things straight here before he took her hard and deep right against the fucking wall so that everyone could see she was his. *Drake, my mate was almost taken. Likely Cyril. Come to the media room. Talk to Tynan, and have someone watch over my female's friend.*

His head buzzed with need. He scented the arousal seeping from her body, and he turned her into the nearest wall, pinned her back and ripped the tie from her hair. He fisted the long chestnut waves, tilting her for his lips. She moaned and opened for him. He plunged inside and took her tongue with his, tangling them as he bumped his hips against her sweet spot. He savored her every bit of sweetness as their tongues dueled. He slid a hand back to her firm little ass. She was trying to ride his cock, and that was exactly how he wanted her. Hot and demanding her pleasure while their friends watched her writhe.

All for him.

Her hands ran along his biceps and shoulders, her sharp nails biting into his flesh. He growled his approval as she attempted to pull him closer.

He moved a hand lower, sliding his fingers beneath the thin material of her swimsuit. He groaned when he hit liquid paradise. She made a soft noise into his mouth as he lifted her higher so that he could dip one digit into her throbbing pussy. Fucking amazing. She was so hot, wet and tight it would be a struggle getting inside. He could feel her innocence and nearly ripped her clothes off and impaled her immediately. Her channel would squeeze him harder than anything he'd ever felt. He almost came at the thought of her untried pussy milking his dick.

His body caged her tight to the wall as his fingers spread her desire all around her opening. He broke the kiss to see her face flushed and eyes glazed for him. His gaze found those big full tits. He wanted to see them, now. He pulled one tiny triangle aside, revealing a taut nipple, dusky and hard, just begging for his mouth. "This is all mine. No one will ever touch these again." He flicked at her nipple while at the same time delving into her pussy with his other hand. Her thighs tightened around him; her pale eyes closed as she moaned. She was so fucking wet.

"Your pussy knows who it belongs to, little one. It's soaking my fingers. Soon all this liquid will be around my dick."

"It's just sex. I belong to *no one*."

Her words hit all of his buttons. His beast was beating at him to prove her wrong, rip off the fabric still covering her and claim her right there while the others watched. He wouldn't, not the first time, but he wanted Tynan and Rain to hear her scream as she came all over his hand. He thrust a finger into her while playing with her uncovered breast. She rode her clit over his denim-covered shaft as he played with her. She was beautiful and wild. He wouldn't be able to keep his dick locked down for long. Her wiggling was driving him mad. "Open your eyes. I want you to see who owns this pussy."

Her moans were getting more heated as they moved together. Her hands moved to his hair, pulling and scratching at his scalp before moving over his back and trying to lift up his shirt.

"Holy shit. That's freaking hot." Rain's groaned words, along with Tynan's whispered response, brought him back to himself long enough to realize how big a bastard he was being, but it didn't stop his thrusting finger. He loved how fucking ready she was. He could bathe in her liquid. He salivated with the need to taste her, to thrust his tongue inside and lap up all the honey.

"What the fucking hell?" Drake bellowed a second later.

Gregoire turned his head and saw his leader standing just inside the room, staring at them. He slid his finger from her body. He was no longer content with her gasps and moans.

He needed to be deep inside her when she came the first time. He ignored Drake and the others as he carried her onto the balcony. He planned to lay her out as a banquet and not let her move for days. There would be no doubt as to who she belonged to. She was better than any fantasy he'd ever conjured, and she was his.

95

Chapter 11

Gregoire's Home, Tetartos Realm

They reformed in front of a big home that looked to be set half inside the mountain behind it. It took a few breaths for Alyssa's body to adjust to being whole again. She was panting, her body clamoring for release.

The desire was consuming her whole. Why did their bodies mesh during a teleport? Her body's essence was itching for another taste of his. It was the strongest pull she had ever felt for anything, ever. She had nearly lost her mind the first time, had tried to prepare the second time, but nothing could fight against the need.

She barely registered her surroundings. The sound of his booted feet was loud on the wood deck, and she bit the inside of her cheek so hard she nearly drew blood. The throbbing need was driving her insane. Fighting against it so that she didn't fall completely in his thrall wasn't apparently an option. He was so damn beautiful, and he smelled like heaven. She wanted to snuggle into his chest and neck, but she refused to show that kind of affection for him. There was no going back from the mating, but she could hold out that one small thing.

She closed her eyes, thinking she'd been so wild with need she'd almost let him screw her up against the wall while Rain and Tynan watched.

Her mother had told her that when she met her destined mate, it would be uncontrollable, that the passion would overtake her, and she hadn't been kidding. She wanted him inside her with a desperation that edged on lunacy. She didn't even know him. He hadn't even wanted to claim her before. Why come for her now, and how screwed up was it that she could do nothing but allow it? His rejection had left her cut open, but her body and beast half didn't give a damn how he'd hurt her. The second he'd touched her, all options were lost. They had to sate the need or it would drive them both insane.

Thankfully, her mother had explained the mental links between mated pairs. The minute she'd registered hearing his thoughts, she'd created a shield for her mind. If her mother hadn't explained, she would have been laid wide open for him. No way in hell was he going to see just how his rejection had affected her.

His dominant and hot thoughts had driven her wild in that room. Hearing how he wanted to make her scream her release as the others watched nearly made her whimper.

She had only gotten bits and pieces of his thoughts and impressions, but that had been so primal she almost begged him for release.

She felt so much heat from him as he carried her. She couldn't help inhaling his delicious scent. Hard, hot male, but with an earthy hint. She knew he would take her in minutes. Her body couldn't wait for his possession, but she would never be his completely until he atoned for the pain he'd caused. She fully intended to keep her heart her own.

He carried her into the gorgeous home. Glass windows covered the front, and log beams formed a high peak and were visible in the ceiling. It was brighter wherever they were. Midday, maybe. The setting would likely feel tranquil, peaceful if she wasn't in such needy

97

turmoil. The sounds of birds fluttering and singing in trees cut off once he carried her inside.

Seconds later he bounded up the stairs and laid her out on the soft dark bedding of an oak four-poster bed that had obviously been built for his size. She could see over a spindled railing out to the two stories of glass that encompassed the front of the home. There were exposed wood beams inside that matched the floors adorned with cozy rugs. It was his home, his scent was everywhere, making her pant, dying to see if he tasted as good as he smelled.

He stared at her from the side of the bed. His shirt came off with slow deliberation, revealing a chest wider and more muscular than any of the male Hippeus she'd ever encountered. The muscled expanse twitched as he watched her. "Take off the swimsuit, Alyssa. I want to see everything."

She groaned at his heated demand and the use of her name. She wanted him because of the damn frenzy, but she really needed to set some ground rules, or the gorgeous ass was bound to think he could run her life. She was breathless with the effect his words had on her. Why did he have to be so magnificent? His eyes were the color of wet leaves in a forest. His brown hair held a tinge of red, and the short beard somehow made him more beautifully male.

He was practically a god to their people, and the old her would have been a little awestruck, easily submitting to his demands. She'd have accepted that this was the way of their world, but the new Alyssa was nobody's doormat. She refused to kowtow to him. She called on the anger and hurt he'd caused and spoke. "I'll do this to feed the frenzy, but the demands end there; do you understand me?"

The big ass raised one dark brow at her, and she swore his lips twitched. Was he laughing at her? He unbuttoned his jeans, and her mouth went dry as she focused on what he revealed.

"Take the suit off, or I rip it off."

She let out a puff of breath. He was so damn huge. Bigger than Kerr and Calder had been. His cock was hard and thick and throbbing high against his taut stomach.

That voice, so deep and seductive, sent gooseflesh rippling over her skin. His eyes were on her face, tracking down to her breasts. If she didn't like the bathing suit so much, she might have let him rip it from her body. The visual was intense. Her breathing was ragged and her hands shook with the intensity of the need flowing in her veins. While he deliberately shucked his shoes, socks and jeans, she pulled the tie behind her head and the one at her back. She'd forgotten that he'd already exposed one of her breasts. She watched his eyes track her hands as she tossed her top aside, and she felt better knowing he was just as needy as she was. The bottoms were next, revealing her newly waxed mound to his gaze.

His eyes heated and then narrowed. "How many?" The words came out dangerously low.

What was he asking? "How many what?"

"How many have tasted your sweet bare pussy?"

Her breath stuttered. He knew what she'd been doing on the island? Was he jealous? She liked the idea of that so much she answered honestly. "Three."

He growled as he crawled onto the bed with her. "No more. No one but me will ever touch you again; do you understand?" His hand trailed up her hip, and she lost whatever response she had. "Spread your thighs wide. I want to see every inch of smooth wet cunt. Every inch that belongs to me."

His deep voice rocked her to the core, and his demands made her ache for his possession. She did as he said, completely out of control. Her skin was oversensitive, and her womb hurt with the need he'd caused. At the island she'd learned that a lot of the races' males were dominant and how that could play out. She had been aroused by it then, but it was on a completely different level with the big male touching her; he wasn't just sexually dominant, he wanted to own her soul. She felt it. He might have closed his thoughts to her, but his feral possessiveness shone bright in his green eyes.

His chest was rising and falling nearly as rapidly as hers. "You fucking smell so damn good. I want to lick up every bit of sweet honey, but you'll need it to take my cock." He bent low, his shoulders crowding inside her legs. He surprised her by catching her thighs with his thick arms, bending them up and back, trapping her with his chest on her stomach, leveling his lips with her nipples. His skin was hot against hers, and she was tilted so that she was slicking the muscled planes of his stomach.

His beard abraded her skin as he nipped at a sensitive nubbin. She gasped and moaned as his tongue flicked out to dampen and soothe the sting. His hot breath wafted over her wet skin. Her back bowed, and he gave her more of his weight. "You're so fucking wet for me, and my skin bears the mark and I fucking love it."

He took his time devouring her breasts. Flicking and licking them as he watched her; then he closed his eyes and sucked deep on her flesh. First one, then the other was treated to the same hot suckling that was bringing her closer to orgasm. She could feel it building as she whimpered in need. Her skin tingled as she tried to move her hips against him. She needed friction against her clit. Desperation was making her ache. Her cries became more frantic as he teased her, backing off every time she thought she'd finally come with just his scorching mouth on her breasts. His abdomen applied just enough pressure to make her throb, keeping her on edge.

"Not without my cock."

"Dammit, let me come." She was flushed and panting. She couldn't take any more torture and could already feel this would be the most intense orgasm of her life.

He looked up at her. His eyes narrowed. "You've never taken a cock."

Her face heated, but he hadn't stated it as a question. All she could do was shake her head. His forest eyes glittered with pure male satisfaction… only far more intense.

"Then, angel, you need to be begging before you'll be able to take me."

She didn't like that his calling her "angel" sent shivers up her spine.

He slid his body down hers, coating his stomach and chest with her desire. Her breath caught as the friction left her panting. It was so hot. He buried his face in her slick flesh. Thick fingers gripped her ass, and she gulped in huge breaths as she writhed and pushed her hips against his face. She would surely die if he denied her again.

"You have to let me come. I can't take any more. I can take you." She wasn't entirely sure that she was telling the truth, but she just didn't care. He was killing her.

He lapped up her cream as he held her gaze. He looked more like a godly beast than a Guardian.

"I could spend days between your thighs. I've never tasted anything so sweet." He leaned down and dipped his tongue back into her fluid, keeping her on a knife's edge.

He moved a hand from her ass and pushed a digit just inside her until she keened for more. "You're sucking my finger, and I can feel the barrier that says you're all fucking mine." His shoulders heaved, and she knew in that moment that he had been torturing them both by making her wait.

He lifted up and leaned over her, devouring her lips until they were swollen and wet, using his tongue in a way that made her writhe. She tasted her need on his lips and loved it, and then he moved again.

Sitting on his knees, he trailed his eyes over her body. His sinew was flexed, and his eyes were glazed with hunger. She watched through lowered lids as he grabbed his huge shaft to guide it slowly into her opening. Tendons stood out on his neck as the thick tip notched at her opening. All she could hear was the pulsing in her head and their heavy breathing as he stilled. She pushed against him, needing him deep, wanting the climax that was waiting to take her over. She felt every nerve ending tune to him.

The odd whirling inside her body became insistent, demanding. Before the sensation had blended with her arousal, but now it pulsed inside her. It was her life force reaching for his. That knowledge made her whimper, her nails scratching at his straining forearms as she tried to pull him toward her. "More, I need more."

He half-groaned, half-growled at her demand, then gripped her hips and filled her hard and fast. Her back bowed off the bed with the sheer force of his entry. She felt a sharp sting that took her breath. He paused, and just as fast the sensation passed, leaving only the feeling of being deliciously full. Possessed. It felt right on an almost frightening level. She refused to let the fairy tale back into her life.

This was nothing more than scratching a biological itch right now. Her stomach clenched. She couldn't believe the intense feeling of intimacy along with the desperate need to come. She shook off all other thought but the pleasure she sought. It had to be the mating making her feel such strong emotion. Her walls stretched around his cock, cradling him deep.

"Breathe, Alyssa. You can take all of me."

A little surprised, she looked down to where they were joined. She was sure she'd taken all there was to take; how could she fit any more? She felt him throbbing deep inside and gasped as her passage clamped down. She heard his sharp intake of breath as she fought for her own. Her body already ached with a pleasure so deep she felt lost in it. His shoulders and every inch of his rigid torso appeared racked with tension, and she thrilled at the sight of it. When she relaxed her muscles and pushed against him, his cock throbbed again, caressing her so deep she moaned. Her heels dug into the soft bedding as she attempted to force him to take her harder. He stilled her hips with a hand and a fierce, almost pained look before slowly inching further inside until she could feel his pelvis against her bare mound. "You grasp me so damn tight. Your pussy is so hot, so fucking perfect." His words and the potent feeling of being claimed pushed her to stir again. Harder. He growled as she fought to maneuver beneath his body.

"I need you to move," she growled right back.

Forest eyes grew heavy as he clenched his jaw tight and pulled out to push back in, slowly. Too slowly. She needed something more, damn him. She wiggled, and her chest heaved as wildness assailed her.

She needed him to take her hard. He paused as his intense gaze grew sharp and primal, assessing. Before she knew his intent, she was flipped to her stomach and entered forcefully from behind. Her fingers dug into the soft blankets; he felt even bigger now. She was so full and aching with need that she cried out for more. She tried to rear back as he began covering her with his weight. Flipping her hair to one side, he licked and nipped at her exposed skin as one big hand skimmed her hip and the side of her breast.

His massive body settled fully against her, blanketing every inch of her under his massive bulk as he moved in torturously slow thrusts. She attempted to buck under his weight, fighting for more, wanting him to move so much faster, but he was too strong. She couldn't take his measured strokes. She needed release and her beast half impelled her to fight for more.

His hands covered hers, big warm fingers twined with her smaller ones, pushing them into the bedding at her sides, holding her immobile, pleasing the animal.

Her breasts were pressed into the surface, her body trapped tight and forced to submit to whatever pace he set. His hips moved and circled behind her and her breath sawed out as she nearly climaxed from the sheer eroticism of the experience. He held her everywhere, from big strong hands to the hot tongue against her shoulder and neck. He'd plastered his muscular torso against her bare back and bottom as his cock thrust all the way inside her pussy. She went wild beneath him. The need to come was driving her crazy. Her juices flowed around him, coating him. Her strength didn't match his, but it didn't matter.

"That's it. Fight me, fight for what you need, Alyssa. Fight for what my cock can give you."

Her mind stopped working at the words said low against her ear. Shivers ran over her flesh, and she used all of her strength and will to take him deeper, pushing and sliding under him. She slammed back against his hold, fought to take him further, harder until he groaned and thrust deep, finally giving her what she so desperately needed. He shifted and sank his teeth into her shoulder, and she came unglued. Crying out in pleasure, she fought him as his motions grew more and more forceful. His big body demanded everything as he shafted deep, filling up every last inch of her channel until he hit a spot hidden so far inside her that it sent her soaring into ecstasy. Her vision blurred as she gasped for air.

He continued to take her hard, hitting the same sensitive area. She screamed as another orgasm hit; her passage pulsed and throbbed around him as he relentlessly thrust. His hot breath on her skin and low masculine groans drove her as she wiggled beneath him. He pushed deep, and she heard a harsh grunt as his warm come bathed her channel.

The sense of rightness was unsettling. She didn't want to contemplate how his claiming had affected her. Didn't dare think about how he'd made her feel while holding her down and demanding she fight for her release.

Her eyes grew heavy as she allowed herself to enjoy his solid warmth against her back. Just for a moment. She was too wrung out to move.

"Sleep now." He spoke the words softly, then lightly kissed the side of her eye. The sensation sent tingles through her. How could he be such a demanding ass one moment and so sweet the next? She didn't have the energy to ponder anything heavy, so she didn't. His big body rolled to the side, taking her with him. The heavy weight of his palm settled over her breast and pulled her to snuggle into his warmth as she drifted off.

Chapter 12

Gregoire's Home, Tetartos Realm

Alyssa hadn't moved from the spot where she'd fallen asleep over an hour before. Gregoire spent a good part of that time holding her, and then he'd decided he had to look at her. Her little nose was cute and pert; long lashes fanned her tanned cheek. She looked so incredibly young, but she was definitely fully grown. He rubbed the side of his jaw.

His beast ached for him to take her again, thrilled at her wild spirit mixed with the sweet innocence he'd claimed. His cock twitched remembering just how snug she was. She'd taken him in, squeezing the entire way, and then pushed that sweet little ass back for more. Everything about her was flawless. He used the blanket to cover her skin against the chilled air, even though he'd wanted to continue looking at her incredible breasts. Her little ass was also perfect, it curved just right for his hands, but those damn tits were a mouthwatering buffet. She was everything he had dreamt she would be. Even untried, she'd fought him. His beast had needed to feel that struggle, that fierceness from its mate.

The rightness of it settled deep and eased part of his soul. At the same time he felt disconcerted by all the newly raging emotions. She'd always carried the potential to unleash a part of him that he wasn't sure should be allowed free, but it was loose now, and there was no going back.

He felt a deep pulsing inside. He knew it was their life forces mingling and pushing to meld. They needed to complete the mating. Until that happened, they'd continue to feel the drive.

Gregoire leaned in and tucked a strand of hair behind her ear, and she moaned lightly and rubbed her face against the bedding. He was entranced by the small movement. Leaning his hands on his knees, he watched her sleepy movements. She was his. His to care for and protect.

Finally.

He scrubbed his hands over his cheeks.

Drake, what did you find in Paradeisos? Is someone watching my mate's friend?

Rain is fine. Tynan had a suspect in mind, which made things easier on the island. It seemed one of the females sharing his bed saw and heard a conversation you had with him before the breach in Lofodes. She's in holding now. Uri and Alex are going through her memories and trying to discern if there's a way to find Elizabeth and Cyril through her. Cyril has people apparently spreading news that he is working to help atone for his father's madness by finding a way around the Mating Curse.

Son of a bitch. Gregoire did not like the way things were heading. This could be disastrous. If Immortals and Mageias went to Cyril for aid, they would be strengthening the bastard's

107

ranks. Matings equaled power to the asshole and he'd exploit the desires of others to get what he wanted.

How is your mate?

Asleep. I'd like you to keep her friend there. She and my mate are close. If Cyril has spies out there, he'll have that information. I don't want her harmed or taken as a way to get to Alyssa.

I'd already come to the same conclusion after talking with her. She's got a room in the manor now. I'll likely have to relocate Rain's entire fucking family. Uri will need to check their minds and make sure they are not a threat first. What of your mate's parents?

Adras and Ava. Gregoire waited for the boom to drop.

I could tell from her scent. You've known for some time, then? Drake growled through the link. He was not one for secrets. *First Uri housing a hellhound on Earth, now you hiding that you had a damned mate?*

Gregoire gritted out, *It was fucking complicated. I wanted her to grow up as normally as possible. And if you'd known about her, I would have gotten constant demands to claim her from the moment she reached majority.*

So sure that is what I would have done?

I was too dominant a male to take an innocent just out of her majority. I could easily have taken her over. I knew my instincts would be harsh and that's a damned understatement. She needed time to come into her own. Adras needed it, too.

108

I get your reasons. I even agree with them. I just wish that my warriors didn't hide shit from me. Drake's mental voice reeked of irritation.

I fucked up.

You were just fortunate Cyril didn't find out about her sooner, brother. The female at Tynan's didn't seem to think Alyssa was more than a plaything for you, but that's likely because no one would ever imagine a Guardian not immediately claiming a fucking mate.

Drake's words grated. He and her parents had been careful, but the thought of Cyril getting his hands on Alyssa made him want to destroy something. Alyssa made a sound in her sleep that forced his attention back to her beautiful face, and the rage settled. She had such an incomprehensible effect on him.

Get the damn mating ceremony done, soon, before Sirena drives me out of my fucking mind. You dropped the bomb that you were leaving to claim a fucking mate and left me with Sirena's excited questions.

I've spent two and a half decades in fucking hell. Tell Sirena to wait. I need time with my mate.

Chapter 13

Private Villa, Tetartos Realm

Dizziness assailed Sam as her body rematerialized. She fell to her knees, fighting the urge to vomit. One moment she was in a million pieces, the next she was somewhere else. It was a different balcony, the air slightly humid instead of crisp and cool. She heard monkeys calling out and birds flitting in the trees. She smelled salty ocean air.

She had definitely teleported. What the fuck?

Taking deep breaths saved her from getting sick, but standing on her shaking legs was a chore. She felt sharp pains in her stomach and head, and it was only getting worse. Touching the door handle, she found it open and let herself inside. How did this happen; how was she able to teleport? It had to be something to do with her connection to Erik. Whatever it was, she was thankful for it, knowing deep inside that he was there.

She entered onto tiled floors. The spacious bedroom was complete with sitting area and raised four-poster bed of what looked like bamboo, but no Erik. She could hear the sound of water running in what had to be an adjoining bath. Pain hit her like a punch to the gut as she quickly entered the bathroom, praying that she was right and Erik was in there. Her heart pounded in her chest. If it hammered any harder, she'd have a heart attack. She moved inside to the stone shower enclosure.

Steam filtered in her nose as she looked inside the opening. It looked big enough for several people to wash without ever touching.

Her breath left in a harsh rush at the sight of him leaning his forehead against the wall. He was beyond beautiful. Water streamed down the taut muscles of his big back. His powerful frame looked incredibly tense as he braced a hand against the wall. His other hand disappeared in front of his hips, and she imagined him stroking his thick shaft.

"You need to go." He wasn't even looking at her but had known she was there. His deep voice resonated with pain she knew he was attempting to hide from her. It was ridiculous. She moved closer. "Sam, don't force me to be a monster. I'm too close to the edge. I need to feel you wrapped around me, but it's too dangerous."

He was in agony. She felt it in their bond, even though he was trying to keep it from her. It was stronger now that she was so close. They needed to do this now. Her heart stuttered, but she wanted him, ached for him. Just the sight of him made her skin heat and her desire flow.

She needed to think, damn it. "Can you contact Vane?" She had an idea, but she wasn't sure he'd be thrilled.

Erik growled low. "Why do you want my brother?"

His growled words trilled inside her body. Everything about him set her off. She closed her eyes against the sight of his broad muscled shoulders and mouthwatering ass, forced away the sight of liquid flowing in rivers down his back. Her breathing was accelerating to panting levels. She wanted to lap up every last drop.

He groaned. "Tell me that was for me, not my fucking brother." He obviously wasn't hearing her thoughts, but it appeared he was getting her emotions.

111

She cleared her throat. "It was for you. Can you get Vane here now? We need his help for my plan to work."

"What plan?"

Shit, was he really going to question everything? "Get him here, and you'll find out." She growled a little of her own.

He groaned deep, and she saw his shoulders shudder. Oh shit. They might not make it, and that could be bad. Vane was right. Erik would never forgive himself if he hurt her with all the immense strength she knew lay inside him.

"What the fuck, Sam? How the hell did you get here?" Vane was fast. His perfect blond hair looked ruffled, and his furrowed brows showed just how incensed and worried he was.

"I need you to get me something to bind him. Is there anything that would work to hold him on that bed?"

Erik turned around slowly. Wet strands of hair fell over his forehead as those gorgeous icy eyes looked at her. Oh, God, those piercing blue eyes held dark dangerous need. Her pussy throbbed in response.

"Now, Vane." Before they ran out of time.

"Shit." Vane looked at his brother. Ran his fingers through his hair as if he was torn. "I'll be right back."

Moments passed as Sam and Erik just stared at one another. Both tense and breathing hard. His cock looked painfully rigid, and she knew just how much he needed her. His gaze burned over every inch of her body. "You need to go, Sam. Chaining me will keep me from hurting you, but what of your memories?" The words were said so low and deep that with the sound of the water, she nearly missed them. Her stomach and heart clenched with deep emotion at his words.

Her chin rose. "Why don't you let me worry about that?" She blew out a breath she hadn't realized she'd held. "Please don't make this harder. The pain is only going to get worse. Sirena said it will start affecting your mind. We need to take care of this before that happens. Putting you to sleep before didn't slow the frenzy's progression, it just delayed it, and I know you're hurting. I can *feel* it." She could tell he wanted to argue with her, so she stopped it with her next words. "The fact that I'll be in control will help. Please don't fight me. It's becoming painful for me too."

It was low, but she hoped to use his damn protective instincts to their advantage. She hadn't really been lying. Her abdomen had been getting pangs the closer she'd gotten to him. Nothing like what slipped through their bond, and she didn't care about her pain as much as she cared about his right now.

His chin dipped to his chest and she knew he was wavering.

His jaw finally locked down tight and he nodded. She'd won.

His massive chest was still heaving with pained arousal, his cock huge and dark. She could see it throb against his stomach.

She returned his nod and took a deep breath. It was time she took back ownership of her body.

With him.

Erik turned off the water and grabbed a towel that had been flung over the stone wall partially enclosing the shower. "Vane said he put everything in the room. I don't like this, Sam." His voice was rough.

"Do it for me," she murmured.

Every muscle flexed with the grace of an animal as he stalked into the room. Metal cuffs were attached to a thick chain that latched onto metal rings she saw under the bed. She wouldn't question why the Guardian called Jax needed those in his guest home.

What she was planning now would be the only reason to need such a feature. It was unreal for her; she'd never done anything remotely like what she was doing to him. He lay on his back, arms and legs spread for her, his jaw tight. "Do it fast. Vane is going to stay outside the door in case something happens. I don't trust myself not to break the damn chains. You need to call to him if that happens."

He closed his eyes, and his tight muscles twitched with the effort he used to hold back. She moved quickly to secure him. It was slowly turning to dusk, but light still came through the curtains at the balcony door. Her face heated knowing Vane was just outside. A big ceiling fan whipped around, stirring the air in the room and helping cool her embarrassment.

She undressed quickly, leaving her jeans, tank and delicate blue underthings in a pile before climbing onto the bed.

His eyes were open but heavy lidded. "I want to taste you first. Make sure you're ready for me."

Her skin tingled at the huskiness in his voice. Did he really want her to bring her pussy up to his face? Her womb clenched remembering how skilled he was with his mouth. She nearly moaned.

"I can feel how that excites you. You taste so damn good. Bring that sweet pussy up to my lips, Sam." His lids were so low she could only see a sliver of crystal blue shining through.

114

She crawled up to his side, not quite bold enough to do as he asked. She was wet and ready, and the situation had gone past the point of foreplay. She really wanted to take him into her mouth, wanted to lick and suck at each dip and ridge of his delicious torso. Take her time with the beautiful man laid out for anything she wanted to do. He was not the type of guy that would let a girl tie him up, she knew that instinctually. This was a unique situation that she imagined no other woman had ever experienced with him and she really liked that. She shook her head; they needed fast this time.

"There isn't time. I'm ready." She heard him growl low. Sirena said they would need to do this often to stave off the pain. There would be plenty of time to experiment later. She was a little dizzy; something deeper than arousal was rippling under her skin. He watched with the eyes of a predator as she slid a leg over his hip, settling herself over his hot erection. She hoped that being in control would stop the memories. Only time would take the shame, but she'd already made leaps in the right direction. She planned to lose herself in the deep, piercing arousal, let instinct take her away, just like Sirena had instructed. She wanted this, could do this.

She bit her lip as she grasped his thick cock in one hand and guided him in. He was so big and hot. Bigger than any she had ever seen, much less attempted to take inside her body. She circled herself on his hot shaft, drenching him with her need, getting off on the silky feel of him. She moaned as his hips pushed up reflexively. She could see his pulse beat at his neck. His jaw was clenched so tight she swore she heard teeth grinding. He'd shut his eyes tight, and she mourned the loss of the sight of those stunning eyes, so incredibly hot and intent on her. She pushed down hard to take him all, but it was such a tight fit, she couldn't accommodate everything.

He moaned and bucked only a fraction as she worked her pussy up and down. She felt every delicious ridge as she leaned over him for a better angle. Hell, it was so good. She'd never felt anything close to how he felt inside her. Maybe that explained why she hadn't enjoyed sex all that much, never climaxing unless she'd taken care of matters herself.

Her body was made for him; it was a silly romantic thought, but somehow it felt right. Her channel throbbed around him. Both were panting by the time she settled all the way down.

Her breasts brushed against his chest. They were not overly large but tended to be incredibly sensitive. She couldn't help but rub them over the smattering of masculine hair. She kissed the hard tendons at his neck because that, too, was more than she could resist.

"Play with those hard nipples for me."

Leaning up, she saw his lids half open and completely focused on her. Mesmerized, she brought her body up and did as he demanded. She heard his pained groan and felt his big frame shake beneath her. She lifted up and started stroking herself up and down his shaft while plumping her breasts and pinching the tight buds. The way he looked at her was if she were the most incredible thing he'd ever seen and it ignited her.

"That's it. Work that wet pussy on my cock."

She pulsed around him, was close, the pleasure so deep it drew gasps from her lips. Beads of sweat were pebbled on his chest, and his skin was so hot she was sure he'd combust. He needed release. She built up a rhythm, circling her hips because she couldn't help herself. It felt so good and full that she knew she was on the edge of coming. She moved faster as he pushed from below to meet her every stroke. She had never felt anything like it. She was going to come all over him without even touching her clit.

How was that even possible?

His breathing was rapid as he filled her over and over. The sounds of their deep moans and heavy pants were all she could hear as she quivered around him. She rode him hard and fast until she was crying out her release above him. He shouted, his hips lifting off the bed, and slammed into her. She felt warmth as his cock emptied inside her.

She fell against his chest for a second to catch her breath. Her body racked with tremors, and she couldn't believe she was conscious. None of the bad memories had invaded. After long moments lying atop his heaving torso, she realized he wasn't softening and looked up. Primal icy eyes looked even more dangerous with a tenderness that she saw there.

"Unchain me, Sam."

Her breath caught, and she stilled for a brief moment at his seductive voice. She slid off the big bed and complied with his request; she wanted his hands on her.

Once free, he pulled her over him, kissing her deeply while his hands caressed her back and bottom. Slowly his hand inched between her thighs and gathered their combined essence and began rubbing it all over her thighs and ass. "Smells so fucking good. So right. I want to rub it all over your body. Mark you before licking it all off. That way I'd have you inside me like I was just inside you. Do you want that, Sam."

Those sexy words sounded like a promise, and she was shocked at how hot they made her. She wasn't capable of answering him, all she did was mewl in what she hoped conveyed her agreement. Her pussy ached with renewed desire and Sam didn't miss the fact that he continued to lay beneath her. She could tell he was a man that was used to being on top, in control, but he was doing it in a way that he thought would be easier for her, melting her heart a little more.

He positioned her so that she straddled him while he kissed and sucked her tight nipples. They were swollen and sensitive, tingling under his wicked ministrations. Big palms massaged her breasts high into his waiting mouth. He sucked on the tight nubs until she was wild above him. She eagerly stroked his rock-hard cock and guided it to her again and pushed down hard. This time her body accommodated his size with greater ease.

His head fell back on the pillow, their height differences too different to allow his mouth access to her breasts while she rode him. He moaned while his hips pumped beneath her. His hands came down, directing her hips. First circling them, then lifting and guiding her back slowly. He took full control over her movements like she weighed less than a grain of sand. A hand came up to stroke her cheek, and he softly pulled her down to his lips. His tongue explored and seduced so that she was breathless and needy above him. Gooseflesh covered her skin by the time their lips finally separated and she was so close, again.

"Rub your clit for me. I'm close, but I have to feel you come all over my cock again. Need to feel you pulse and squeeze me." He watched as she touched herself, appeared mesmerized by the sight of what her fingers were doing. "Fuck yeah, that's it, *beautiful*, give me more of that sweet honey."

She came hard around him, crying out to the ceiling. He pushed deep and groaned. Warm jets of his seed bathed her womb as she fell onto his chest again. Sirena had said this wouldn't result in pregnancy, not for years, and she was grateful not to worry about that right now. The warm slide of his come and the soft skin of his cock felt too incredible.

118

He lifted and settled her against his side. She was thankful because she couldn't have moved on her own. Strong hands held her against his warm chest, rubbing circles in the center of her back, and the tears came. His movement stilled and his body went rigid. He leaned and kissed her hair before holding her tighter as the pent-up emotion flooded out of her. He was so freaking perfect, and she was such a basket case. She knew her tears were probably freaking him out. Guys were known for panicking at that, but she couldn't seem to stop them. How could she find something so perfect after everything; he deserved so much more than her damaged ass.

Chapter 14

Gregoire's Home, Tetartos Realm

Alyssa woke hot and aroused. Her skin was flushed, and she already ached for release. When her eyes opened, she saw the source of her body's neediness. Gregoire's dark warm brown hair was inches away, and his lips were suckling at her breasts as thick fingers toyed with her slick opening. "So wet and already wanting my cock."

She couldn't speak, instead moaning at the heated words. One hand fisted in the blankets while the other dug in his thick, messy hair. The soft strands felt amazing as they ran through her fingers. She pulled at them as she bowed her back for more of that dizzying suction.

He groaned against her flesh and gave her harder pulls as his fingers became more demanding. At least three digits filled her while his mouth devoured her tightened buds, leaving her in a state of pure euphoria. "Sometime soon I'm going to fuck your tits."

"Why does everyone want to do that?" she mused dizzily, floating in pleasure. His movements stopped, and she made a needy noise of disappointment. Lifting heavy lids she hadn't even realized she'd closed, she was met with his furious forest gaze.

His voice was dangerously low. "Did you let someone fuck your tits?"

She swallowed at the look in his eyes. "No." Her words were breathless. The jealousy sparkling in his eyes made something deep inside itch to taunt him, just to see what he'd do. "That's in my next lesson."

He growled, his eyes flashing. She knew instinctually that anyone else would have run from him, but it was like she was purring inside.

"You want a *lesson*, angel?" His words were spoken with an edge of challenge.

Mmm-hmm. Desire flooded her channel. She liked him growly... Why? Maybe a small part of her wanted him to suffer in some way for rejecting her. Whatever the reason, his possessiveness turned her on like nothing else ever had.

He was up, opening a big wooden armoire by the bed. "I had things prepared for your arrival. I didn't plan on using the items in this cabinet so soon, but I can smell how wet you are at the idea of a lesson." He was nude, and his muscular back and ass drew her complete attention. She wanted to explore his body with her tongue. The delicious male belonged to her.

She shook her head. The frenzy was making her ridiculous. It was only sex, she had to remind herself. That was all she could afford to feel. She had planned to give herself to Kerr and Calder... at some point. So there was no reason she couldn't enjoy doing the same with the big Guardian.

She sat up, covering herself with the blanket as she watched him. His muscles rippled as he moved his hands in the cabinet. She couldn't see what he was doing. She was too focused on the way his body strained and flexed. Her mouth watered at the mere sight of his magnificent form.

Before she completely lost her mind, she decided to distract herself. "Did they catch the people that attacked Tynan and tried to take us?"

His back stiffened before he spoke. "Not yet. They were Cyril's. Drake found out how they got the information on you."

She was a little surprised, then realization hit, and her jaw clenched. "They found out I was your mate. How did they know?"

"Your father contacted me when you left. I've known Tynan for centuries and went to him to find out where you were. Unfortunately I was called away before I could get to you. One of the females in Tynan's bed heard my telling him to watch over you until I could return." He said the last as a low rumble.

She should have realized, but she hadn't been thinking since the moment he'd touched her.

"So that's why you finally decided to claim me?" The words tasted bitter on her lips. "Because I finally decided to leave home and find some independence? Because I dared leave my father's watchful sphere? In making Tynan babysit me, you inadvertently outed your dirty little secret. And got Tynan attacked."

She felt disgusted at the fact that he likely would never have come for her otherwise. She got out of the bed and headed toward the bathroom, not liking the insecurity and pain that assailed her. It was tightening her stomach and chest, making it difficult to breathe. She refused to be in the same room as him. If she'd been thinking clearly, she would have realized that he'd come looking for her because her parents had told him she was gone, not because he'd *wanted* her.

She'd just stepped inside the big bathroom when she was lifted and settled on top of a cold counter. She flinched in surprise at the speed with which it all happened, then tried to jump down.

He lifted her again and sat her back down on a towel that he must've telekinetically positioned beneath her.

His brows were narrowed, and he looked furious as hell. For some reason that just set her off. "I'd like to take a shower. Privately." Her voice was as calm as she could make it. She didn't want him to see her emotional upheaval, and she needed to get his scent off her skin. It was making her traitorous body want him more.

"No. You're about to explain to me why you're so concerned with Tynan."

Seriously? "What are you talking about? And why would you care who I'm interested in? You *only* came for me because my father called. Not because you wanted to claim the precious mate you could have come for at any time during the last five years." Her stomach clenched tight, and she squirmed to get away, but he'd effectively caged her with his arms on the counter and his hips between her spread thighs.

"It doesn't matter if you're interested in Tynan. The only male that ever gets to touch your hot little cunt is me." The thumb of one hand came to toy with her clit, and her damn body responded to those soft circles. He pushed two digits in deep and hard, and her hips ground against his palm.

"This belongs to me, Alyssa." She clenched her teeth and tried to still her movements when he continued, "I'd planned to come for you when you could handle my nature. I gave you fucking years to have a normal, quiet life before completely making you mine. I watched you from the time you were old enough. I knew I'd demand every inch of you. Could you have handled this any sooner? Fuck, no, you couldn't have. Not to mention how your father would have dealt

123

with the fact that his old friend was taking his innocent little daughter away from him."

She sat there fuming at his arrogance, and then the words set in. "You're friends with my father? He never spoke of it." She crinkled her brow, not sure she believed him and didn't like that his words somehow eased some of her pain.

"Your father and I have been friends for longer than I can remember. I found out you were my mate the day you were born, little one."

"How is that possible? Mating frenzies don't start unless you've hit your majority." She was attempting to head around what he was saying.

His features twisted. "Of course they don't. You were a babe. It was an instinctual feeling, not sexual." He looked thoroughly disgusted by her question.

"I can understand about my father, if what you say is true."

He growled at her, "Are you saying I'm lying?"

She didn't think he was. "Why would I discount the possibility? I don't know you." He got up in her face, his fingers still inside her body, holding her there. It was hot and it took everything she had not to move on them.

"I don't lie." His voice was low and challenging. "Waiting for you has been hell."

His thumb moved around her clit slowly, and his fingers started pumping inside her body. The conversation might be over, but that didn't mean she was letting anything go.

Right now she wanted him, and she'd take him. Her wet passage clenched around his thick fingers. She was thankful for her minimal experience. It gave her confidence that she'd lacked before. The fact that he had somewhat valid reasons for staying away relaxed her upset stomach, and she allowed herself to fall into the pleasure his fingers provided. He'd set up a slow and seductive rotation on her clit as his digits plunged deep.

"You think I was able to completely stay away? I've been living a half-life since you were born, getting reports on you since you were a babe." He growled while adding another finger inside her tight channel. She gasped as his movements grew harder, more demanding. "I know everything about you. I also know that I only give a fuck that you're *mine*." He pushed in deep, curving his fingers and touching a spot that made her squirm and writhe against him. "There will be no Tynan or anyone else but me. My hands, my mouth, my dick are the only ones to touch you from this moment on."

She was on fire for him, dying for more while he held her firm, preventing any movement, any relief. "This possessiveness you've unleashed isn't tame. Keep that in mind when you poke the beast. If you let anyone touch you, they die." His gaze was as harsh as the words that vibrated from his lips. The muscles and tendons on his neck stood at attention. His fingers started moving again.

She released the breath she'd been holding and fell into the pleasure he wrought; she was close, to the point that one more caress of her swollen clit would push her over. He watched with a feral glint in his eyes, holding her gaze as he pushed her closer and closer until she was finally screaming her release. His lips and tongue took her mouth like his fingers owned her body. She throbbed against his hand as he lifted away. She saw scratch marks on his shoulders she hadn't even realized she'd been making.

He continued watching her as he brought his hand up to her

lips. She smelled her sweet release as he caressed it over her mouth. Her lips parted on a gasp, and he slid inside the opening. "Suck it off. Taste your sweetness." She did as he said, completely in his thrall. He removed his hand and licked the rest before leaning in to lick her lips. He groaned, fisting her hair and tilting her for his mouth's possession. She moaned and reached down to stroke his hard cock. Her fingers were unable to span even a fraction of his girth. He was so damn big and she was dying to know how he tasted.

She broke the kiss to demand it. She wanted to make him squirm like he'd made her. "I want to taste you."

"Then suck your come off my dick, angel." He used both hands on her hips and slammed fully inside. It took her breath and bowed her back. He was so damn big her body took a second to adjust before he slammed harder inside. "Fuck, you tighten around me like a vise. I can't wait to get in your ass, see just how much you can strangle my dick."

She was so hot and wet. All she could hear was a buzzing in her ears as he lifted her off the counter and slammed her onto his shaft over and over. Her legs gripped his hips, and she held on.

His mouth found hers again as he took her with a force that edged with a kind of pleasured pain she loved. She screamed her release into his mouth. Her body was racked with spasms. She was down on the floor a second later. His eyes were glazed with desire. "Now, taste yourself all over my cock." Her mouth watered as she got on her shaky knees. A stack of cushy towels awaited her. Again, he'd used his power to make sure she was comfortable. She didn't want to acknowledge that she liked it.

He tilted his long shaft so that it was in front of her lips. She lifted up as far as she could to take him into her mouth. He was so thick. It felt erotic and empowering to suck her desire off of him. She made a mewling noise when she tasted the pleasure seeping from the tip. It was so good she lost her way until he began pumping shallowly between her lips, only giving her the head. His hands were in her hair, and she looked up to see his eyes were focused on his cock as it disappeared between her lips.

She wanted to drive him as wild as he'd made her. She sucked hard and rolled his sac in her hand as the other pumped. She sucked and swallowed around him over and over, working her way lower as his hands tightened in her hair and his breathing grew erratic. He grunted as she sucked and stroked until she had almost all of him down her throat.

"Fuck."

She kept up her ministrations, breathing through her nose, knowing she could take him. Her jaw ached, and her pussy wept as she inched him in. She finally swallowed him all the way, and she heard him shout. She felt his hot come sliding inside her. She licked him lightly as she slowly backed off, bathing him with her tongue while he finished coming down her throat. He was right. The combination of their pleasure was incredible. She didn't care that her jaw ached; she wanted him again.

He lifted her up into his arms and took her back to the bed, where he kissed her with a tender abandon that left her feeling wide open. She felt exposed and disoriented by the sweet caress of his hands and mouth as they worshiped her. She was taken over, could do nothing but fall into it and hope she came out of the other side whole again.

Chapter 15

Cyril's Compound, Tetartos Realm

Reve, one of his Kairos, returned with an unconscious Kane and no female.

Cyril was not happy when he asked, "What happened?"

"The Guardian got there right as we found her. Kane was blasted into a wall in the fight, and there was no way to get her."

Cyril came within a foot of the male, and using his powers over the body, he stopped Reve's heart. The fool's eyes widened, and then he dropped Kane's unconscious body. Cyril felt rage so strong and deep he wanted to do permanent damage, but he forced himself to rein in the desire to kill. Kairos were rare, and he had so few in his employ, but he couldn't deny the need to do harm. He lifted his power from Reve's heart, allowing it to beat once more. The Kairos gasped and held his hands to his chest as he tried to get his breathing and heart rate to even out. He was Immortal; he would be fine. For now.

"Go to your room to await your punishment," he said through clenched teeth.

The fool left the lab as fast as he was able to manage. Cyril watched in disgust. His lab assistants had quieted around him, attempting to look busy as far away from the scene as possible. Rage was boiling up inside. He looked down at his second in command and repressed the urge to kick him in the head. He already needed to repair enough damage. He saw blood tracking down Kane's neck, and his hair was matted with more. The blow had to have been a strong one. Kane's skull looked fractured. Fuck.

"Get him on a table," he bellowed at his assistants. He couldn't believe they'd failed. Having a female of interest to the Guardians would have been all he needed. He could have taken out his body's needs on her. Used her for his pleasure, knowing the Guardians would be furious. They never showed any particular interest like that. The thought made his teeth clamp down tight. What if she really was Gregoire's mate? He shook off the thought, as he had before. It wasn't likely now that Urian was mated. The odds of two Guardians finding their mates just days apart was doubtful. Information of another mated Guardian would have spread like wildfire within the Realm. That didn't mean Kane and Reve's failure was any less upsetting. He would make the Kairos suffer. Punish them both in ways that wouldn't take away their usefulness.

After he'd alleviated his anger, he would get back to his research. Something was missing. He felt it had to do with Subject Nine, the blonde female had held some potential. There was a niggling in the back of his mind. He would find out what it was trying to tell him after he healed his idiot second in command.

At least his other plans hadn't been affected. Soon, things would be set in to play that could change the tides back in his favor.

Chapter 16

Gregoire's Home, Tetartos Realm

Gregoire woke to a sense of peace that left him feeling lighter than he'd ever felt in his long life. Alyssa was tucked into his arms, and her sleepy, well-fucked scent filled his nose. Her soft ass was pushed up against his cock, making him want to grab her hips and slide his way inside. He forced himself to leave the bed, rubbing his hands over his beard. If he didn't move away, he'd take her again. Light filtered in through the big windows blanketing the front of his home. He hadn't bothered to close the blinds the night before.

He took another look at his sleeping mate. She was covered in thick blankets, her chestnut hair in wild disarray. Her beautiful face and pouty lips were all he could see peeking out. She needed her rest. He'd been rough with her. They'd spent nearly two days between the bedroom and bath. He would take her to refuel her energies when she woke up.

Immortals needed to feed from the world's energies to keep up their strength. They didn't need a boost of energies as often as humans required food, mainly because they received small amounts daily. To get fully recharged, they'd need to be within. Most of their kind had private caverns for that purpose. His was located inside the mountain behind their home.

His life force was etching a constant tattoo under his skin. They would complete the mating soon enough, but until then he would feel the whirling under his skin as it sought to connect with hers.

For the moment he was enjoying keeping her all to himself; the ceremony could wait. He looked down at her sleeping face. Her eyelashes curled against her smooth cheeks. She was so fucking perfect. She might be tiny, but she bucked and fought against him, and he fucking loved her strength. She had become more demanding with each taking. He shook his head at how his tiny mate ruled him. At least she didn't understand how much power she had over him, yet.

He strode downstairs naked. If he stayed up there, he would wake her again with his mouth and dick. He grabbed a remote and brought the blinds down a few feet so that the upstairs loft wouldn't get so bright.

He started coffee and leaned against the cool island, waiting for it to brew. He rotated his neck and shoulders; he'd never felt so damn good. It was like a soothing boost. Was the melding of their powers already starting, or was it just having her near?

Conn, did anyone get my mate's bags from Paradeisos?

Yeah, they're here. Want me to drop them off?

That'd be great. Gregoire was glad he wouldn't have to put on any clothes and go get them. He owed his brother.

Expect it out there in a few.

Thanks, man.

He poured his coffee into a big mug and went to the front of the house and stared out over the meadow that led down to a sparkling lake below. It was a beautiful morning.

He saw his brother port in with the bags, sporting a big grin. Stepping onto the cool deck, he grabbed Alyssa's things, easily shrugging the straps over his shoulder. "Appreciate it."

Conn laughed. "Next time, appreciate it with clothes on." Conn shook his head with a smirk. "I'm happy for you, man." There was genuine warmth in his brother's gaze. Conn shook his head and was gone a second later.

He scented her as he entered the door with her bags over his shoulder and his steaming mug in one hand.

"I smell coffee." Her voice was rough from sleep and sounded sexy as hell. He threw down the bags and watched her. She wore his tee shirt. It reached all the way to her knees, and it filled him with satisfaction that she was covered in something of his. She already smelled like hot fucking sex. Her hair was in wild waves around her beautiful face and stunning pale green eyes. He'd never seen such a unique color. His cock stood at attention as he tracked her movements.

His lips twitched as he watched her open cabinets until she found a mug and then poured some of the brew inside. If he was concerned with her feeling lost in her new life, her new home, he should have known better. She was Adras and Ava's daughter. His tiny mate owned the space, filled it. She opened the stainless fridge next and let out a little noise. He tilted his head at the happy sound. She came out with containers of Carmel Macchiato and Thin Mint creamers he'd picked up, knowing that Adras had been getting the shit for years in the supplies Bastian and Sacha provided Tetartos Realm.

Pale green eyes ensnared him, and her lips tilted in a tentative smile. "Thank you." Her words were spoken softly, but he heard them clearly. She focused on the treats, finally pouring the Thin Mint into her cup.

"Let me know if there's anything else you'd like me to get for you," he told her.

"Thank you. Were those my bags you brought in?" She came around the couch, eying him.

"Yes."

"Thanks for getting them." She nodded as she said the words and then turned to look out the windows, sipping her coffee. She made a little moan of enjoyment as she curled up on the big leather couch, tucking her feet underneath her. She put her nose up to the cup and closed her eyes as she inhaled, making more noises that went straight to his cock.

He telekinetically brought a blanket down from upstairs. He sat next to her, pulling her small feet into his lap before covering them. She'd held tightly to her cup and frowned until she settled into the new position with her head and shoulders on the armrest. He sat back and enjoyed the view outside while feeling her smooth calves and feet on his thighs. He felt her eyes on him, studying him. He knew she was hesitant, felt it. He understood that she didn't know him yet and had felt rejected. She would learn how far from the fucking truth that was. They sat quietly, drinking their coffee and relaxing. His cock was hard, but that was nothing new.

Her soft-spoken words drew his eyes. "How long have you lived here?" He saw how uncomfortable she was talking to him. It made sense, as their only other conversation in the last forty-eight hours was when she'd asked why he'd needed to leave the island before going to her. He'd explained about the hell beast attack, which led to her mentally contacting her parents to make sure everyone, including Rain's family, was okay. She'd been noticeably relieved that they were

133

fine. After the distraction, he'd managed to keep her occupied on his cock for hours.

He took a breath and answered her question. "It took about a decade to finish it the way I wanted. I've lived here for fifteen years." He watched as she did the math.

"I'll take you to refuel in a bit; there's an underground lake with hot springs deep in the mountain. I won't need to patrol for at least another day. And you can buy things and decorate the place to make things how you'd like them. Unless you'd rather we live somewhere else." He really didn't care. They could live here part of the time or not at all.

"What?"

He looked over to find her brows furrowed and her cup suspended just below her lips. "What are you questioning?" he asked.

"You'd build something else if I didn't like this? You spent *years* building this." She looked so adorably confused he found his lips tilting.

"I've lived here for years, Alyssa." He rubbed a small foot with the hand not holding his coffee. "We have many more to go, so if you'd rather live on a beach or in the jungle, it doesn't matter. I'm not sure which powers of mine will meld to you. My ability to teleport came from the Creators, so I don't know if you'll gain that power or not. You might wait to see what you are able to do before you decide how remote you'd like to live."

He looked at his coffee and contemplated adding whiskey.

She made a little moan as he massaged one of the small feet in his lap. He looked over and noticed that her eyes had grown heavy as she lay there with her mug resting on the swells of her breasts.

She was getting comfortable in his company. They would likely have bonded more rapidly if they had left themselves mentally open. She had quickly pulled up a shield, and he'd done the same. It was a knee-jerk reaction that would not be changing on his end. He had a difficult time imagining allowing anyone inside his head.

He owed Uri for explaining that you were wide open mentally at the start of a mating frenzy. What had surprised him was that she'd known to shield her thoughts. Her parents were a rare mated pair, so it was likely her mother or father had shared some of the specifics. It hadn't sat well with him that she'd closed herself off so quickly.

Chapter 17

Gregoire's Home, Tetartos Realm

Alyssa wasn't sure what she was feeling. Intense emotions had been waging a battle within her since the moment she'd accepted him inside her body. It was possibly because he was the first male she'd ever slept with, but more likely a side effect of the mating. She felt exposed. Her mind was her own, but her body completely belonged to him; she couldn't imagine experiencing that crazed intensity with another male.

His hand at her feet felt soothing yet arousing. He was forging a sensual assault to her senses while relaxing with his coffee. The damned male overwhelmed her without even trying. She lay with her head and shoulders on the cool leather of the couch's arm, letting him lull her as her skin heated.

She watched through heavy lids as he drank from his mug. He was looking out the massive windows to the meadow and tree line leading down to a lake. She allowed herself to sink in and relish the innocent touch while tracking the way his lips touched the ceramic and his throat moved when he swallowed. She stifled a moan and realized she was jealous of that cup.

Thoughts of the past two days threatened her peace. He'd spent the time alternating between hard, dominant sex, and soft, tender lovemaking where those same lips had been her downfall over and over again. She held onto her resolve that she would never again live under someone else's expectations. It was a fine line she was dancing, one that would set the stage for the rest of their lives. His rejection still stung, but not as much now that she understood his reasons and had so many hours immersed in him. It was the small bit inside her that had fantasied about her mate being out of control for her, tossing her over his shoulder the minute he could. Claiming her in front of the entire Realm, damn her innocence or her father's feelings.

In reality she was glad that he considered her father's feelings and had tried to take her needs into consideration. The part she balked at was that no one gave her the choice or bothered to ask what her *needs* were. Both he and her father had made those decisions for her based on their ideas of what she could handle. That was what made her tread carefully with him. She would not be taken over.

She planned to enjoy the sex, making sure to hold her ground whenever dealing with her business and her day-to-day life. The fact that he enjoyed coffee, quiet mornings on the couch and hard crazy sex was no reason to get sappy.

There was no forgetting being left under the watchful eyes of her parents for *her own good*. Even though she just knew her father had his hands all over that. That male could work guilt like nobody else. She planned to have a chat with him and her mother about that when she went to pick up her things. Never again would she let someone think they should decide what was right for her; she had been considered a grown female for five years. Enough was enough.

It would take time to get to know him and for him to get to know her. She would set ground rules as soon as she wrapped her head around exactly what those needed to be. She was totally on board with some things she'd learned about him. She thrilled at his possessiveness. Even his jealousy did it for her. There was no going back from a mating, so she would enjoy the perks while being smart.

He changed feet, still staring off toward the lake below. Tingles ran up her calves, but she didn't dare move or say anything. She was afraid he'd stop, and the feeling was too damn good to relinquish.

The living room was big and cozy. She hoped there was another room to set up as a work space; otherwise he might regret telling her to arrange things as she liked. Her lips kicked up at the thought of him coming home from patrol to see the entire living room set up for her business. She shook her head. It was still technically her vacation. She had a little time to figure out where to put her things.

She liked how open and light the house was; he'd explained at some point that the glass was infused with metal and the house was protected with intense spells. She had been a little relieved because they were in the middle of nowhere and the Guardians weren't without their enemies. That thought sent a little chill up her spine, but she pushed it away. She would be safe, and she was not powerless. She had to admit that she loved his home; it felt comfortable.

She'd been happily surprised he'd put in a kitchen. It was open to the living space, separated by a stone-topped island. Immortals didn't need to eat, but some enjoyed sampling small bits. Her mother had been a Mageia before mating her father, so her love of cooking had started well before she was turned into an Immortal.

She almost smiled, remembering how her mother had taught her to cook. When Alyssa was growing up, her mother baked for the enjoyment of it, and when Rain and she had become friends, her mother had been ecstatic. It was her way of relaxing after working alongside her warrior mate all day. She was always thrilled when Rain would come over and they all whipped things up together. The majority of the creations would get sent home with her friend. The smell of cookies and bread felt like home to Alyssa. The thought of doing that in her own home gave her a fluttery feeling. Would Gregoire like that? Was the kitchen something he enjoyed, or was there more to it?

She took a drink of her coffee. It tasted delicious. She remembered the little twinge in her heart when she'd seen her favorite creamers in the fridge. Since they'd been unopened, she knew he'd bought them for her. He'd obviously made the effort to find out things that she enjoyed. She stared at his beautiful features, wondering if all was as it seemed.

His hand moved over her calves, and she closed her eyes, enjoying his touch.

They'd spent the majority of their time in the bed, shower, on the stairs and now in the living room, and she needed him again. She was wet, no matter how she fought it. Their soft quiet time was ending. His hands stilled on one calf and the air charged around them.

"You want me back inside your hot little pussy again, angel?"

The sound of his voice brought her focus up to his sexy lips, firm and inviting inside his shortly shorn beard. She remembered how the hair had abraded her skin so deliciously in their play.

Looking higher, she was held by his forest gaze. Seeing the depth and hunger there made her breasts swell and her pussy ache. Her breath caught as he grabbed her cup and stretched back, settling the mugs on the high table behind the couch. His muscled chest and shoulders flexed and rolled with the motion. Her eyes caught at his ridged stomach, and her foot moved of its own accord, sliding the soft material down his legs to show his massive erection. He had been hard and wanting her while he drank his coffee. When he turned back around, the blanket was tossed on the floor.

"You want my cock, angel; I can smell it. Take the shirt off; get on your hands and knees with your ass in the air. I'm hungry for your pussy."

She felt desire seep from her body as she moved to follow his command. The shirt hit the floor beside the blanket, and she leaned her forearms against the arm of the couch. She turned to see him crawling toward her.

His palms came up to her hips. "Spread your thighs wider and tilt your hips. Show me every inch."

The sexy demand in his voice caused her juices to flow. She wanted his mouth. He was talented and knew just how to make her wild. He'd used his tongue to drive her out of her mind several times in the last couple of days, and she was becoming addicted. She felt his hot breath first, teasing her cheeks as he massaged and spread her for his enjoyment.

You smell so damn good. I want to spend the entire day covered in your slick, edible scent. Then I'll cover you in my come. The scent of us together is fucking intoxicating.

Anticipation set her nerves on end. She let out a deep moan when he finally put his lips to her, lapping her juices and then flicking her clit with his tongue. Her entire focus settled on what he was doing. He liked to tease, get her good and desperate for release. He spread her pussy wide and licked deep, spearing his tongue inside. She wiggled to get more, and he smacked her ass, which only made her ache. She made a noise of protest when he moved again. His tongue lapped at her back entrance; it felt so good and wicked as he pushed at her and got her all slick before blowing against the skin there. By the time he pushed a finger in her ass, she was out of her

140

mind. Growling his approval, he proceeded to eat her pussy like he would never get enough.

She was reeling by the time he let her come. She cried out her climax while pushing against his finger. It was so good, but she needed more.

A moment later she was flipped around over his lap, facing the massive windows. He positioned her over his shaft and slammed her hips down hard. He filled her to bursting, and she panted as her body throbbed around him. She was wide open, her knees straddling his thighs, her bottom against his stomach. She circled her hips, thriving on the stretching sensation of being taken. He flipped her hair to one side and pulled her bare back against his heaving chest. Lifting her up, he set his tongue and lips to her neck, and gooseflesh rose all over her arms. He angled her head so he had the access he needed as she moved on the tip of him. One hand massaged her hip up to a swollen breast.

Do you like being open and on display for anyone that might come up to the house?

Desire flooded her at his words and the implication and then he slammed her back down. She was spread and impaled on his cock, her back tight to his chest, as he caressed her in front of the open windows. No one was around, but the idea was there, and it made her hot.

I can feel that you do. Imagine all they would see. Your bare pussy sucking my cock deep as I lift your breasts and play with your pretty nipples.

He kissed her temple as her movements became frantic, attempting to lift up and ride him.

The only movement he allowed was the grinding of her hips and ass. She pushed hard, trying for more, when one of his hands left a breast and gave a sharp smack to her mound. She jumped at the unexpected action. It hadn't hurt; the slight sting moved quickly into delicious warmth.

You like when I slap your pussy, angel? Like the sting? He spread his thighs beneath her, forcing her knees wider. *Look out the window and imagine what they'd see. Your beautiful body spread wide, my cock buried deep inside your pussy, and your mound pink from my hand.* Another sharp smack landed. This one lower, right against her clit. She cried out; she needed to come and almost did as heat flooded her. *They'd see you come as I slap your pussy, marking your skin as mine, and only mine. They'd watch what only I can do to you. They'd know you were mine in every way.* One more hit landed, and she came apart. He held her down, the hot words and heat of his hand were too much, she just kept coming.

"You're fucking perfect." His voice came out raspy, and she felt his chest rising and falling against her back. His cock twitched inside, and she bit her lip, thinking he might set off another hot orgasm.

"I want your ass, angel. Are you going to give it to me?"

She thrilled at his groaned words. He needed her, and she was more than willing to experience everything with him. The fact that he wanted her so badly, that she heard it in his voice left her feeling hot and empowered all at once.

His fingers massaged her clit, and she wiggled against him. He lifted her to nip at her neck. "Tell me you want me in your ass, angel."

Yes, she sent in their mental link.

He growled and pulled from her body, and she made a noise of protest as he flipped her over. "Fuck, your pussy milks me like nothing else. I can't wait to see what your ass does to me."

She was suddenly positioned with her knees on the arm of the couch, putting her hips up higher than her body. She turned her torso and neck, watching as he stared at her exposed body as if he'd never seen something so wonderful. His hand lifted, and a jar came from the air; he'd telekinetically retrieved it from somewhere. He looked nearly out of control and so magnificent she felt her breath leave in a rush. His eyes caught hers, his massive, muscular chest heaving so powerfully she couldn't look away. He opened the jar, and she felt as he slicked her back entrance. The lube was tingly and felt amazing, like little flutters were filling her flesh.

"Push out onto my fingers so I can stretch you."

She did as he said, her body wanting more of that delicious sensation.

"Fuck, you look incredible with my fingers in your ass. It'll look even better with my cock tunneling in."

She wiggled against his invading fingers, loving the stretch and feel of him there. Her clit pulsed, and she felt her fluids rushing as she braced her hands and pushed back for more. He growled and smacked her ass, which only made her ache for more. The stretch of her ass and the warmth from his slap made her whimper.

Creators, if he didn't get inside her, she was going to come without him. He smacked the other side of her ass. "Not yet."

She groaned. "Then stop spanking me and get in my ass." She was frustrated. Couldn't believe he wanted her to wait, and he wasn't even inside her. She wanted to feel what it was like, and she loved his fingers to the point of madness.

"Push out. If you want it, take it deep, Alyssa."

143

She felt the tip as it stretched her so damn wide. She was breathing hard, and she felt a bite of pleasure-pain so intense her clit pulsed, and she wiggled her hips. Soon it was too much and not nearly enough. He was moving too slowly. She felt the bulbous head but needed all of him.

"More. Harder." She swore she felt his need through their bond. Not the thoughts, the desire so great it was near insanity, and she pushed back.

"Fuck," he shouted, and then slammed all the way inside.

She felt owned. Full in a way that was addicting and wild, making the animal inside her nuts.

"So hot and tight, like a damned vise clamping down on me."

She moaned and circled her hips in front of him. She felt his sac hitting her pussy, and she wanted more. He held her hips in a bruising grip as he started thrusting. She cried out for more. He brought one hand around to her clit, and she climaxed in a rush. She heard his shout in the background as she gasped for breath and fell face-first into the soft leather. She felt his big hands massaging her cheeks as he gradually receded from her ass. She felt strung out. That had been her most out-of-control experience yet. She felt a little sore, but she liked it. She'd made her big, powerful mate lose his mind.

He caressed her back and trailed his fingers in along her crack. "I love seeing my come all over you. In you."

She closed her eyes as he petted her flesh and moved the fluids all over her ass.

"You need to get refueled, angel. We both do," he said before lifting her into his arms. She snuggled in, thinking sleep would be nice, but he was right, she was running a little low.

Chapter 18

Cyril's Compound, Tetartos Realm

Cyril had the answer... His body nearly vibrated with
excitement he was attempting to leash. He'd finally figured
out the problem with his prior formulas. The answer had been with
Subject Nine all along. He'd known she was the key. He clenched his
teeth tight. He only wished he still had her, but eventually the damn
Guardians would let her go to live in the covens of Tetartos, and then
she would be his all over again, in every way. His cock pulsed with the
thought of what he would do to her. She had the most delicious
ability over metal. She was currently limited, as was the case with all
mortal Mageia. The race itself was made of only slightly evolved
humans, weak unless enhanced or they found an Immortal mate.

It had all rested on her rare offshoot of the common earth
ability. He shook his head, thoroughly disgusted that he hadn't
figured it out sooner. He no longer needed Cynthia to acquire Nine's
family members. The Earth Mageia needed to be informed not to
waste her coven's paltry abilities acquiring and sending them. He
would instruct Elizabeth to inform her. The family would be useless.
It wasn't in Nine's bloodline but the anomaly in her, a mutation that
was not common in Mageia. The race tended to hold very basic
elemental abilities with one of four elements: air, earth, fire or water.
Nothing exceptional, but *she* had power over metal, a rare variation.

He filled a few vials with the new formula. The clink of the glass
sounded loud in the quiet lab. He'd dismissed his assistants hours

ago. He trusted no one, so much that it had crossed the border into paranoia. The breach to his old facility had started it, and it had worsened with time instead of abating.

He wouldn't think of that when success was finally his. He only needed a new candidate to inject. Soon.

For the moment, he intended to make much-needed preparations. First he needed to set up a private lab, somewhere he could test his new formula away from prying eyes and potential deception. He wished he had the ability to take blood memories like an Aletheia so that he wouldn't suspect everyone around him as being the traitor that had tipped off the Guardians. He balled his hands in irritation. Not knowing who had betrayed him was slowly driving him mad and indicated he would be completely without assistance going forward.

Setting up a bedroom in his hidden lab was a must, along with relocating his most important research. Decision made, he gathered the vials and put them in his pockets.

Fortunately he was able to teleport, a power from his father. He'd gotten his most prized gifts from being the son of Apollo. He would be even more powerful once he achieved his goals.

He only had a few days before his latest plan went into effect. He needed to move fast in order to get everything arranged. His new place would be special. Hidden where no one would be able to hear the screams of the mates he planned to claim. Where he would harness the females' abilities, gaining more power than Drake or his mated Guardian ever dreamt of acquiring.

Chapter 19

Gregoire's Home, Tetartos Realm

G regoire cradled his small mate in his arms and never felt
so... much. He didn't want to ever let her fucking go. He
hated the idea of leaving her while he patrolled.

She was snuggled up into his chest as he carried her through the
door next to the fridge. Once in the pantry, another door slid open,
and they were in one of the tunnels behind the house. It was dark
except for the fluorescent rock embedded all through the mountain.
It made a soft greenish glow, lighting the path to the lake. He already
felt the energies blanketing and seeping inside his cells. Relaxing and
meditating made the process faster, but the small amounts were still
more than he felt when above ground.

He looked down at her plump breasts and bare mound. Her hair
trailed over most of her chest, offering him teasing peeks between
the strands. He'd waited so long, and now she was finally his.

"It's nice and cool in here," she mumbled into his chest. "How
far are we going?"

"The lake is still a bit further. The water will feel good on your
aches. I was rough with you." He clenched his teeth at how angry he
was with himself for taking her so hard. He'd left marks on her hips,
and her tiny ass had to be sore even with the special spelled lube. He
was too large to take her like he had. He'd never lost control like that;
then again he'd never felt anything so incredible. Her body stretched

for him, was fucking made for him. He'd gotten balls deep and wanted to somehow get further.

"I liked it."

He grunted. She'd bucked against him, begging for him to take her harder, so he was sure she was telling the truth. It was the fact that the frenzy was making him lose his mind that threw him.

They'd finally rounded the last curve in the tunnel and walked down steps leading down to the lake of the domed cavern. He loved the space. He looked down at her when her breath caught, and she turned to look around. "It's gorgeous."

"It's one of the main reasons I built on this mountain." The cavern ceiling was high. Rocks jutted out in groupings around the big lake. More of the glowing stone filled the room, making it seem lit by candlelight.

"You said there were hot springs; do they feed into the lake?"

"Yes, it'll feel warm."

He carried her straight into the water and felt her twitch and cling to him before her body accepted that it wasn't cold. His lips tilted at the little sigh she made while relaxing into the water. He took them in until her hair fanned out in the water and her nipples softened from the soothing liquid. Her eyes were closed as she let the water caress her skin.

He bent and kissed her temple. Pale green eyes looked up at him and held while he moved further in the water, keeping her face above the liquid. "I'll hold you while you refuel."

She looked up at him, wide eyed and beautiful. He couldn't take his eyes off her. "I've got you. Take what you need." He saw her inhale before fluttering her eyes shut. Her brow smoothed out as he watched his mate taking in energy. He opened himself to refuel his own cells, but only enough to slowly let it glide inside. He was too intent on watching her to focus on himself.

They stayed like that for a long time, him moving with her so that her hair floated around them.

He finally settled on a ledge that was the perfect depth.

Her eyes opened after another minute. "You bought the creamer for me."

He furrowed his brow, wondering what made her think of creamer. "Yes."

"Thank you."

"You're welcome." He felt his lips tilt at how much a small thing seemed to make her happy.

After a long while where she seemed to assess him, she relaxed even more.

They were both refueled when she spoke again. "I should really check on Rain. I know you said she's fine, but I feel terrible for leaving her like that."

"She's staying at the Guardian compound. Drake's arranged a room for her."

"For how long?"

"Indefinitely, she's important to you, and with Cyril still out there someone could easily use her to get to you."

He saw her lips firm when she understood how true that was.

"Her shop... I'll have to talk to her and help her figure things out. I don't want her in danger because of me, but I guess it doesn't really matter what I want. I've already been targeted once." She blew out a frustrated breath and tried to get out of his hold.

"Stop moving," he demanded.

She gave him an exasperated look. "I need to get up so I can think."

"The rock is rough. You'll stay were you are."

"A little stone won't hurt me, I'm Immortal."

His lips twitched. "I remember."

He carried her out of the water and dried her with a towel he had in a hamper near the two-person lounge he'd set up knowing he would be claiming her. He'd picked it because of its strength and the comfort of the thick green cushion.

The blustering finally subsided, and she asked him questions about his brothers. Something had changed while they'd been in the cavern. She wanted to know more about the manor, which had to do with her worry for her friend. She asked how close the house was to the Guardian compound and Lofodes. He'd explained it all, yet the questions kept coming. Once she'd started, there was no stopping her, and he found he enjoyed it. His female was learning all she could about his brethren and what he did every day. She was learning about him.

He watched her use the air currents to blow out her hair. He was mesmerized by how easily she called up the power and used it. Her hair was in wild waves around her delicate face, and he loved it. As he carried her back to the house, he explained that he was on Earth Realm rotation. She seemed quite interested in the fact that Uri had

151

hidden a hellhound on Earth and that they were starting to use the beast in the hunt for demon-possessed in that Realm. He told her about Alex coming to Uri for help with her brother and finding out they were mated.

"So Cyril had a Mageia on Earth sending him females to test on? Why would she send her own kind to be an experiment?" She looked up at him with a scowl on her beautiful face.

"The mortals on Earth don't know that the Immortal races exist. They're obsessed with Immortality, and Cyril had been providing her with Aletheia semen. The regenerative components were making her look and feel younger." In order to stay that way, she'd needed a constant fix. She was likely addicted, so Cyril had her.

"Oh, Creators. Those poor females. So they're staying at the Guardian compound, like Rain?"

"Yes, until Sirena feels they're up for going to live in the covens."

"And Erik's mate?"

"Yes." He nodded. He hadn't been around to hear if Sam and Erik had ever finished their mating.

"I need to get over there," she said and he frowned, hating leaving the sanctuary of their home. Hated sharing her yet, but he felt how much she needed this. When they got into the house, she wiggled to be put down, but he wasn't ready to let her go.

She gazed up at him with a frown of her own. "I'm not weak, Gregoire. I can walk." She blew out. "And I won't be taken over. I need to have a say in my life and right now I need to see my friend."

"I intend to take you to see Rain and I don't think you are weak." He growled. He wondered where the hell that had come from and

152

cocked a brow in confusion.

She snorted. "You may be the only Hippeus not to think that, then."

He frowned at her. "Explain?" He loved her pale green eyes. They were such a unique and soulful shade.

"I don't think there is one Hippeus, at least in the clans around Lofodes, that doesn't see my size as weakness."

He frowned again, getting irritated. "That's ridiculous. Yes, your size is unique for a Hippeus, but that has absolutely nothing to do with weakness." He was offended. His mate was anything but weak. "You slammed a grown Aletheia into the wall so hard he lost consciousness."

She shrugged at his words, but he watched as she closely assessed him as if she didn't believe what he was saying.

"With your ability over air, you're more powerful than your father's warriors." Her obvious worry wasn't making sense. The whole thing wasn't adding up. Unless… Her father had to have done something. Damn Adras. She'd masked her features, but her eyes didn't lie. There was pain and hurt there. It made him want to rage. He'd kick Adras' ass if he wasn't concerned about it upsetting her.

He hated the fucked-up clenching in his heart. Full understanding of how she must have felt when finding out that he knew she was his, but he hadn't come for her… She'd somehow been made to feel inferior to her own kind and he was the most powerful of their race. When he hadn't come for her, it would have been a harsh blow to her confidence, as if feeling rejected hadn't been enough. He stroked her cheek with his thumb and shifted her so her legs wrapped around him, because he wasn't setting her the fuck down. He was finally able to hold her after decades and he planned to do it as much as fucking possible. He took the stairs to their room and closet as he claimed her lips, stroking and soothing. He wished she wasn't so damned determined to leave or he'd take his time making her forget the way their damned race had made her feel.

Meeting in ten minutes, Drake ground out through the Guardian telepathic link. He was still off duty, but if Alyssa needed to see Rain, he'd see what was going on.

Chapter 20

Private Villa, Tetartos Realm

Sam woke to a sweet, gentle kiss and a whispered, "I'm going to lift you up. Just relax for me. I need you on my lips." His voice was a deep rasp. The frenzy had worsened with the time Erik had been kept unconscious. Sirena had explained that he would need massive doses of sex to get him leveled out.

Knowing that and experiencing it were two entirely different things, but thank God she'd had some warning. She wondered what a normal frenzy was like. Shit, she hoped her body would survive the crazed marathon they were running. She was only slightly sore, made less so by some special balm Vane had left for them, courtesy of the healer. She'd heard bits of the brothers' mental conversation. Enough to grasp the gist of what it did as Erik had gently caressed her aching opening with it after the first couple of times they'd had sex.

That small jar saved her ass. She wouldn't have made it through the last couple of days without it. He'd needed to have her almost hourly at first, and he was ginormous. She wondered how long she'd slept after the last bout in the shower. It didn't matter.

She opened her sleep-fogged eyes and saw the pain and sorrow reflected in his gorgeous icy gaze. Her heart clenched. She could easily love him; damn, she already felt like she did. In their short time together, she felt like they had been through more than most couples were forced to conquer in all of their years together. She saw in his tensed muscle that the experience was taking its toll on him. She just needed to get beyond the feelings of unworthiness that plagued her. She knew there was no way out of what was happening.

Only pain and madness lay ahead if they tried to fight the bond. That knowledge had made things much easier. They were both caught up in it, and she'd been told everything would be easier if she trusted her instincts.

They were telling her this was right and she was beyond caring about whether her feelings had stemmed from his rescuing her. The whole white-knight thing just didn't matter.

She kissed him sweetly, attempting to reassure him with her lips that she wanted everything, wanted him. She skimmed her hands along his muscled chest to his hard brown nipples. He groaned deeply. How much more fucked up could she be that some part of her loved his needing her. She knew it was wrong to be happy while he was feeling pain and guilt. She mentally shook her head.

Before she could do anything more, his big hands lifted her up so that she was straddling his face. He'd moved so fast and effortlessly that she was forced to grab the headboard for support. It thrilled her that he could so easily lift and arrange her above him, like she weighed nothing. He took possession of her pussy like a man starved. Her mind completely derailed as blinding need assailed her. She moaned as her hips moved against his torturous mouth. He licked so far into her body that her eyes rolled back. Damn, but his mouth was lethal. Her fingers clenched tight to the wood, grasping to stay grounded while his mouth ruled her. His tongue pumped in and out until she was a wanton mess above him. She was actually riding his lips, not feeling the least bit self-conscious. His fingers dug into her ass as he pulled her closer, burying his mouth between her thighs as if he didn't even need air.

She was overcome with sensation. Felt pleasure like nothing she'd ever known or thought possible, but she wanted to taste him too. She attempted to use the headboard as leverage to turn around, but he only held her tighter, growling against her wet flesh. The primal sound against her pussy caused her to crash over the edge in a rush. She screamed and held tight to the wood while he drank her, not stopping until she was limp and her channel finally stopped throbbing.

She was still struggling for breath when she heard him groan deep. Warm jets of semen hit her back, and she turned to see him stroking his slick erection. He looked so damn sexy with come still pumping from the tip onto his slowly moving hand. She lifted a shaky thigh over his head and waited for their breathing to even out.

She noticed he wasn't softening. "Doesn't that help?"

"Tasting you eases some of the ache." He said the words low, his eyes seeking hers; it was like she could fall in the icy surface and end in a heated abyss. There was nothing cold about his eyes. They held so much. Her heart stuttered in her chest. She had made the choice to fight for him, and it felt completely right. She would slay her demons for him, be the woman he deserved. The one *she* deserved to be. He was hers, and he needed and wanted her with more intensity than she'd ever known. She felt the thrumming inside. It was her link to him, and she enjoyed the pull.

"Are you still tender?" He caressed her leg and looked into her eyes. She shook her head; she only felt a little sore. He pulled her into his side as a towel came from the bathroom. She would have to get used to his abilities. He brought the soft cotton to his shaft, and she pushed it away. She was dying to taste him. He groaned deep as she leaned over and licked him gently, unsure if he was too sensitive. He groaned, and his cock bobbed against her lips. "Your mouth feels incredible." He was beyond perfect, tasted amazing, nothing like anything she'd ever tasted before. She could get addicted to the sweetness that seeped onto her tongue. Poor thing, he hadn't been soft since before she'd gotten there. Was that really days ago? He'd had Vane bring her food at some point.

His back bowed as she swirled her tongue on his crown. She pumped him in her hand and savored the taste and feel of his big shaft. There was no way she'd be able to take him all.

"Fuck, Sam, suck it." Crap, his voice was so deep she could likely come from listening to him. She looked up to see the eyes of a predator looking back. Her body clenched, and she felt arousal slide from her. She wanted so badly for him to understand how much she loved this. He growled deep and closed his eyes. "Your shield is wide open. I'll have to show you how to put it back up, but damn, I love hearing your thoughts when they're like this."

She tried speaking in that link. She wasn't sure if he would hear her, but she concentrated, not wanting to lift her mouth from suckling at his cock. She was enjoying it too much to let go. *I don't need the shield now. Stay with me.*

"Gods, you are amazing." He groaned as his hips thrust, and he dug his fingers into the bedding.

You don't have to be so gentle. Tell me what you need me to do.

Keep talking, keep your mind open, and let me feel how hot you're getting sucking my cock. His voice in her mind was a hot seduction that added to her arousal. She sucked and licked, loving the silky feel of his flesh, the heat and the way his erection bobbed in her mouth. She took him deep into her throat, sucking and pumping with her hands. He moaned. His hand came up and stroked her hair, but didn't pull or grab. He was holding back, worried he would hurt her.

I love being in your mind. I love what your mouth is doing to me. Suck me as hard as you can, beautiful.

She moaned at his words, her cheeks hollowed as she pulled hard, getting more of that sweet taste in her mouth. Loving every bit of it. She gained speed and used her hands. She looked up to see him watching every movement, his tendons tight, chest shining and beautiful. She loved the beautiful man. His head shot back; she heard him shout as his come filled her mouth. She drank deep and then cuddled into his side to sleep. He covered her with a blanket and held her as she drifted off. She felt intense emotion coming through their bond.

He'd heard the declaration in her mind.

Chapter 21

Guardian Compound, Tetartos Realm

Alyssa and Gregoire teleported to the balcony of the Guardians' compound. They still melded together while teleporting, but, thankfully, it didn't create as much blinding lust as before. It was still a little brutal though.

She took in a bracing breath, nervous about meeting the other Guardians. Her insecurities were making themselves known, but she held her head high. She had changed during the last week and had no intention of allowing anyone to make her feel lacking again.

Gregoire looked down at her. "You have nothing to worry about."

She didn't doubt for a second that he believed that. Her big gorgeous Guardian likely never had a reason to feel insecure in his long life. He couldn't possibly understand what it was like.

She, on the other hand, had been quite intimate with feeling self-conscious. She used to bury herself in her work, avoiding uncomfortable interactions, but that was not who she was anymore.

He looked down at her with furrowed brows. They were getting each other's emotions more and more. He opened the door and led her inside, tucking her tight into his side when they were in a big room with couches and a wall-size TV. His heat settled her. Bastian and Sacha, the darkly beautiful Kairos, came to greet her first with

Brianne, a vibrant redheaded Geraki. Brianne had on a brown leather halter top that left her back free. From what she knew of the race, Geraki did not like their backs covered, even when their wings were retracted. Gregoire had just introduced her as his mate. His deep rumble against her side did things to her body, and she felt tingles running along her skin at the sheer headiness of being introduced as his. They all smiled warmly, and Brianne made an excited noise and moved to hug her, but Gregoire would not let her loose from his side.

Brianne raised an eyebrow and then burst out laughing. Her laughter filled the room, and Alyssa couldn't help but stare up at him, shaking her head. Gregoire was being ridiculous, but something inside thrilled that he'd taken possessiveness to a whole new level.

He scowled at them all, and she felt his arm tense around her. She looked up and put her hand against his tense abdomen, wondering if her emotions were messing with his instincts. She smiled at him, and he eased his hold but didn't let go. Instead, he lifted her up into his arms so that she was level with his mouth. He took her lips in a soft seduction that made everything around them fall away. She reveled in his strength and touch. Her arms came around his neck, and she held on as their tongues tangled.

"Again?" Rain's voice penetrated her aroused daze, and Gregoire's irritated grunt indicated he'd heard her as well. She started chuckling against his lips, and he peered into her eyes. His forest eyes held something beautiful and intense, maybe with a touch of arrogance.

He set her on her feet, and she heard the others talking around her again. She met Conn, the amber-eyed half wolf, next. She liked him instantly. There was a warmth and playfulness about him. He was the type of male used to setting people at ease, maybe before pouncing on them. Gregoire's little show had somehow relaxed her. Conn was gorgeous like Bastian and the two females. Of course they were… Immortals were attractive as a rule, but Guardians were nearly Gods, and their powers filled the room around them.

Gregoire squeezed her side, and she started to calm in a room full of Guardians.

"I'll find you after the meeting," Gregoire growled, apparently not pleased to be separated from her at all.

Before she could respond, she was lifted up and kissed as if he were leaving for days not hours. He left no recess unexplored, and she was wet and wanting by the time he set her down. She felt dazed and heated.

I love the fucking scent of you wet and hungry for my cock. I won't be long. His words rumbled through the link, setting off even more heat. Then he was out the door. The room was empty except for Rain, who was laughing and shaking her head. She felt cheated. She had to shake off the arousal before her friend grilled her for details on what had been going on.

Chapter 22

Guardian Compound, Tetartos Realm

Gregoire gritted his teeth hard. He hadn't wanted to release Alyssa from his side. The mingling of their life forces was distracting and making him possessive as hell. When Brianne had come forward to hug her, he couldn't make himself let her go. The thought of anyone touching her set him off.

He'd loved making her wet, knowing everyone could smell just how much she wanted him. Hippeus were known for their "look but don't fucking touch" fetishes when it came to any female they considered theirs. Gregoire had never experienced that need. Until now.

Her scent was fucking incredible, and letting his brethren get a hint of that ambrosia had nearly gotten him off. The thought of baring her and fucking her in that room was almost too much temptation to resist. Now, he was stuck waiting for a damn meeting instead of being deep inside her cunt. He was surly as hell knowing how much she'd needed to see her damned friend.

She'd worn a low-cut peach tank top that set off her golden skin and tiny tan shorts that he'd wanted to rip from her body. Her small stature made it so he could look down and see the gorgeous swells and deep crevice of her cleavage, making him want to bury his face and cock there. He hated that every blushing mark he made on her soft skin had faded with her Immortal healing. Fuck, all he imagined doing was marking her skin and slamming her hard on his cock on display for their entire world to see.

He sprawled into a chair in the war room, hard as steel. He, Bastian, Sacha and Conn were the first to arrive. Dorian came in and pulled up the chair next to his. Alex, Uri's mate, and her brother Vane had walked in a few minutes later. Slowly all of the other Guardians had taken their seats while Drake started. Gregoire barely heard his leader's words. He'd been reporting the same thing for centuries. The Gods were still sleeping. Drake personally monitored them to ensure that never changed.

Dorian shifted in the seat next to him. The Nereid kept looking around the room. Gregoire wasn't sure what was agitating him.

Drake's voice was a low boom as he spoke to Uri, bringing Gregoire's attention back to the meeting. "Tell the others what you've learned about the containment spell from Tetartos."

"Havoc is still able to get to Earth with a passenger. If it ever got out that he can do that, it would be a fuckfest here." The others nodded.

"Sirena said the hound can clear the Creators' confinement spell because of my blood, but the fact that he can actually take a passenger makes no sense. *I* can't even do that shit," Uri added, running fingers through his hair. If it got out that blood-bonding with Uri was the answer to Immortals clearing the confinement spell on the Realm, his brother would have a target on his back. And the pup being able to take passengers was fucking crazy. Something they'd likely never have known if Uri's mate wasn't so damned powerful. Alex had been the one to figure it out.

Sirena spoke up. "I'm still trying to learn how Havoc can do it. I don't dare test on a hellhound that was sent over by the Tria, since the beasts are all blood-bonded to the demons. The bastards might figure out what I was doing. That means I don't have any way to see if it's unique to him unless we find another pup that hasn't been tainted with Tria blood." She sat back in her chair. Her fifties look was complete with horn-rimmed glasses that she didn't need.

"Alex, have you gotten through the confinement spell again?" Sirena asked Alex. She was sitting next to Uri, her dark hair in a ponytail, sapphire eyes shining. Gregoire felt their mingling powers even across the table.

"So far I can't get back to Earth on my own. It feels like I might be close. I just need more practice." Alex had a determined set to her eyes as she spoke the words. They were all wondering if the Demi-Goddess would get Uri's Guardian abilities now that they were mated. She'd gotten through the confinement once, but Url had been badly injured. A mate bond could do crazy things during dire circumstances, because the souls were bound to each other.

Uri looked less than thrilled. "Even if she does get through, she might not be able to take out demon-possessed like she used to. If she gets my Guardian abilities, who's to say she won't be bound by the curse against harming humans?" his brother said through clenched teeth.

"I'm sure I'll figure it out pretty quick," she said, cocking her brow at her mate. When Alex and her brothers had been avoiding exile in Earth, they'd taken out their fair share of demon-possessed, which was part of the reason Drake never had them hunted down and exiled. The Guardians had needed the help.

Uri shook his head in irritation. Alex was a warrior at heart, and her reckless streak was currently driving the male crazy.

Gregoire repressed a grin at his brother's irritation. He noticed

Vane smirking across the table, no doubt enjoying that his sister was tormenting her mate.

He pondered his own mating. They needed to complete it soon, but he wasn't looking forward to the blood-bonding. He sat there grinding his teeth. There was no way around her seeing his past, and that grated on his nerves. She was too damn innocent for some of the horrors he'd seen.

"Vane or Sirena, any news on Erik?" Drake asked.

"Sam's still with him at Jax's place. I'm still surprised the little mortal was able to teleport herself there, but he was in bad shape by the time she got to him. Things seem okay for now," Vane said before leaning back in his chair.

"She teleported?" Gregoire asked, aghast. Sam was a mortal.

"Yes," Vane growled. "I don't know how she accessed Erik's ability, but she had to have. Their connection is strong." It was another example of the power of a mating bond, even one that wasn't completed.

"Shit." Gregoire seemed to be the only one who hadn't known this, but he had been gone for days.

Gregoire caught a heated glance Vane sent in Brianne's direction a moment later. He raised a brow at the catch in Brianne's breathing. If he hadn't liked the male so much, he would not have handled that look to his sister well at all. He might owe Vane for getting him out of Mageia hands the week before, but he wasn't sure just how far the debt went.

Gregoire noticed Dorian stiffen next to him. A glance at the Nereid confirmed Dorian had also seen the interaction. His muscles were tense as he glared in Vane's direction. They all liked Vane, but

Brianne was their sister, and even though they were all very aware that she was capable of taking care of herself, that didn't mean the Guardian males were any less protective. In the early years, that protectiveness had gotten every one of them bloodied by Sirena, Sacha and Brianne. It was for that reason he would not be having a chat with Vane, yet.

Sirena cleared her throat. "This is good, but Erik and Sam still need to finish what Cyril started for her mortality. It's that or they start the process all over again." He could see that Sirena's announcement killed a little of Alex and Vane's joy. Being filled with Aletheia semen was one step in the complex process for a mortal mate to gain their Immortality, and that process had been started before Sam's rescue. Uri pulled Alex's chair even closer to his and tucked her further under his arm. Alex was close to her brothers; it had been the three of them together avoiding exile to Tetartos for centuries.

Drake's voice rocked through the quiet that had descended. "What have we found on the breach in Lofodes?"

Uri's jaw tensed. "It was some sort of deteriorating spell on the shielding for the city. Adras went through the hidden video surveillance on the wall and rounded up anyone that passed the area in the last few days. It seems that we, in fact, have a problem. It was caused by a Mageia that Cyril gave the spell to. An Earth elemental around sixty years old, brought over when he was twenty. No family. His memories confirmed that he was to blame." Uri paused, his eyes showing how much those memories pissed him off. "He's bitter, felt coerced into coming to Tetartos. He was angered when he didn't find a mate and Immortality, though it wasn't like he knew that was an option when he chose to relocate here." They all knew Sirena never told Earth Mageias about the potential of Immortality in Tetartos. "He's just an old fucking idiot. Cyril's people had him convinced that he could make the male more powerful and give him youth after he completed the task. He didn't count on the city's lockdown, and he didn't know that there were hidden cameras throughout Lofodes." Uri shook his head in annoyance.

"We also checked the bitch that went after Gregoire's mate in Paradeisos. Cyril was behind that, too."

A rumbling from his brothers started. They were nearly as outraged as he was that Cyril had tracked his mate so quickly after word leaked from one of the females Tynan had taken to his bed. This was something Drake had already shared, but it didn't make him any fucking happier. This was why they had these weekly meetings, not all the information went out between nearly constant patrols.

Once the others finally settled down, Uri gave them the information they sought. "We checked her mind and confirmed that she heard Gregoire telling Tynan to watch over Alyssa while he went to the breach in Lofodes. She didn't know Alyssa was his mate though, so that's good." Gregoire listened as Uri shared the rest. "Tynan said to inform you that he intends to start doing mental scans on all of the guests before permitting them entrance into the resort. He expressed his apologies and offered to help in any way possible. He wasn't any happier than we are about this shit."

More talk filled the air, and Gregoire tuned out most of it. He was getting restless, wondering what Alyssa was doing.

*****

"Out with it. When you left with him, the media room was so hot I almost jumped Tynan. So?" Rain had taken Alyssa to the big bedroom that was given to her. It was beautiful with dark wood and eggplant walls. A fireplace and seating arrangement were to the side. That was where they were curled up while chatting. Alyssa grinned at her friend and told her some of the details.

"I'm really happy for you. That mountain of a Guardian looks at you in the way you deserve," Rain said with genuine warmth in her aqua eyes. "You've been hiding from the world long enough. I'm glad you've come out and started living. You needed something to shake up your solitary existence, and he definitely fits the bill."

"Thanks. How is it here? Are you okay?"

"Everything's fine. I'm still trying to get settled. Conn took me to check on my parents and the shop, so I picked up some things. Mrs. Lewis decided to keep the store open. I told her it would be fine if she wanted to spend time with her family, but she said it gave her something to keep her mind off the scare. The hell beast attack rattled everyone, but they seem to be okay otherwise. I can't believe it happened." Rain's features were tight, remnants of worry for her family. Rain's parents were sweet and scholarly. Her friend liked to shake them up a bit with her humor, but they all loved each other. There were many layers to Rain that her friend never let the outside world see.

Gregoire had told her about the breach, and she'd briefly checked on her parents and knew Rain's were fine as well.

Rain rolled her neck before talking again. "Drake said I would have to live here."

She felt instantly guilty that her friend's life had been upended because of her. "I'm sorry, Rain. What can I do?"

Alyssa could see the stubborn glint to her friend's eyes. "I'm good now. I had words with the dragon, but I've had enough time to get used to it." She could only imagine the huge leader of the Guardians going up against her tiny Mageia friend. Rain was stubborn as hell. Yes, she enjoyed her life and greeted new experiences with open arms, but she loved that shop. That particular thought took away some of Alyssa's amusement.

"What happened?" Alyssa cocked a brow in inquiry.

"I might have gotten a little heated when he suggested I close my own damn business... Did you know that smoke comes out of his mouth when he's annoyed? I would likely have peed myself if Conn hadn't started laughing," her friend said, shaking her head. "He's right. It's probably too dangerous for me to run the shop. If not now, it will be when the Realm learns you're Gregoire's mate."

Alyssa felt like crap that her life had done this to her friend.

"Don't get that look. I've already figured it out, and living with a bunch of sexy Guardians won't be a hardship." Rain winked before continuing, "I have a temporary plan. Contrary to what that big badassed dragon thinks, I'm not stupid. It truly amazes me that these big males think that just because I'm mortal and a little on the petite side that I have no brain." She shook her head in annoyance as Alyssa laughed.

"What'd you figure out?" she ventured, trying to come up with some solutions of her own to help out with the situation. Unlike Rain, who had an actual storefront, Alyssa was able to run her business from anywhere.

"That staying in Lofodes isn't a good plan. The Guardians are careful in their dealings on Tetartos for a reason. There are those who believe the Guardians can get them out of the Realm. It really is shitty. After all they do to help the inhabitants here." Rain shook her head, looking thoroughly disgusted. "Astrid even gets my stock for the shop through them. She hasn't told me exactly how it works, and I've never cared about the semantics. That being said, I wouldn't want some idiot trying to use me to get to you. I crunched the numbers, and I can afford to hire someone to work the store for a bit. I know Mrs. Lewis likes the part-time work, but I really need to find someone that needs a place to live too. That way I could trade room and board for work at a smaller wage. I think I can get by with that, and I have a couple of people in mind. It won't really leave me much, but since I need to find another occupation, that particular problem should solve itself."

Rain chewed on her bottom lip as she looked off, thinking. Alyssa had a lot of respect for her friend's ability to go with things. "I would have offered rent here, but since the big-ass dragon annoyed me with his assumptions about my mental capacity, there will be no rent for him." That would likely change. Rain would eventually find another way to make the Guardian leader suffer since he probably didn't need the money. Alyssa smiled.

"Well, you're welcome to be my assistant. I still need to talk to Gregoire about where to set up my stuff once I get it from my parents' house, but there is plenty of work. My lingerie designs have been selling really well," she offered.

Rain cringed. "Sorry, Lis, there's not enough booze or money for that. I honestly don't think I'd be capable of sewing a straight line and you'd hate me in days."

"There are plenty of things to do besides that."

"Thanks for the offer. And in reality I may end up taking you up on it, but you'll completely regret it," she said, smiling and getting up. "Let's get out of here. Stop worrying. I don't want you stressing that this is your fault, because it's not. You know I like change. It'll be an adventure." Rain grinned wide at her as she tossed a pillow. "But you know what? We're technically still on vacation, and there are a ton of places around here to get drinks and have fun while we wait on your hunk of a Guardian. Let's go see what we can find. There are pools, hot tubs and little seating rooms with fully stocked bars. Conn gave me the short tour, or so he called it." Her eyes glittered when she spoke about the Lykos Guardian with amber eyes and tattoos.

Alyssa raised a brow. "Conn?"

"He's a sweetheart, and I could easily go there. He's got some impressive pheromones, and he's hot as hell with those tattoos... I just don't know... I've been in a weird place mentally since I got here. I'm sure once I get my new path figured out, I'll be all over him." Rain chuckled, but Alyssa could see her friend's heart wasn't in it.

"We'll figure it out."

"Lis, please stop worrying, I fully plan to make the most of it. You know how I am. I'm excited to come up with something new to do. I've had the shop for over five years. I really do think I'm up for the change. Worry about that massive male of yours. Shit, I can't believe he didn't break you in half with his big Guardian equipment."

Alyssa flushed with embarrassment and desire, her mind instantly going to that particular portion of his anatomy.

Her friend burst out laughing as they exited the room and walked down the hall. "I'll take that as confirmation and start looking for a Guardian of my own to tangle in the sheets with." Her friend started chatting about the amenities in the compound, going on to describe how secure it was. She said she'd met a few of the staff, but the place was huge, so she was sure she'd only seen a small portion. They entered an area with cozy oversized chairs and a big window and French doors leading out to the courtyard.

"Hi, Pela. Meet Alyssa, my best friend in the world. We've known each other since we were kids," Rain said to the bright-eyed blonde cozied up in a chair by the window. She had a book in one hand, wine in the other and looked like a picture the way the light hit her.

Alyssa smiled as they said their hellos, as Rain began opening cabinets and pouring them something to drink. Pela grinned and set her book aside, unbothered by the interruption. She was in a pretty halter dress of pale blue cotton that perfectly complemented her light hair. Alyssa enjoyed making dresses, but she preferred wearing cargo shorts and tank tops for day-to-day stuff. That was a lie, she just thought it'd be ridiculous wearing dresses while she worked, and there were rarely other occasions for her to dress up.

Her mind wandered to how Gregoire was doing in his meeting. She looked forward to touching him again. The thrum of their life forces trying to connect was getting more distracting as they spent time apart.

Was he feeling the same?

Two other females came in a moment later, a redhead and a brunette. Pela greeted them. "These are my friends Areth and Thala. Ladies, this is Rain, she's been living here a few days, and this is her friend Alyssa," Pela said, pointing at each of them. It felt awkward correcting the female's assumption, so she let it go. All three of the females were Geraki, part of the Immortal race able to change into large birds or partially shift to produce wings on their human form. Brianne was of that race. All were stunning with willowy figures and delicate features. They poured their drinks while Rain brought theirs over and sat down.

"What do you do here?" Alyssa asked politely as she sipped the sweet drink Rain had given her. It was truly decadent, so she took a longer draw, hoping it would calm the escalating need to search out her mate.

"We are in charge of everything from cleaning to helping with guests," the dark-haired one, Thala, said thoughtfully before a soft almost dreamy glint came across her face. "We were even honored to have been asked to prepare Alexandra for her mating to Urian."

Their eyes lit as they spoke of the mating preparations and Alex, who, from their description, was stunning. They were obviously in awe of the Demi-Goddess, and Alyssa felt a pang of what others would think about her mating with Gregoire. She was nowhere near the level of Uri's mate. The females' excitement was palpable. A mating was such a rare occurrence, and it gave all the Immortals the hope that they would someday find their other half. Curiosity was getting the best of her and she couldn't help asking what they knew of the mating ceremony itself. Her parents hadn't shared any of the details though she and Rain had heard salacious rumors over the years.

"What happens?" She noticed Rain's eyes lit with curiosity as Alyssa asked her question.

The Geraki shared a grin of pure enjoyment at being able to impart their knowledge. Thala explained, "It's all very carnal and beautiful. In Immortal pairings like Urian and Alex's, last week, they do the first ceremony in a hidden temple where the male gets branded with the mating mark." Thala put her hands up to her chest and her cheeks flushed as she spoke, making Alyssa all the more excited. She and Rain leaned forward in their seats. "He then takes his female off to the Temple of Consummation, where they blood-bond while someone watches over them; then they spend hours consummating the bond in whatever way brings the *female* the most pleasure. Some males bring in several others to ensure all of her fantasies are met in that one night, no matter how possessive the male may be. It's an incredible honor to be invited into something that sacred. There's a great deal of trust and reverence involved. I was invited participate only once, many centuries ago. It was beyond beautiful. I heard Gregoire was brought in for Alex and…"

Alyssa stopped hearing anything that was said after that point. Her ears buzzed, and she felt like she might actually throw up the wine she'd consumed. It was like everything blurred into slow motion as the walls around her came crashing down. Sounds were quieted by the pounding in her ears. She felt as if a knife had speared into her heart and was twisting slowly.

Rain jumped up, stammering something, probably excuses; Alyssa couldn't seem to process any of it. She took Alyssa's glass from her weak grasp and urged her out of the room. A cold stillness came over her. A kind of blessed calm after feeling as if she'd been flayed wide open.

Are you okay? What's happening? Cold fury filled her at hearing his voice, but she blocked it, blocked him. Gregoire had slept with Urian's mate a week ago? Had he just been whoring around while she was kept untried the entire five years? With a damned Demi-Goddess?

She was sitting back in Rain's room, although she remembered little of the walk there. Her friend stared down at her with worried aqua eyes. "Lis, sweetie, I'm so sorry. I should never have introduced you to those women. I had no idea that happened."

"He slept with his brother's mate a week ago, Rain. He could have claimed me any time in the last five years and instead he sleeps with someone else? A *week* ago." Her voice sounded dangerously low. She'd never felt pain or fury like it. If he came for her now, she wouldn't be responsible for her actions. It wasn't as if she were ignorant about the sheer eroticism surrounding Immortals and she'd heard wild rumors about the mating ceremony itself. She and Rain were fully aware of all the sharing and orgies that went on everywhere. Hell, she'd made her fair share of lingerie for those going to sex parties. But she'd never considered that *her* mate would be willing to participate in something like that during a time when he could have been with her.

Her heart felt like it was breaking in half, yet at the same time she felt cold inside.

Chapter 23

Guardian Compound, Tetartos Realm

G regoire stood outside of Rain's room with Alex and Uri. They'd come with him when he'd gotten her surge of emotion at the end of the meeting. They'd wanted to meet her. All three of them stood, tense and still, in the hallway after having heard what she'd said. The door was shut, but with their hearing, it didn't matter.

You've known she was your mate for five years? Alex demanded of Gregoire, using the Guardian mental link she shared with Uri. He heard the fury and saw the tensing in her muscles as they stood there.

Yes, he responded.

I never took you for an idiot. You better fix this, now. You betrayed her by even showing up at our mating. You sure as hell better tell her I didn't know you had a mate. I'm going to be around her, and you've made her hate me before we've even met. I could kick your ass right now, but I'll leave that honor to your mate. She gave him a scathing look before spinning on her heel and walking back in the other direction. He closed his eyes and rubbed the back of his neck. He was fucked.

Uri held back a second. *I don't envy you, brother.* Uri gave him a sympathetic look before following after his mate.

*****

She felt him, knew he was outside the door, but made no moves to open the damn thing. He could wait, but at the same time she wanted to let her fury loose and didn't want to do it in front of anyone else, even Rain. This was private, though the whole Realm seemed to know.

A mating was for all eternity and she felt the length of time like a chain around her neck at the moment.

She got up. "I'm going to go have a talk with my mate." She said the last word as if she were talking about hell beast dung not a male.

Rain's eyebrows lifted. Her friend's eyes held concern and maybe a little respect. "Take no prisoners, and come get me if you need backup."

She opened the door to see him standing right there. He looked like he was just about to open it before she'd flung it wide. "Let's go," she said through clenched teeth. She focused on the fury not the pain because the hurt would only tear her apart. Her heart felt bloodied and broken, but she'd be damned if he saw any of that. The anger kept her whole as they walked the halls and made it outside.

Porting made her ache for him, and that just set her off more. She was wet, hurting and seething by the time they got inside his home. He'd been silently watching her, waiting her out.

She turned around and used air currents to lift her up into his face. "Why is it that you could fuck the world and I was kept chaste? Hmm?" Her voice got higher pitched as she let the fury fly. "You fucked your friend's mate while I was living a confined life with my parents. Well, screw you!"

"Alyssa," he growled.

178

She wanted to scream at the fierce look on his face. "No! You listen to me. How the hell did you think that would make me feel? Oh, that's right, it doesn't matter what I feel or want. It's all up to the big-assed Guardian to make all the decisions for my life while he gets to do whatever and *whoever* he wants, right? It doesn't matter that I've been made to feel inferior by just about everyone in our race; let's add to it by fucking a damn Demi-Goddess, that I could never possibly compare to, days before screwing me and acting like it meant something." She was nearing a roar by the end, and she punctuated it by using air currents to slam his ass into the wall, shaking the building around him.

She'd felt her powers expanding in the last couple of days, but that held a punch she hadn't expected and she was angry at herself for resorting to violence. His green eyes flashed before he stalked toward her. She set back down on her feet and turned to leave the room.

"You got to talk. Now it's my turn." His tone was dangerously low and she didn't care.

"Don't. I can't." She was angry and brittle at the moment. She needed a moment alone to think. "I'm going to shower, alone, and then I'm going to figure out what *I* want to do with *my* life."

He appeared in front of her a second later and lifted her into his arms, her own held firmly behind her back. Smart male, she was still tempted to do some damage.

"You will listen," he gritted out. "I already explained why I didn't come for you before now. I did what was best for you."

She narrowed her eyes at the presumptuous ass. Yes, they'd discussed this before, but it didn't make it better now mixed with everything else.

"Until you said something, I had no idea that the others treated you badly and I have no problem bloodying them for their stupidity. In fact, I would love to do just that, but I suspect that your father may be behind it because I cannot believe those of our race are fucking stupid. I can, however, see your father doing something to keep them away from you. Probably to save their damned lives, because if any had touched you, I would have killed them." He growled, "I want to go and kill the males at the island that you allowed to touch and suck on your beautiful breasts and sweet little cunt. I may end up doing it one day if I lose control. You have too much fucking power over my beast. Too much power over me, Alyssa, and it's a dangerous place for both of us."

Her traitorous body clenched in desire at his tone and words. He set her on the ground in front of him. His hands went to his hips and his muscles flexed as he spoke.

"That you are small only makes you more unique," he gritted out before going on, "I didn't have sex with Alex. Yes, I was there, and yes, Alex is a Demi-Goddess, but I don't care. In my mind there is no comparison between the two of you. You are my world. She is Uri's." He stared into her eyes.

She didn't know what to do with this information, she was dying to believe it, but could she? It didn't help that she was still hungry for him because of the damned frenzy, no matter that she felt splayed open. He'd hurt her so badly she didn't think she could forgive him. "What did you do with her?"

He growled low. "Don't." After a second he bit out, "I'd kept you a secret from everyone, so neither Uri nor Alex knew at that point that you existed. I was invited to join in Uri's mating consummation, and yes, I went because it's a huge honor to be asked. Uri is my closest friend and brother. The mating consummation includes giving the female every pleasure she desires. The tradition started with

Immortal males' need to cherish their females and atone for the horrors they'd been a part of as forced studs in Apollo's labs."

His jaw clamped down tight for a moment before he continued. "Alex's fantasy was to be taken by two males, so I was invited. But when I watched over their blood-bonding and saw their connection, it changed things for me. I'd been denying my need to claim you, but after seeing what they went through, I planned to call it off. Alex stopped it before I got the chance." He paused before going on, "My need to claim you proved impossible to curb from that moment on and I immediately started making arrangements to come for you."

He'd been there though. At some point he'd agreed to screw Alex. The thimble-sized relief that he hadn't was hollow because the intent had been there. "Do mated males usually participate in that *honored* practice?" she challenged.

He clenched his teeth and she saw him battling for an answer.

She shook her head. "How many others did you *honor* with your cock during the last five years?" she spat out.

A muscle ticked under his beard as he growled. "Immortal males need sex just as they need earth's energies."

"What does that mean?" She'd never heard that. Yes, Immortals were incredibly sexual, that was obvious, but saying that he *needed* sex seemed ridiculous to her. "I obviously didn't need to screw every male I met since I turned twenty."

He growled low, "I know, or I would have come for you before you were ready. I will not lie to you, Alyssa. Males need a mutual release to stay fucking strong. My hand was never enough." He sounded disgusted. With himself. With biology.

"Then you should have come for your mate!"

181

She hated feeling the truth in his words.

"You were not ready," he growled.

"How many females did you fuck for my own good?" She was vibrating with fury.

He sat her on the island still holding her hands behind her back. His hips forced their way between her thighs so he was against her. "Don't, Alyssa." There was anger and a hint of torment in his tone when he continued, "I was forced to endure the touch of human females for the last twenty-five years. I won't lie to you, but I also won't make excuses for doing what I had to do." His gaze was intense.

"Let me down," she demanded, and for a moment he held her impossibly tighter before growling and setting her on her feet to stare up at him.

She felt sick to her stomach. Endured? Gods, how many were there? Her hands were shaking when she paced toward the kitchen and closed her eyes against the hurt in her chest.

Hadn't she intended to have sex with someone else, knowing he existed? That hadn't been the same... It was all convoluted and painful. They hadn't known each other, but how could he claim to have wanted her while having had sex with others?

Creators, this was all so messed up. Just when she'd started to think she might get the fairy tale, it turned into something ugly. When she turned to face him again, she asked, "So if I want to be taken by two males? If that is my deepest desire for our bonding, you'll play along?" She saw his whole body tense. She didn't desire that, but what if she had? The way he answered that question would define how they moved forward. She needed to know what he was willing to do. He'd ripped her wide open whether he'd meant to or

182

not, and she just couldn't let it go. How the hell did she get past any of this?

"Do not ask that of me, angel." His bit out words were so intense they practically vibrated through the room.

"Then what do I do?" she asked as he stalked her.

"I can feel your hurt, Alyssa, but do not ever ask that of me." He warned.

When he reached for her, she moved. "I need air and to think. Don't follow me. This isn't a hunt." His beast better fucking curb the desire to chase, because she desperately needed space. Turning, she shook her head at him. "You could have had me, Gregoire."

He pulled her into his arms, his muscles tense as he lifted her back up, "You weren't ready for *me*, or for this life. I gave you what you needed whether you want to believe it or not, Alyssa."

He set her down by the front door a split second later and eyed her.

She spun and exited without another word. The second she felt cool air, she was able to fight back the desire she still felt. She sucked in a deep breath and headed for the lake below, feeling his anger and frustration. She swore she felt pain in there too, but it could have been the echo of her own. He seemed to be taking her need for space seriously because he didn't come after her.

Chapter 24

Private Villa, Tetartos Realm

Sam felt cherished in a way she'd never thought possible. Of course she'd never imagined Demi-Gods walked the Earth, that there were more Realms than Earth, or that Immortals existed. She shook her head as she finished one of the sandwiches Vane had procured for her. She set the wrapper aside and snuggled back in the bed.

Erik was starting to even out, though they were still making love like bunnies. They'd gone to a cave not far from the villa the day before and sat in the cozy seating area by a spring as he'd fueled his body's needs. He'd shared energies with her and taught her how to take them in. It was a heady experience that left her feeling amazing. Unfortunately, nothing she'd said helped dispel the guilt he was constantly feeling.

"I think we should get back to the compound. Jax was nice enough to give me access to this place and cave, but we've been here for days. We have the suite in the compound until we decide where to build a place of our own." His voice was a seductive rumble against her chest. He was holding her against his chest. She felt incredible. It was like she was stronger, felt his strength inside her. His power?

"Okay. Can I try to teleport us?" She lifted her cheek off his warm chest and looked up at him.

Some of the tension had left his beautiful features, but he stared at her intently before speaking. "Are you sure you feel up to it? You are wielding power that your body isn't yet accustomed to; maybe we should stick to trying to enhance your power over metal." His voice held a note of concern.

"I'm sure it's fine. I got here on my own. I was nauseated, but that was it. I really want to try again."

He was quiet while his hand traced circles on her back. She loved the gentle touch. They'd both been leaving their minds open during sex, and it had given her an added feeling of connection with him. He hadn't said he loved her, but she felt it from him. She knew he had his own struggles with guilt, and she wasn't sure any man enjoyed spouting their love. The time between having sex was spent discussing their pasts.

They'd spoken of families and the fact that hers might soon be in Tetartos. She'd passed some notes back and forth through Drake, and it looked like they were planning to relocate. They said they could easier be in hiding there or in a Realm with their daughter. She'd gotten teary eyed when she'd read that last message from her mother. Drake had put them in a safe house on Earth because the Guardians had detected that Cyril was interested in them, which made her anxious. The monster hadn't gone after or watched any of the other girls' families that had been taken and used in his experiments. That thought left her unsettled. Why her family?

She shook off the worry. Her parents were safe and likely settling things in order to drastically change their lives in a few months.

"Okay, you can port us back after you rest." He kissed her forehead and tucked her head back to his chest. She grinned at his comment. She was wide awake; there would be no sleeping anytime soon. She wanted him. She kissed one hard nipple and felt his deep inhale. He was so big and gorgeous everywhere; she wanted to lap up every inch of him. He made a rumbling noise as she nipped at the tight brown nubbin. That vibration made her so hot.

Chapter 25

Gregoire's Home, Tetartos Realm

Alyssa woke up in Gregoire's arms, cradled into his chest. At first she felt content and safe, snuggled up in his warmth; then she remembered what had led them there, and her heart ached. She'd only had an hour at the lake before the frenzy became too much. He'd taken her so damned slowly and she knew It was him trying to atone with his body. She took a deep breath and was assailed with his scent, which only made things worse. She still wanted him. His answers might have eased some of her fury. Making him think she wanted another male in their bed wasn't a move she was proud of.

She tried to move out of his hold, but his arms tightened. She looked up to see his green eyes shining under heavy lids.

"I want coffee."

He released her from his grasp, and she watched as he stretched his arms high over his head before getting up. Her breath caught at the sight of his muscles moving with the motion.

"I also need to see if there is somewhere I can set up a work space here." She needed to bury herself in work.

He grunted at her as he moved around the bed toward the stairs. "Come with me."

He headed down the stairs, gloriously nude, and she closed her eyes for a moment. His ass was a work of art, and she followed it past the kitchen to a doorway that was set at an angle, giving it a hidden effect. When he moved aside so she could finally see around him, her breath caught in her throat, and she almost choked.

The room was huge, set inside the mountain but with a large floor-to-ceiling window that matched the living room and let in a lot of natural light. She stepped deeper into the space, her fingers sliding over soft fabrics set inside shelves designed to fit them perfectly. There were hundreds of bolts from delicate silks to denim. She saw tables for cutting, sewing machines and soft fabric-covered mannequins. A huge rack held every bobbin and needle or trim her imagination could come up with. It was a seamstress's dream. She wasn't sure how long she stared at the contents of the room, finding more and more she hadn't seen until she set her sights on the machines she had no idea how to use. She was too overwhelmed to look at him. This had taken time and a considerable amount of coin, she was sure of it.

She turned to him. He had been still and quiet, stalking her with his eyes as she rounded the room. She felt his gaze on her skin as she stole glances of him leaning against the doorway. She cleared her clogged throat. "Thank you. When did you do this?"

When he spoke, it came out gravelly. "It's stayed empty until recently." She walked to him, comfortable with her nudity but at a loss with how raw she felt. She wanted to love him with everything she was, like mated pairs should. She wanted to get lost in him and chase away the flicker of sorrow she'd seen when he hadn't guarded against it fast enough. She also wanted him to pay for making her care for him after hurting her so much.

"When I built the house, I wasn't sure why I put this room here. There are bedrooms on the other side of the stairs and ones inset in the mountain for the young I hope we'll have. There is also another master bedroom set behind the loft for that same reason."

Her mouth dried up as she felt a deep intense craving from him. He wanted a family and he'd planned for her, for the children they'd one day have... She'd never given much thought to having young. Children necessitated having a mate, and the chances had been slim of ever having one. The fairy tale had always ended with her mate finding and claiming her.

The first time they conceived wouldn't likely be for at least a decade, she knew that much of matings.

All she could visualize now were small children climbing all over her strong Guardian mate. Him holding them in the safety of his big arms as they slept. She wanted that more than she ever imagined, and it made her angry. She pictured wild little boys with piercing forest eyes running all over their home while she sewed them tiny clothes. Shit, she needed to find a way past what happened. She wanted the good there could be in finding her mate. She took a deep breath.

"It hurts... Knowing I'd been kept a virgin for you while you were out fucking the world's female population. I want to believe your reasons. But I feel possessive of you too. Think about how you would have felt if I'd gone to be a part of Uri's mating, intending to fuck him? Or if I'd given myself to any male I could find, knowing you were out there oblivious to the fact that you were mine."

His eyes narrowed, and he growled deep. His muscles had tensed. "I did not lie, Alyssa. I would have waited if I could have. It hasn't been as easy as you believe."

"I'm not sure that's enough... Did Alex want you specifically or the experience?"

"Don't." His tone was harsh.

"I don't know how to just get over all of this. I have to face Alex, Uri and everyone else that knew you went to their mating ceremony and that you'd been with others before that. Help me not to hate you for this."

His jaw was tight, and she saw the frustration in his eyes, but she also saw understanding and a kind of resolve set in.

"Come here... If I'd had any idea you would feel like that, I would have declined to go to Uri's ceremony, no matter how big an insult that would have been. I should have." His deep voice was full of emotion. At least he hadn't slept with Alex.

She walked toward him.

"I never would have intentionally hurt you, Alyssa. Your parents should have explained more about the ways of Immortals."

"I'd heard rumors about the mating ceremony, but it's different when your mate is the one *honored*. As for the fact that you need sex, I wish I would have been given a choice between having my mate fuck around or claim me. I understand my father probably made it more complicated, but I should have been given the option to choose. If you needed sex, it should have been with *me*."

His eyes flashed with desire and regret.

He leaned in and took her lips in a sweet caress that left her breathless before breaking away to run his hands over the back of his hair.

He touched her cheek and looked into her eyes. "I watched you on your twentieth birthday and it nearly killed me not to come for you.You deserved time to grow. If you'd have known and said you wanted me then I wouldn't have turned you away. I would have claimed what was *mine*. I would have been the bastard that took you before you were ready." He growled, "Your life will never be the same now that you belong to me, Alyssa."

He really believed what he said. And maybe he was right. If she'd been given a choice at twenty she would have chosen the fairytale, and being a Guardian's mate was more than that. It was potentially dangerous. A fact they'd discussed in his cavern.

Even Rain's life had been affected.

Knowing that didn't make the hurt go away. She couldn't stop imagining him with other females.

He took a deep breath. "Why didn't you come to me when you overheard your parents?"

She shook her head. "If I'd come to you, we would have gone through the frenzy. I would never have known if you'd have chosen me. I wanted for once in my life to be picked because I was what my mate wanted most." She was being completely honest even though it was painful to admit. She really needed to find her way through all of this.

"If we'd met after you'd hit your majority, at an Emfanisi, it would have been the same." His brows were furrowed.

"But we hadn't, you knew about me, so I wanted you to choose to come for me. Whether it was logical or not didn't matter."

He stood there staring at her as if he were searching for something. Probably understanding. Finally, his jaw hardened as he seemed to come to some kind of decision.

His strong hands pulled her to him. "I'm going to open my mind to you, Alyssa. I can't think of any other way for you to understand how I feel about you without you second-guessing my words. It goes against everything in me to be open like this." He nearly growled those last words before she was hit with it.

She felt the minute he opened to her; she saw herself through his eyes. Such intense, overriding emotion assailed her, and it was almost too much. He lifted her into his arms, fisted a hand in her hair and devoured her lips. Her legs wrapped around his hips, and she lost herself in him, mind and body. Felt how he loved the sensation of her breasts against his chest, her nipples hard and tight.

He couldn't get enough of her taste; his tongue tangled with hers, taking all that he could. He wanted so many things. He wanted her laid out as he ate her pussy. Wanted his tongue to plunge deep inside and lap up all her juices while his fingers probed her ass and made her ready for his cock. She was more than anything he'd imagined she would be.

He spoke in her mind. *I'm laid bare for you, angel. I've only ever wanted you safe and happy. Now you know how much control you have over me?*

The day you were born, you brought me to my knees. And the first time I saw you fully grown, I watched as you ran in the hills; I knew then that you were too young, even without your father pointing it out, but just the fucking sight of you brought light into my life again. I felt peace for the first time. From you. Not any other female. You, angel.

The raspy words in her mind made gooseflesh rise along her skin. He lifted her higher and pulled her hair back to lick and suck her neck. Tingles ran down her body; she shivered, wanting his lips on her swollen breasts as he spoke to her. His emotions were raw, untamed, and she was getting blasted with them. And they weren't all sexual like she'd expected. This was far deeper than just lust from the frenzy.

I've fucked too many humans imagining it was you. Your pussy, your mouth as they took the edge off my need. It was your beautiful green eyes I saw every fucking time in the last five years. You were a hunger that ate at my gut every fucking day. Now that I have you, it's even more intense. It's not enough to have you. My beast wants everyone to know you're mine. I'm obsessed.

She moaned as he splayed her out on the cutting table, her bottom was at the edge, and he spanned her legs wide. He was mesmerized by the sight of her bare pussy glistening and begging for his cock; she knew his thoughts, loved hearing them.

"What if I wanted to claim you like that? Tie you up and let everyone see that you are *mine*," Alyssa asked. The thought had come, and now that it was out there, she felt how much she wanted it. She wanted to lay him out and take him. He was so dominant she wasn't sure he'd be able to do that. He stilled and stared at her.

She felt his thoughts before he spoke them aloud. "Would that fix this, Alyssa? Would it heal the pain if I gave you leave to bind and claim me?" She was surprised that he hadn't protested the idea outright. "Let me inside your mind, angel."

His hands caressed her thighs, and she felt odd emotion mixing in his mind. His knuckles petted her lower lips and clit. He planned to tease her, coax her into letting him inside her mind. He loved her. The words weren't in his mind, but the emotion was.

"Let me in, love. I need to know what you're thinking."

Allowing him to see her pain was asking a lot.

I need to know.

She watched him for a few moments. He was letting her feel his emotions, how much he needed to know what she was struggling with. He wasn't going to let it go.

Let me see how to make this better.

She lifted the shield and moaned when she felt him slip inside. It was intense sharing minds like they were. He knew all she was feeling or thinking in that moment. His fingers tempted and teased as she gasped. He stared at her, and she felt how overwhelmed he was. There was so much; the pain had lessened a little with understanding of how much he truly hated touching others. How much he'd yearned for *her*.

If you want to tie me up, angel, I'll let you. He lifted her back in his arms, still in her mind, feeling her roiling emotions. Her legs wrapped back around him. His cock was hard and heavy between them. *I'd let you tie me up in the middle of Lofodes if it'll make your pain go away. I hate that I hurt you, love.* Gods, he hated it, it was all there for her to feel.

It was a whirlwind as he carried her to the bed and followed her down. *I'm going to try to make it better. Let me stay in your mind.* His big body was cradled between her spread thighs.

He licked and sucked at her bottom lip as he ran the head of his cock over her slit until she was panting and gasping beneath him. His mind caressed hers as his body blanketed her. She loved when he gave her his weight, let her feel him. He was so warm, and the caress of his mind, seeing such heavy, intense emotion, set her on fire. It was hot and crazed, and she loved it, loved him. Her strong and possessive Guardian saw her as special.

He growled above her. She knew her thoughts were setting him off. She writhed as he stroked her. She felt his determination. Her big

194

strong mate was set on seduction, planned on using everything in him to ease the hurt inside her. She melted at his thoughts. He kissed and touched, gliding his lips and hands over her skin.

She felt cherished. The hurt slid away, desire and love slipping into its place, at least for the moment. She moaned as he spread her wide and ate at her, first gently, then more demanding. Her hands were in his hair, tugging at the soft strands, wanting more of him. She felt how much he wanted to impale her with his cock, ride her hard and fill her with his come. He looked up at her smooth stomach, and she felt how much he wanted her to give him a child. She gasped as his mind conjured pictures of her stomach full and round as he used his mouth to bring her off. A climax hit her hard and rode her as his lips gentled, slowly bringing her down. She felt just how much he loved her taste as he used his tongue to clean her. The pain was temporarily forgotten.

He spent hours loving her. Taking her with his mouth over and over and then finally his cock. She was dizzy and spent by the time he curled her into his side to drift off.

She was still snuggled into his chest when she opened her eyes again. She felt warm and secure in his arms. She lifted her head from his big chest and saw his forest gaze watching her. She instantly felt the loss of his mind.

"It's a struggle for me to keep it open, Alyssa."

She lifted her own mental shield, knowing he'd heard her emotion. His eyes narrowed. "I liked hearing your thoughts."

She grinned up at him. "I liked hearing yours too. Any time you want in, I'll ask that you do the same."

He growled a little, and her smile widened. She felt lighter. She refused to think about any of the rest. She planned to do her best to move forward.

"Are you okay?" he asked before kissing her temple.

"Better. I'm not sure the hurt won't hit me again at times. Let's just leave it at that for now," she admitted honestly.

"And, Gregoire, never again. No other female touches what's mine." She knew he didn't want others, but she couldn't stop from warning against it.

He growled his approval. "And no male touches you."

She nodded with a smile and they just looked at one another for long moments.

"Coffee, angel?"

"That sounds wonderful." She moved to get up but was lifted into his arms again. "I can walk."

"I like carrying you." She liked it too. His hands caressed her butt as he moved, and she snuggled her cheek up against his big chest. He smelled so damn good.

All too soon, she was settled onto a towel on the island. She watched as his muscles rolled as he moved around the kitchen, setting the coffee up to brew. The grounds alone smelled amazing.

"Let's run down and around the lake," he said while selecting a couple of mugs out of the cabinet. "I've never seen your animal."

She cringed internally. Most Immortals needed to allow their beasts free on a weekly basis, but she'd thankfully been able to keep hers locked up for much longer before it beat at her to be free.

"I'd rather just run in my human form."

He cocked an eyebrow at her in challenge. Damn it, he'd have to see her beast eventually. The animal had been pushing for freedom for days as it was.

She felt somewhat confident he wouldn't laugh at her, but she'd never allowed anyone but her parents to see it. He poured their coffee and pulled the creamer out of the fridge as she stewed.

"Which one?" he asked, pulling out the creamer options.

"Thin Mint, a lot." He grinned in amusement as he poured until she nodded.

Her cup was so full it nearly spilled as she brought it to her lips.

"Okay, I'll run with you, but one word about my other form, and I won't be responsible for the chunk taken out of your ass."

He nearly choked on his coffee. His eyes lit with mirth, and his mouth kicked up into a stunning grin. His beauty made her breath catch, and she lost track of what she was saying.

His voice was a deep rumble. "Why would you say that?"

"I'm small in all my forms. The other Hippeus would have had a field day with that knowledge, so I've managed to keep it hidden. Chuckle all you want, I'm not kidding."

"I have no doubt you are small, and I won't laugh. I'll let my animal out as well." He grinned at her as he took another drink.

"That'll make me more comfortable... I'll be the pony standing next to what I imagine is your huge-assed warhorse. That's so much easier, thank you." She infused the words with as much sarcasm as she could manage. She was dreading the experience, but at the same time she looked forward to seeing his beast.

Meeting now. No battle, but all five cities have breaches. Drake's angry voice sounded in her mind, and she jumped.

"You heard him?" he asked, his gaze assessing. The beautiful grin was gone, leaving his normal stoic features fully in its place.

"Yes."

"Then you have access to my Guardian telepathic links now." She looked inward and her mouth gaped at all the connections she could see.

A moment later, both were in their bedroom, dressing. He frowned at her. "You don't need to go."

"I want to."

"Before you see Alex, you should know she's furious with me. She and Uri were with me outside Rain's room because they'd wanted to meet you."

"What are you talking about? Why didn't you tell me that before?" She narrowed her eyes at him.

"I was more concerned about you." His answer settled her.

"She heard what I said to Rain, then? What exactly happened?"

"Yes, and she wanted to make sure I told you we didn't have sex. And that she didn't know I had a mate. Then she threatened to kick my ass."

She nodded. She needed to let it go now; Alex hadn't even done anything wrong. They were all going to be around each other for centuries and she'd rather pretend the past didn't exist in any form. "I appreciate her sentiment. Right now, I need to know what's going on in Lofodes, so I'm going to the meeting with you. If there's a breach, I'll also need to get to Rain's parents."

He only grunted.

They quickly donned the rest of their clothes, and Gregoire added a blade at his side.

They ported to the Guardian manor, and she took a bracing breath to clear the arousal and get her mind together before heading into the meeting.

They walked through the media room she'd been in before, down a hall and into a big room with all kinds of electronics and a huge table. The seats were mostly full when they arrived.

Brianne came in behind them, and she was glad for that because the redhead greeted her warmly with a smile and a wink. "Hello, Alyssa."

Gregoire had her tucked tight to his side as a few more people trickled in. Drake was already talking, so she wasn't forced to meet the others.

"All five cities have small breaches set in their shielding. According to the warriors in each city, each breach was made by Mageia females that left notes saying they were defecting to Cyril's side. All notes stated that he was providing them with mates and Immortality." Rounds of "fuck" went through the room.

"All the cities need help getting the shields repaired. We need to see if it's the same fucking spell the asshole used in the hell beast breach. I will send you all my mental notes, but I'm guessing it's the same one that we haven't been fucking able to find a way to counteract." Smoke was billowing from the leader's lips.

I'd like Lofodes, she heard Gregoire informing Drake. She was definitely on the same channel as the Guardians now.

That's fine. Drake's mental voice sounded in her head in response to Gregoire's request. She spotted Uri and knew the beautiful female next to him had to be Alex. Both were looking at Drake as he finished discussing the details and assigning Guardians to cities. They made a beautiful pair. Alex was gorgeous, with her nearly black hair and flawless features.

They all got up a second later and started quickly exiting, so again she was spared meeting the others. Most nodded and gave her a quick smile as they moved out. Alex glared at Gregoire before nodding to her. It actually made her feel a little better even though it was still awkward as hell. At least that initial contact was over with. Dorian came up beside them. He was assigned to Lofodes with Gregoire. The other Guardian was about as tall as Gregoire, but not as bulky. He was much bigger than the other Nereids she'd seen. His blond hair was spiked up, and he was beautiful to look at even with the furrowed brows.

"Dorian, meet my mate, Alyssa."

Chapter 26

Cyril's Compound, Tetartos Realm

Cyril walked down the hall to his lab, inwardly thrilled. He couldn't wait to examine his new test subjects for the anomaly that would allow him to trial his latest formula. He'd been spending a good deal of time setting up his secret lab. It would work beautifully. He just needed to keep his excitement tightly leashed under his usual mask of scientific indifference.

First he planned to see if any were at the right stage to inject with the drug for his other experiment. It was even more important than before. If all was successful, the entire Realm would fall at his feet.

He couldn't wait to enjoy the spoils of his latest genius. He had no doubt the Guardians were worried that there would be mass defections, with the letters the females would have left. Cyril smirked. He planned to keep any that sought him out in a separate facility his males were currently building at the other end of the Realm. He did not wish to have true defectors near him, even after their blood memories were assessed. Kane and Angus were making those particular arrangements under the eyes of the spies he had watching the two top-ranking warriors. It really was planned out well. They were kept busy and away from his labs.

He saw Reve in the hall, and the male refused to look at him as he passed. The Kairos' punishment had been distasteful for them both, but necessary. It was obviously effective. All twelve of the women his males had targeted were in his lab, awaiting their examinations, and so far there were no Guardians beating down his doors.

His senses stayed on alert the entire time the Kairos' steps echoed in the tunnel behind him. He refused to look back, but tracking the male was prudent.

Excitement washed over him when he walked in to see six of his twelve females naked and laid out for him to examine. There was much to do, but he was closer than ever before.

Chapter 27

Lofodes, Tetartos Realm

"Where is the breach?" Gregoire's voice was low and dangerous as they came up on Curran, one of the Hippeus warriors under Adras' command. He didn't like the look of familiarity the guard sent Alyssa's way. There was another warrior with him that Gregoire didn't know by name.

"It's up around the left of the main entrance. The others are there already. Did you need me to have someone escort Alyssa safely home?" The male said it as if they were talking about a weak child.

"No," Gregoire growled. He wanted to kick Adras' ass for whatever he'd done to make this Hippeus see her as weak and possibly addled, because he saw just how right she was about that.

He ignored the Hippeus as he, Alyssa and Dorian stalked up the rise. He could practically feel his brother's confusion at this tension.

The only reason he hadn't informed the imbeciles that she was his mate was because of the threats in the fucking Realm. He hated that fact, but it was necessary for her safety.

He'd discussed keeping the mating secret with her again before they'd come here because the last thing he'd wanted was for her to think he didn't *want* to claim her for all their world to see. It still grated though. He wanted to yank her into his arms right then and let her feel just how fucking happy he was to have her as his mate.

Cyril might know Gregoire was interested in her, but if the bastard thought Alyssa was a Guardian's mate, the target would be far larger. Neither he nor his beast could handle taking any more risks than they already were when she didn't have his power. He might calm if and when she was able to teleport. That would be an advantage for her against any other attempts to take her, but not fucking now.

Until then, her parents, she, Rain and all his brethren were keeping her status fucking quiet.

Thank you. I understand why we're doing this, Gregoire, she whispered softly into his mind and he finally allowed his mental block to go back up.

"That was just fucking weird," Dorian said after they'd put some distance between them and the warriors.

"They've always associated my size with weakness."

Dorian raised a brow at that. "Is that a Hippeus thing? Because they obviously haven't met Sirena." Both males snorted at that truth. Sirena was only a few inches taller than Alyssa and her power packed a fucking punch.

Gregoire appreciated that Dorian was making an effort with Alyssa. The Nereid distrusted most Immortals and Mageia and only relaxed with his brethren. He looked over and nodded at him. Dorian acknowledged it with a subtle nod of his own. They finally came up to the others. Gregoire gave harsh looks to the other warriors, indicating for them to stay back. Adras came up, looking both fierce and concerned. Ava was right at his side, appearing mostly nervous at seeing their daughter for the first time since she'd left. They'd only spoken briefly through their familial connection.

"Who's missing?" Alyssa asked her father, getting straight to the reason they were there.

Adras relaxed a little. "Her name is Delia. Are you okay, sweeting?"

Gregoire tensed at the indication that Alyssa wasn't safe with him. Bastard. His mate ignored the question. "I know Delia. Not well, but I can't see her defecting to that monster. She worked at Rain's shop here and there and she hadn't even gone to her first Emfanisi yet. Why automatically take drastic action to find a mate at barely twenty?" Alyssa said, turning from her parents to frown up at him.

He nodded sharply. This was an abduction and they all knew it. "How far have you gotten with sealing the breach?" Gregoire demanded.

"Halfway. It's the same as last time. I still have no idea how to counteract it so this doesn't happen again," Adras growled, the male's muscles tense.

Gregoire telepathically sent the information to Drake immediately. *Adras said the Lofodes breach looks the same as the last one.*

It's the same here in Ouranos as well. Drake was not pleased. *Get the breach sealed, and check any video. I can't believe young females are defecting on their own.*

No.

He felt his female's tension as she spoke. "I need to check on Rain's family, unless I can help any here."

"Go. This shouldn't take long," Gregoire told her.

"They can handle it. I'd like to go with you," Ava said to her daughter.

Everything in Gregoire rebelled at letting Alyssa go, but she needed time with her mother.

Gregoire fisted his hands as they silently moved to the breached shield. Adras had pissed him off and he couldn't even call the male on his bullshit. He had work to do. That didn't stop him from tracking Alyssa's every move through their link; he didn't like having her away from his side.

She sent him soothing energies through the bond and that eased him somewhat.

He turned to her father and knew Adras felt just as frustrated that they weren't alone. It was going to be a long fucking task.

Chapter 28

Guardian Compound, Tetartos Realm

Erik headed down the hall back to his suite with Vane at his side. Everything was changing so quickly, but at least his family was together.

He had a *mate*.

His stomach clenched at all she'd been through and how he'd been fucking adding to it. She was strong, beautiful and fit him perfectly. She'd been through hell, yet still wanted to fight. He was proud, but concerned that she was so damned determined to wield his powers. He understood her need to be able to protect herself.

His sister had been obsessed with protection after her experience all those centuries ago.

Rage clawed at his stomach, but he managed to keep his beast leashed around her. She needed gentleness, and he made sure to do everything possible to make sure she felt safe. She thought she wanted to kill Cyril, but in all reality Erik would never allow her near the bastard. Cyril would die a bloody and painful death under Erik's claws. His animal wanted to bathe in the bastard's blood. He'd never be able to stomach Sam getting close enough to the male that caused her suffering.

"Did Drake ask you to work with the Guardians?" Vane asked as they headed toward their rooms.

Erik felt need burning under his skin. It had only been a couple of hours since he went to help Alex and her mate. He felt marginally better after spending some time with them. He'd wanted to give Sam some time without him pushing to be inside her; he still felt like a bastard for being so damn demanding. He rubbed the back of his neck because he was about to do it all again; there was no preventing it. He just hoped she'd gotten some rest.

"Yes."

Getting away for a while had been a good plan. He'd never been to Tetartos, and if it was to be their new home, he wanted to get a lay of the land and its inhabitants, and assess potential threats to his mate and siblings, which he'd done when helping reconstruct the shield in Limni. Much as he expected to dislike his sister's mate, he hadn't. The male obviously cared for Alex, and he was powerful enough to ensure her safety. He'd also provided Erik with a good deal of information on the Realm.

"Good. You better have agreed to work for them. There is a never-ending amount of shit to do, and I, for one, would appreciate the fucking help." Vane grinned at him.

"Yes, I agreed." He wasn't thrilled with being in Tetartos, but at least they had purpose. The Guardians needed the help, and Vane and Alex were already a part of their fold. Watching out for his siblings was ingrained. Alex might be taken care of, but it didn't stop him from wanting to be there if she needed him. Vane had never needed him, but it didn't matter. He wasn't sure how well he'd take orders, but Drake hadn't questioned him on that.

"You still screwing the Guardian?" He asked Vane the question that was the elephant in the room. He knew his brother and Brianne had been secreting away for more years than he could remember. He'd always been aggravated at Vane's recklessness, but his twin was fucking stubborn and wild. He wondered if the two had continued now that the danger element was lost.

"Yeah. Let's not go there." His twin ran his fingers through his long hair. He could feel his brother's agitation. He shook his head. He knew more about the situation than Vane probably wanted him to. Buckets full of booze had loosened Vane's tongue a few times over the decades.

"Careful, man," he told him. The races didn't blend, so Brianne could never be his mate.

"Not my style."

Erik's lips tilted at his brother's humor, and he slammed him into the wall, making his grin widen.

Vane righted himself before asking, "Did Sirena tell you all that you needed to know about the mating ceremony?" His brother looked uncomfortable asking, and Erik understood why.

"Yes. I'm going to talk to Sam as soon as I get to the room." He rolled his neck. "We need to do it tomorrow evening. Sirena told me the details." His jaw clenched almost to the breaking point at what the healer had said. They needed to have the ceremony that would complete her Immortality, and they were running out of time to finish what the bastards had started when they'd taken her. There was a lot for them to talk about, and he was dreading the fuck out of it.

She'd admitted to loving him, and he'd felt like shit. It went against everything he was to be forced to use her body like he'd been doing. He shook off the thoughts. He knew he'd be inside her shortly after going into their suite. He wouldn't be able to help himself, and she would sweetly take him.

There was so much he needed to accomplish, but finishing the mating ceremony was priority. After that, he planned on finding and killing Cyril, and then he needed to provide his mate with a home of her own, not an apartment in the Guardian compound.

It was the mating that concerned him; the rest was easy enough to accomplish.

Sirena's instructions had been clear. Sam wouldn't be able to blood-bond with him without adding Aletheia blood. He'd been forced to ask Urian for some of his. It grated having to ask for anyone's help, but he couldn't stomach the thought of her ingesting blood from someone he didn't know. The whole thing turned his stomach, but he couldn't imagine her staying mortal. Parting with her in a few short decades wasn't an option. She was his, whether he deserved her or not.

Blood-bonding was going to be a nightmare for him, but Sirena had been clear that there was no way around it. Seeing her rape was going to haunt him for eternity. He clenched his teeth, hating that he hadn't gotten to her sooner.

"You good, man?" his brother said, snapping him out of his thoughts. Vane looked at him, understanding shining in his eyes. They'd made it to their suites. He was on one side of the hall, and his brother had been given the one across the way. Something was off. It was a weird dizzy sensation that made him worried. He shook his head at his brother and quickly opened his door.

He instantly knew something was wrong. Fuck, he just hadn't felt right for a while. He thought his body had been fucking with him for going too long without her. He'd wanted to check on her through their link, but hadn't wanted to wake her if she was sleeping. His heart rate accelerated.

He found her lying in their bed. Her tanned skin was flushed. He brought his hand to her forehead. She felt warmer than before. He didn't have much healing ability, but he gave her a little boost of his energy.

She opened her eyes and smiled. "I think I may have overdone it practicing with the powers I'm getting from you. I even teleported again."

He didn't like the glassy look in her eyes at all.

Vane, go get Sirena. Something is wrong with Sam.

Chapter 29

Gregoire's Home, Tetartos Realm

"In the shower, angel. We have somewhere to be in an hour," Gregoire said as they walked into their home after a very long day. First the breach, then a detour and hours spent with Rain, because Alyssa had wanted to tell her about Delia's abduction personally. The girl had worked for Rain on occasion.

He'd told them what the video surveillance had shown. Delia had been compelled to leave, and the damn note she left was only advertising. Cyril was likely hoping that others would believe the females were getting mates. If even a few of the inhabitants of Tetartos believed the bullshit, Cyril would increase his ranks. Plus, he'd just acquired more females to experiment on. Drake had ordered all the cities on lockdown until they figured out a way to counteract the spell that was used in all the breaches. Sacha and Bastian were doing the political rounds.

"Where are we going?" she asked him.

"To the beach." He'd made arrangements when she was talking with her friend.

"Nighttime or daytime beach?" She looked so beautiful, her eyes were shining up at him, and he couldn't help lift her into his arms to kiss her. Her lips yielded instantly under his, and he took it deeper as he carried them up the stairs.

He mentally turned on the shower, still holding her. He'd never kissed as much as he did with her. He couldn't get enough of her lips and the sweet taste of her mouth. Light moans uttered from her lips every time, and he wasn't sure she even knew she made them. Those little noises went straight to his cock. He set her down on the rug.

"Evening."

She frowned at him and shook her head. "Cold or warm weather?"

He liked the crease the frown made on her forehead. "What are you trying to figure out, love?"

"I need to know what to wear."

"Anything you want to." She was killing him. He'd wanted to be buried inside her for hours, but they'd both been busy. He found he enjoyed listening to her questions. It was her voice. It had a soft soothing cadence. He also liked that she was loyal to her friend. He'd wanted to get the hell out of there much sooner, but the look in her eyes told him that wasn't going to happen. He'd gotten a whiskey and settled into a chair and listened mostly.

"I'll also need to know what we'll be doing and if there will be other people there," she said with a grin. He was glad that things had lightened between them. He hoped what he had planned might help atone for hurting her.

"We are meeting a couple of my brothers at one of the Guardian beach homes."

"Which brothers?" she asked, and he could tell she was curious about his plans.

"Conn and Bastian."

He stripped them both and carried her into the shower. She moaned when the warm spray hit her breasts. "It feels so good." He spun her around so that her hair got wet.

"It was such a whirlwind today I never got to thank you for your restraint with my father." She shook her head.

He grunted. He and Adras would likely always have issues. She wrapped her arms around him and kissed his chest lightly. It was soft and meant to be sweet, but his cock throbbed between them. "And I appreciate you not rushing me with Rain. She was pretty upset over Delia, and she's in a new place." She ran her hand over his aching cock. It had been too many hours since he'd last been inside her slick pussy.

"If I take you now, angel, it needs to be fast."

She moaned and kissed his chest again while pumping his dick in her small hands.

He lifted her with his hands cupping her ass. She kissed his lips and neck as he dipped a finger inside her. "You're already nice and slick. I wish I had time to eat that sweet pussy, but I'll have to wait for my meal."

She moaned into his neck. Her fingers were tunneling in his hair, pulling to get him closer.

He groaned. "Can you take it hard, little one?"

"Yes," she said on a moan.

He lifted her higher. "Guide me in." She complied immediately, her small hand moving between them to position him at her entrance.

"Fuck, yeah, you suck me up." She felt so damn good. So tight, yet she yielded to hold him deep; it was like nothing he'd ever felt before. "Your pussy was made for me."

They didn't have much time, only enough to take the edge off. He slammed her hips down on his cock. Her thighs tightened at his hips, and her neck fell back. He couldn't reach her breasts with his mouth like that, but the hard nipples rasped his chest so damn good. He pushed her against the shower wall and pumped hard and fast. She wiggled and moaned her desire. "Take it, angel. You like it hard. Like my cock slamming deep. Roll your hips, and let your clit slide against me until you come all over my dick." She started panting against his chest. Soon, her pussy pulsed and throbbed, and she was screaming her release. That drove him, loosed his control until he was pounding into her over and over. His balls tightened, and he groaned as he came deep inside her.

She kissed his neck. He wanted to stay like that, with her wrapped around him, but they needed to wash and get ready.

"Better, angel?"

"Mmm. Yes."

"Do you have any dresses?"

She looked up at him, her eyes searching for answers. "Yes."

He filled his palm with shampoo and worked it into her hair. Her eyes closed as he massaged her scalp and neck. He forced himself to move quickly through washing her and then himself.

She used the air currents to dry her hair again as they walked into the closet. He picked some jeans and a plain blue tee shirt. He rarely wore anything else, unless it was fighting leathers. He could have gone naked and it would be fine. He turned, and she was still looking at her clothes. A short off-white dress with a flared bottom sat among her other clothes, and he pointed to it. "Wear that one."

She tilted her head to the side, pondering, and then grabbed it. When she went to the drawer with her lingerie, he said, "Don't wear anything under it." His cock pulsed at the thought of her naked under that sexy dress.

*****

Alyssa slipped the dress over her head. She'd never worn it. She'd never had a reason to. It was beautiful and fit her perfectly. The cotton clung to her breasts and stomach, then flared at her hips. The neckline was cut straight and low, showing the swell of her breasts. When she looked in the mirror, her breath caught at the look in Gregoire's eyes.

"You're beautiful." His voice was low. "If we don't leave now, I'm going to toss the skirt over your ass and fuck you in front of that mirror." Her skin heated; she wanted exactly that.

He groaned, and the look on his face could only be described as tortured. She furrowed her brows in confusion.

"We need to go." He grabbed her hand and started walking down the stairs. They were both barefoot and on the way to the beach. She had an idea of what he planned to do when they got there, but her nipples hardened and she wasn't sure she could make it.

"Fuck, you smell so damn good. Tonight is going to be torture."

She frowned, wondering what he meant, but they were out the door and ported before she had the chance to ask.

She moaned when her feet hit soft sand. The mingling of the life forces always intensified when teleporting, and it took her a couple of deep breaths before she settled down and shook herself out of it.

The sun was setting on the horizon, and the salty breeze felt wonderful on her heated skin. A huge home sat above the beach, and she saw through the massive windows into the lit rooms inside. Clay-colored stone steps led from where they stood. She saw Conn and Bastian on the patio above, sitting at a table with drinks in their hands.

A nervous fluttering started in her stomach. Anticipation licked at her. When they'd made it up the steps, she saw a filigreed iron bed with white bedding, all set up outside.

Conn winked at her, and Bastian nodded. They were the first Guardians she'd met, and seeing them eased her nerves a bit.

"Tonight is yours, angel. Anything you want, you can have. My brothers are here to witness my submission to you."

"This is something I never thought I'd see." Alyssa heard Conn speak, but she wasn't sure she heard right.

She licked her lips and looked up at him in confusion. She'd thought he was going to take her, claim her in front of his brothers like they'd constantly fantasized about. Instead, he planned to play submissive to her. She'd said the words when they were in the sewing room, but she hadn't thought to follow through with something like that.

He lifted his shirt over his head. He'd asked what to do to make her not hurt, and he thought this would do it. Her big dominant Guardian planned to give himself up to her. She stood in shocked silence.

He unzipped his pants, all the while assessing her. His jaw looked tight, and his muscles were tense by the time he stood nude in front of her.

"Tell me what you want, angel." She looked at Conn and Bastian, and both featured the same stunned expressions.

She wanted him. He'd arranged this for her, but she had no idea how to start.

Anything you want, Alyssa.

She sucked in a breath. She was so turned on she had to breathe through it.

Okay, on the bed. If she was going to do this, she intended to drive him wild and completely out of control.

He got on the bed and lay with his head on the pillow, looking at her. She understood why he'd suggested a dress. He was giving her the ability to claim him while keeping her body covered. She mentally shook her head. He was making such a monumental effort, even if it was misguided.

She needed to think. Her heart swelled when she saw the fierce look on his face. He was a predator not used to being at anyone else's mercy, yet he allowed it of her. In front of his brothers.

She pulled the dress over her head and tossed it aside. He growled low, and the sound made her pussy weep. She heard groans of approval from his brothers, and that encouraged her more. She watched as his lids lowered and his cock bobbed against his stomach. Yes, she would claim him; he was hers. She knew it was making him hot seeing her body on display. She couldn't believe how bold she'd become.

She crawled up on the bed with him. He watched her breasts

sway, and she knew she had him. He'd wanted his brothers to see her; well, they would see everything. She arched her back as she moved near him.

"Is there lube?" she asked and watched his breathing accelerate.

"I'll get some," Conn offered, and she heard him leave.

She crawled over Gregoire's body and nipped at his lower lip. She let her breasts trail over his chest; her tight nipples rubbed against the hard muscle.

"Do I need to cuff you to the bed, or will you stay still?" she taunted him when she saw the metal cuffs that were attached to the headboard. It would dampen his power, but she had no doubt her strong Guardian would be able to get free if he wanted.

"The choice is yours, not mine, angel." His jaw flexed as he said the words.

"Hold on to the headboard, but if you try to touch me without permission, I'll have to cuff you." She heard Conn's footsteps as he returned to the patio. She looked up to see both he and Bastian standing there with raised brows.

"Did she just threaten to cuff him to the bed?" Conn asked Bastian, sounding shocked. She heard every word along with the sound of the waves hitting the sand.

"Yes. She's a sight to behold. I'd never have thought he could allow this," Bastian answered his brother. Gregoire's hands were fists around the iron filigree and he looked resigned and heated all at once.

Conn set the container of lube on the bed while she planned what she would do.

"You two will get a better view at the head of the bed." Her voice came out sultry, and both males looked at Gregoire, who nodded. She was getting the feel for it, and she found the challenge wicked.

She bit her lips, then grabbed an extra pillow from the top of the bed. "Lift your hips." Gregoire narrowed his eyes at her, but did as she instructed. She couldn't believe how wild she was being. She was naked outside with her mate, with witnesses to all the dirty things she wanted to do to him. His brothers' faces looked shocked when she tilted his hips higher. She was getting wet with all her wicked ideas.

Angel, I know I said anything, but what the fuck are you planning? I can smell how wet you are, his voice growled in her mind.

"Spread your thighs." He narrowed his eyes, but did as she said. She was dying to taste him. "I want your come in my mouth. You want that, don't you? To come down my throat?" All three males groaned at her words. Gregoire watched as she set her lips and tongue to his cock. His lids went heavy as she sucked on the tip. Alyssa held him out and up while she knelt in front of him. First swirling her tongue around him and then taking him deep. Breathing through her nose, she swallowed, again and again until she had him down her throat. Her fingers massaged his sac, and she pumped her other hand before she started feeling bolder.

Turning her body around, she straddled him. It was the perfect angle to take him to the back of her throat. "Fuck, I can see how wet your pussy is." She wiggled her ass in the air and bobbed her head on him, sucking hard and deep. It took time to get him all the way inside. She finally got all of him, until her nose was at his sac. She kept swallowing and twisting her neck.

"Damn, she took his whole fucking dick." She thought Conn said the words, but she wasn't sure. She was engrossed in the sweet taste of her mate's pre-come as it slid down her throat. He tasted so damn good.

"Tell me to touch your pussy. Tell me to finger your pussy and ass while you're swallowing my cock." His voice was a raspy growl, and his hips were twitching beneath her, but he held onto his control. He was barely managing, and she loved it. They'd only just begun, and he was already trying to take over.

You can use your hands, but only until I come. She moaned when his hands spread her wide and thick fingers spread her desire all over her lower lips, then up to her ass. "Fuck, I'm close," he said. "I want your come all over my hands when I fill your throat." He pumped his fingers, and she met him with every sucking pull she took from his cock. Her jaw was getting tight, and she scented the arousal of the males near them. It set her off, and it took everything she had not to clamp down. "Fuck," he shouted behind her, his warm come filling her throat. She felt his fingers leave her body as she licked her way off him. She lifted her body on shaky limbs.

She heard heavy breathing. Hers was still evening out when she looked at his flushed face and knew his submissive state wasn't going to last. She licked her lips. "I love how good that tastes. It's still on my tongue." She couldn't wait for him to come unglued, and she thoroughly loved her role as seductress. His chest heaved, and his glittering eyes held hers.

"Fuck, I don't think I can take much more of this." Conn's voice sounded strained to the point she fought a grin of satisfaction.

Gregoire wiped his hand down his chest. Her nostrils flared, knowing he'd just marked himself with her come. She crawled over and situated herself between his thighs again. He watched her, waiting. She knew he was close to snapping his leash, and she knew just how to push him.

She smelled the arousal of the other males. Knew Gregoire scented it too. It had to be driving him to the brink. She focused on him while she opened the container Conn had set on the bed. She took the lube and caressed it over her breasts as he growled deep. She loved that noise. Loved that he thought to give her control, but loved even more that he would soon take it from her. Her nipples were tight and achy. She pinched and pulled at them, loving the tingles that fluttered over her body. Closing her eyes, she caressed her breasts, pushing them together and high, hearing more groans. "I thought I could do this, angel, but I don't know how much I can take watching you do that."

She opened her eyes. Never had she felt so sexy and empowered. Male arousal scented the area, but her focus was on her big mate. He looked feral, and she knew he'd come for her soon, take her. That was what she wanted. She grabbed his cock in her slick hands and caressed him up and down before crouching between his thighs. Spreading her knees wide, she sat on her bottom and leaned forward, rubbing his shaft over each hard nipple, then into the valley of her cleavage.

She heard Bastian say, "Son of a bitch, she is exquisite."

She rolled her torso and caressed him between the soft mounds. His hips thrust as soon as she pushed her breasts around him. The silky skin of his cock slid along her skin. She watched him with lowered lids as he thrust. The sound of metal bending under his strength made her juices flow. His muscles were taut, and his jaw was clenched tight. She lowered her head and licked at the tip of his cock when he thrust up. "Fuck, I want to come all over your tits." He looked desperate like he couldn't hold out a minute longer. In a blur of motion she was on her back and his come was painting her tight nipples. He held his cock above her, running it over each breast, then rubbed the turgid tips aching for him.

"I'm sorry, love." He looked down at her, shaking his head, but his hands moved over her. He was massaging his seed into her breasts as she panted beneath him.

I wanted you to lose control. I wanted you to claim me like you've talked about.

He groaned low, and she knew she'd won when his gaze snapped to hers. "I'm going to take you every way possible while my brothers watch."

"Yes."

"Son of a bitch, this isn't cool. I want to fuck so bad my dick's turning fucking blue," Conn said.

"Then jack off, but no one touches her. No one else's come gets anywhere near her." She watched him growl at his brothers. She was so aroused that she made a whimpering noise, and his gaze shot back to hers.

"I'm going to mark your skin and fuck you hard, love."

She moaned. There were no words to describe how ready she was. He smacked first one breast and then the other before caressing away the sting. She moaned and writhed as her back bowed off the bed. *I need to come,* she told him, and a second later she was flipped and slammed down around his cock. His back was against the pillows, and her thighs wide. She watched as Bastian and Conn focused on her breasts and the huge cock of her mate they had to see was buried all the way inside her pussy. She bucked on him, needing friction.

"I love that they can see and smell your perfect pussy and know it belongs only to me." His hands massaged her come-covered breasts while she circled her hips on him. "Shit, it's so damn tight and hot." He moved his hands on her hips and shafted her on him fast and hard. She cried out, holding on to his hands. "Rub your clit and come all over my cock." At the first touch of her fingers to the tight nubbin, she came unglued, throbbing and pulsing until he slowed. Her hand fell away, and she felt a sharp smack to her pussy, which forced a cry from her lips as she came all over again. "Fuck, I love when you throb like that." He moved her hair and kissed her neck and nipped at her ear. She didn't think she'd ever been so wildly turned on. "I want in your ass, love. Will you give it to me?"

"Yes."

This time she was lifted off his shaft and lay with her hips over a mound of pillows. She didn't know how they got there and didn't care. Slick lube was caressed over and inside her ass. "I can't wait to get inside you."

"I don't think I can take much more of this, G." Conn groaned.

Soon, she felt his shaft pushing inside. All three males groaned. She knew they watched as Gregoire tunneled inside. The bite of pleasure-pain felt incredible, and she arched her back for more. "Fuck," he said. That the others watched only made the experience hotter. They'd witnessed her mate go wild for her. Witnessed how much he needed her. How he laid himself out for whatever she wanted to do to him, then completely lost control. She didn't care that his beast needed this. Apparently hers needed witnesses as well. Wanted the world to know he belonged to her.

Chapter 30

Mountain Temple, Tetartos Realm

Erik felt like he would go insane if he was forced to wait one more fucking minute for his mate. When Sirena had gotten to his room earlier and said they needed to complete the ceremony immediately, his heart nearly stopped. He'd growled when they'd taken her from him. The healer gave him a jolt to his chest with her healer power, snapping him out of it.

Sirena then assured him she was taking Sam to get ready and give her a boost of something that would get her through the ceremonies. He paced the golden temple, waiting. His twin stood to the side next to Uri, and both looked wary. Everything had happened in a blur. The healer had taken her. Uri had come with the black silk pants for the ceremony and gave him instructions and a vial of his blood. He wanted to beat the male, but instead he'd donned the silk and waited.

His head shot to the doorway as Drake walked in. "They will be here any moment," the Guardian leader said.

Erik's jaw was tight. This was his fucking fault. Sirena said that Sam had overused his powers and her mortal body couldn't handle it. His fingers tunneled in his hair. Fuck.

Flickering light from the chandelier trickled over the gold walls of the mountain temple. There was something about the place. It felt alive. Sacred. He just wanted to see her. Finish this so he'd know she

225

was safe and couldn't be taken from him.

When he heard the sounds of her arrival, he stilled. His breath caught in his throat at the sight of her. Her skin glistened under the pink of the flowing silk gown. Her cheeks were flushed. Blond hair flirted with the skin of her bare shoulders.

He moved to her as Drake said something he didn't hear or care about. Nothing mattered but touching his mate, feeling for himself that she was okay. His pulse was pounding in his ears as he touched her cheek and scrutinized her face; she didn't appear sick.

She smiled at him. He caught her up against his bare chest and took her lips. He needed to feel her. Taste her. Her tongue dueled with his, and he tasted wine on her lips. He broke from the kiss. "Drake, finish this," he demanded. He wanted the first ceremony over with. He was worried she would get sick again. Drake spoke words in the old language, and he felt compelled to repeat them. It was odd, as if the room buzzed, and he heard nothing.

Her small hands covered the skin of his chest. She felt so soft and warm touching him. Sirena fitted her hand over his mate's and began funneling her power through Sam and into his flesh. It was heaven and hell all wrapped in one. Pleasure and pain mixed to make it an almost euphoric experience. This mark would stay with him for eternity. Even if his flesh was separated from his body and regenerated. It would always regrow with the double serpents entwined in double eternity. He went to lift her off the ground when it was complete, but she stilled him.

She shook her head. "I want a mark as well."

His brow furrowed at her request. His sister held the mark on her chest, but he was told it was only tradition for the male to be marked. He spoke in her mind. *You do not need to do that. I wouldn't want you to mar your beautiful flesh if it's not what you want. The tradition is that the male is marked. I'm happy to be marked as yours. I planned to give you a wedding ring.*

She smiled beautifully for him. "I thought I would mix traditions." She entwined the fingers of his right hand with her left, and then he felt Sirena's cover his as power again flowed. When it was done, her face flushed even brighter, and he could smell her arousal. He growled when he looked down and saw the mark circling her left ring finger. It was the same mark of the two serpents only smaller, more delicate. He brought it to his lips and kissed her softly as he held her gaze.

He lifted her up and kissed her before carrying her out of the temple. Uri had given him instructions, and he knew they were finished with only one section of the ceremonies. She settled into him. Her arms went around his neck, and a soft sigh left her lips. He felt her warm breath on his neck, and his cock pulsed. He tuned out the sound of the others as he exited to the tunnel. He needed her. Vane would meet him at the other temple to watch over the blood-bonding, even though he didn't want anyone with them. These traditions were driving him mad.

He felt her lips on his chest. Her tongue followed the lines of the marking. He closed his eyes and groaned deep.

"Does it hurt? Mine just tingles, but it's smaller."

"Mine tingles too. I need you. I need you to be mine and safe, Sam. You scared the shit out of me."

"I scared me too." She said the words against his skin, and his heart clenched.

"You're safe now. I've got you."

He just hoped someone had clued her in on what they would be doing. He would be careful with her, as gentle as possible no matter how badly he needed her. He clenched his jaw as they ported.

Chapter 31

Cyril's Compound, Tetartos Realm

Cyril was obsessing over his soon-to-be mate. She was perfect, and he couldn't stop thinking about her. She was young, just out of her majority, and she had a thick mane of red hair and rare fire ability. She was everything he had hoped for. After his Aletheia had finished filling her with semen, he'd gone to her, moved her to his hidden lab. None of the guards dared question him when he'd taken her from the labs. Word must have gotten around about Reve's punishment. Many would not even look at him, and even his assistants seemed even more nervous around him in the last few days. Good.

He was having trouble concentrating on what Kane was saying, because he would much rather be with her. He'd only had her for a few hours before being forced to come back for this meeting with his second. He could have cancelled it, but he hadn't wanted to do anything out of the ordinary.

He hated this facility. He still got the itch at his neck when encountering others in the tunnels. He'd already set up a room in his new mountain, away from the prying eyes of his people. Close to where his fiery-haired female would sleep. Where she now lay while her body fought through the effects of his formula. He needed to get back to her. Couldn't wait to see the results. He already felt that it was right.

"What is the news on the new compound?" He tried to be interested in the underground facility he sent Kane and Angus to work on. The one that would house the defectors they assumed would be trickling in soon. "It should be sufficient while we vet new recruits to our cause," Kane said.

Elizabeth was crouched in the corner, looking more and more feral as the days went on. He had no use for her, and he could not be more thrilled. He truly hated her. Would find true joy in killing her, but he was not one to waste. He wouldn't dispose of her anytime soon. He was pleased enough that Kane was still keeping her in line. If all went well, he would have little use for her ability to contact the other Realms. He planned to have his own enhanced abilities soon. Cynthia would be left to deal with her own Guardian issues on Earth. The Tria would still be there if he found he needed them for something. For now, he could forget all about them and focus on the only thing of importance. Gaining power.

His beautiful Delia would provide him a nice new power. He was enamored enough of her beauty and stunning ability that he'd found out her name. A first for him. He couldn't wait to sample her, and he would. Soon. He needed to do one more test of the serum first. He had finally chosen the perfect person to make that happen. Someone he could easily afford to lose.

"Has there been any word on old test subjects? Are they in the cities yet?" If he could get his hands on Nine, he would have fire and metal at his disposal. His cock hardened at the thought of all that beautiful power at his fingertips.

"It doesn't seem so, but I can't imagine that the Guardians would keep them for much longer." Kane's dark brow creased, and the Aletheia looked decidedly uncomfortable when he added, "The cities are still on lockdown, so I don't have much information. We've lost two contacts. The one we used for the hell beast attack on

Lofodes. I'm sure the Guardians know we gave him the spell."

"Yes, I'm sure they do, but there is nothing they could do about it. They have more problems to worry about. The fool didn't hold any knowledge of true importance."

"We also lost the contact that told us about the female in Paradeisos. Elizabeth cannot seem to connect with her."

"I'm sure she's dead. The Guardians would have tried to get information and killed her as a traitor when they found nothing." Pity to lose two contacts when they had so few; he liked being informed on what was going on in the cities.

"I acquired information on the female the Guardian Gregoire was interested in. I find it unlikely that she's more than a possible plaything to the Guardian. If she was his mate, he would have known and claimed her when she was presented at her majority. The female's twenty-five and the daughter of Adras, so it's possible Gregoire was only looking for her at her father's request."

Cyril thought about that. What Kane said made sense. No male would leave a mate unclaimed for that long. Especially not a Guardian. He would still like to get his hands on her. Her father could pose a problem... The family link would have to be severed, but that was easy enough. Taking her would be sweet vengeance if there was even a slight chance that she meant something to the Guardian.

"Keep an eye out for her. Take her if you see her." The current formula wasn't made for an Immortal, but it didn't matter. He would take from the Guardians like they took from him. He would have her for an eternity. Plenty of time to gain retribution any way he liked. He suppressed a shiver of delight at the thought.

He had one other task for his warriors. Kane and Angus were cleared as loyal by his spies. That information had better be correct.

His fists clenched.

"Monitor the cities when they open back up. I want my old test subjects back. Also, I want you to find me any female Mageias with an offshoot ability to experiment on. Find me as many as you can. But they have to have something other than the basic four elements." Cyril would not let his second in command know just what those females could mean. He had no plan to share the power he would harness. At least not until he had all the power his own body would take.

The serum was not exactly what he'd hoped for, but it had intriguing potential that he had not even touched the surface of. He just needed to find more Mageias with rare abilities. Like Nine, with her power over metal, an offshoot of the earth ability. Or his delicious Delia, who was able to produce fire within her body. Also incredibly rare. Most Fire Mageias needed a spark or fire to manipulate. Elemental Mageias, as a general rule, were not able to create the actual element itself, only wield it. His Mageia could produce fire from air. The ability was weak, but that was likely due to her mortality and possibly her age. It didn't matter. It was there, and it would be his.

Chapter 32

Guardian Compound, Tetartos Realm

Gregoire woke with Alyssa snuggled in his chest and Drake in his head, informing them that there was a meeting where he wanted Alyssa to meet his brethren officially. He considered attempting to ignore his leader, but Alyssa mumbled and started stirring.

"I want to check on Rain, anyway."

He pulled her up for a kiss, savoring her sweet taste until she was soft and moaning beneath him.

Half an hour later, he was stuck in a sitting room, half-listening to Alyssa and her friend talk about nothing and everything at once. He drank the coffee they'd made as he considered the meeting to come. He wasn't fucking looking forward to it. It would be Alyssa and Alex's first true meeting and he wasn't sure how she'd feel.

Rain looked drained, like she hadn't slept all night, and he felt sorry for the female as he watched Alyssa give her a hug. He tensed at the contact; he fucking hated her touching anyone but him. He stifled a growl as Alyssa narrowed her eyes at him. He clenched his jaw, knowing those instincts weren't likely to change anytime soon. They headed down the hall and up the stairs toward the war room.

Are you going to be okay doing this? he asked as they got closer. He felt her tension through the bond.

I'll be fine. I might be more uncomfortable dealing with the fact that your brothers watched us have sex. She shook her head.

Nothing in what we've done is out of the normal for Immortals, love. I really hope you understand that. That was not shameful. It's the way of the Hippeus. Something ingrained in our beast makes us need to display our mates, usually while the male holds them down and fucks them hard.

Why didn't you ever explain that's why I wanted it so much? And please tell me that my mother and father didn't do that. She looked thoroughly horrified to the point that he laughed.

I won't tell you that. You have nothing to worry about with Conn and Bastian, love, he added.

Gregoire and Alyssa made it two feet into the room before being swarmed. Alyssa had only been introduced to a few of the Guardians, which hadn't included Sacha and Jax or Sander and P. Congratulations were issued, and she was greeted warmly by his brothers and sisters, and all too soon he was given shit for growling when anyone attempted to touch her. Even his little mate was laughing about it with Brianne, feeling comfortable and relaxed. It eased some of his tension.

He noticed Dorian frowning as he walked to the doorway and back. Pacing? He caught his brother's gaze and quirked a brow, and Dorian shook his head. Something was up with him.

Alex and Uri came up with Vane. He tracked Alyssa's emotions as best he could while they were introduced. She smiled politely and accepted their congratulations and he finally eased up.

Dorian finally moved from the door as everyone was taking seats. His brother came near them and leaned down and smelled Alyssa's hair. Gregoire growled low and pushed her behind him.

"What the fuck are you doing?! Ever try to inhale my mate again, and I'll remove your sinus cavity."

Dorian paled and looked horrified. "Fuck, I think I'm losing my mind. I keep smelling something that's getting to me. I'm sorry, G." The Nereid ran a hand over his neck and sat down.

Gregoire looked over at Sirena, and she nodded. Shit, something was definitely wrong with the male, and he knew only Sirena could figure shit out about the male's sense being out of control. He didn't like it.

Is he okay? Alyssa's worried voice came into his head.

Sirena's going to check on him. That wasn't like him.

He grabbed two seats at the table, pulling hers close to him so that his arm rested over the back, his hand in her hair.

"The cities are still under lockdown, but one of the warriors in Limni thinks he may have a way to prevent the spell from working on the shields again. I also got a report that a Mageia in Efcharistisi might also have a solution. The two are now working together in hopes that we'll find answers. Bastian or Sacha, what have you got?" Drake was in his usual stance at the end of the table. He never sat at a meeting.

Bastian spoke. "Each city is having Aletheia come in to go through at least the Mageia's memories. They aren't taking blood memories because the inhabitants threw a fit. Instead they are taking surface memories while questioning everyone on what they know of the females that were taken. I'm not sure it'll be effective, but they're concerned, and the victims' families are in an uproar. They've tried to keep the information on the notes quiet. They believe as we do that the females were taken, not defectors."

"In other news, Erik and Sam were mated last evening," Sirena said.

The room erupted with conversation until Sirena explained what happened. That Sam had sickened from using Erik's power, and they'd needed to complete the ceremony quickly.

The air charged with power and Alex suddenly stiffened.

"Get the fuck back!" Uri shouted, and he acted on instinct and pulled Alex into his arms. Everyone ported from the table to the back of the room at Uri's warning. The Guardians knew all too well what Alex's shield could do and what it meant.

"Shit," Vane said, running his fingers through his long hair. Both Alex and Uri were on the floor, a translucent shield covering their bodies. Chairs had launched away from them and toppled to the floor, leaving them in an empty space.

No one else spoke as Gregoire brought Alyssa into his side. *What's going on?* she asked.

Remember when I told you about Alex's ability to hop into others' minds.

She nodded.

That's likely what's happening.

How long will they be there?

I don't know. I've never seen it happen.

After long minutes where everyone seemed at a loss of what to do, the shield finally dissipated. "Fuck!" was all Uri said as he lifted his mate into his arms. Her delicate face looked pale and furious. To be forced to suffer with the victims and be unable to do anything

236

would be an infuriating experience that Gregoire wouldn't wish on anyone.

"Suffice it to say, Cyril has a new serum he just injected into one of the females. We didn't get much but the pain of her fighting whatever the fuck was in it. I was able to get a little into her mind and saw that the Aletheia have already raped her. So far that was the only part she was conscious for, other than the injection he fucking gave her that is like fire in her veins." His brother cuddled Alex as he continued, "We weren't able to figure out where she is; she wasn't conscious when he brought her there. It's a fucking cave system. That much she can see from the cell. Shit, that was so fucked up."

Uri got up with his female. "Alex and I are going to need energy if we're going to have any success trying to get back to her."

Gregoire could see his brother Guardian was exhausted and tense. Uri's jaw was tight as he held Alex in his arms. They were at least able to delve some into the female's mind, which was an improvement. Alex used to only see what was happening as it occurred or if it was spoken in the victim's forethoughts.

"Go." Drake's jaw was clenched, and smoke was billowing around him now. Conn telekinetically kicked up the exhaust fan.

"Everyone, get going. Do spot patrols, and make sure to get some fucking rest and energy. We'll hopefully have a fix for the cities' shields soon and who the fuck knows what will come of Alex's contact with the female."

"I wish I knew who she went to. I'm really hoping it's not Delia, but no one deserves what the monster is doing." Alyssa's eyes shone with concern and anger.

"I need to talk to Drake and patrol. I won't be gone long if you want to stay and spend time with Rain." He didn't fucking want to leave her but, shit. He had a really bad feeling things were going to get worse.

Chapter 33

Guardian Compound, Tetartos Realm

Sam stretched her arms over her head. She felt incredible. She hadn't realized how drained she had been getting. It seemed like it had gotten ugly so fast, but looking back, she had been getting more and more tired well before hitting bottom. She assumed it was just the crazy amounts of sex. She knew she was overdoing using the powers, but she was dying to feel stronger.

She felt Erik's weight next to hers and opened her eyes. She inhaled deeply. He smelled incredible, and she wanted to lick his skin. They were back in their suite at the manor. He was on his side, one hand propping up his dark head so that he could stare at her with those enthralling icy-blue eyes.

"Morning," she said with a grin.

"How are you feeling?" His eyes were full of concern. He'd been so worried about her during the consummation and gently loved her in every way possible.

"Really good." She smiled up into his gorgeous face. The memories of all of the things they'd done made her head spin.

The blood-bonding had been painful, yet cleansing somehow for her. She'd seen so much in his memories and come back to herself secure in his strong tensed arms. Rage had poured through their link.

Unfortunately, sharing the memories of what happened to her was horrible for him. They'd held each other and talked for a long time after and then they'd spent the night replacing bad memories with nothing but happiness. She loved him so deeply it didn't seem possible.

"We should get fueled so that you know what it's like for an Immortal." His voice was so low and sexy. His lips met hers, and she melted into his taste. It was intense, just like his scent, so much more potent and alluring. Her core pulsed, and her skin tingled like it was tracking his touch. He was hers for all eternity. She felt strong, like she could accomplish anything. She flipped him over and straddled him, grinning wide.

"I feel wild inside. I can't explain it," she said, and his eyes searched hers, assessing.

"Let me in, so I can see what you're feeling."

She sighed and let him inside her mind; the sensation of him inside her head was beyond incredible.

There was wildness in her, though, that needed to get out. She wanted to play. She wanted to make love and roll around with him.

"It's your cat." His voice was a mix of satisfaction and concern. She'd manifested a beast mate to his lion. Knowing it would happen was so different than feeling animal instincts and desires like she was now.

The thought of transforming was intoxicating and scary as shit. What if she couldn't do it? Or she did and got stuck; had that ever happened?

"Shh, I'm here. I'll get you through it, and you'll be fine." His voice soothed her as he sat up. "No one has gotten stuck, Sirena

240

assured me. You won't be alone, focus on me." He was still in her mind, relaxing her with his presence. She'd known this would happen and had been looking forward to it, but now that it was real, she felt panic eat at her.

"You'll still be you. You'll know everything that's going on. I'm going to help you through it. Feel me, and I'll show you what to do," he said, and she took a deep breath. His hands were on her face, and he stared into her eyes, grounding her as his mind walked her through. He loved her.

"I do love you, and I'll never let anything bad happen again." He growled, his icy gaze growing fierce. "It's okay, don't fight it. I can feel your instincts working for you, telling you what to do. Let go, and fall into me."

She struggled to do what he said. It was like she was split in two. One half wanting freedom, the other fighting for control. She took a deep breath and relaxed, feeling only Erik, knowing he'd never let her lose herself. Her body needed it, needed the release she felt coming. It was like everything vibrated around her, and she was whirling, almost like teleporting, a million pieces and then one again, but so different.

"Gods, Sam, you're beautiful." He looked at her with soft icy eyes, and then his fingers ran over her head, but she felt so much more. He smelled intoxicating, and she wanted it all over her. She tilted her big head, pushing her face into his hand. He ran his palms over her neck and down her back until her body shivered in delight. The sensation was intense and needy. She rubbed her face against his, wanting to have him all over her. It was so good, scary good. She pushed at him, and he grinned at her. He hadn't budged, and the knowledge of his strength was setting her off in a disturbing way. She saw pride and humor shining in his eyes, and she took a big huffing breath.

241

You'll need to mind speak when you're in cat form, beautiful. Your fur is incredibly silky. I hadn't realized how it felt like this.

Her heart rate was accelerating again. She tried to fight past it.

It feels right somehow to be on all fours. That didn't come out right, and I see your lips twitching, she responded to his chuckling inside her mind.

She tried for deep breaths to calm herself. It was scary and amazing, but fear was winning. *I'm still panicking. Can you help me get back so I know I can do it? It helps having you with me, but I think I just need to know I can get back,* she said, trying hard to calm down. She was excited to have the abilities, knowing that she finally had the strength to protect herself, but it was all so new, and what little bravery she had was faltering.

He continued rubbing her body, and his eyes held such love that she settled. "Follow my lead," he said, and she found the spot inside where it all stemmed from and pushed herself back through; the same feelings assailed her as the first transformation. As soon as she was back, he caught her up in his arms and held her as her body shook from the adrenaline spike. "I've got you. You did really great. Just breathe now and let me hold you." His chest was warm and comforting against her cheek. She held on tight, her hands running over his muscles, wanting to rub herself all over him.

She finally evened out a little, but the wildness was still there. "I still feel that crazed caffeine high. The need to go back. Will I always feel like that?" she asked into his chest.

"Usually it happens after several days or a week of keeping it locked up. You'll feel better once you let the beast run for a bit."

Shit, she was going to go insane before she got used to it.

"I think you need to let her back out. It's only going to get worse until you do. I'll take you running in the forest." He held her as she relaxed a little, but she felt that same need. She just needed to let it free, he felt that instinct, but damn, the knee-jerk reaction was to stay in the form she knew, the one she understood and was real to her.

"It'll all be real; it's a big adjustment. I can't even imagine. Your courage and strength shocks me at every turn, beautiful." He kissed her forehead and kept her tucked into his body.

He spoke again. "I've never been without my other form, so it's natural for me. I can't imagine what it's like without it. Someday you'll feel the same. Do you want to try again? This time I'll change with you. Your lioness has needs, love." Her face reddened as he chuckled.

"She's gorgeous, just as you are. Regal." He put his hand on her chin and tilted her face up; he searched her eyes. "I know it's a completely new world for you. Let your instincts guide you, they won't let you down, and don't be embarrassed. I know she wants me all over her. She knows I'm hers, and he wants me to show her I'm worthy. It's animal instinct. I don't want you to be scared of anything you feel or need in either form. Let's start with a run through the forest. I want to stay in your mind. My beast is dying to get out now and scent her."

God, it was all so much. He was right. Her pussy clenched, and she wanted him, but her lioness was beating to be let loose again. Shit, she was an animal, one that wanted to be claimed and dominated by her mate. Her breath caught. The need was only getting worse; she needed to finish it. She took a bracing breath and nodded at him. His eyes heated, and the roiling sensation started; she knew she was going to do it.

Chapter 34

Cyril's Hidden Lab, Tetartos Realm

His formula worked so well the effects were making his cock twitch. The pheromones his Mageia was putting off were highly potent. It had been a full evening of waiting for the mating to complete. He hadn't liked that. Cyril gazed into the cell to see Delia curled naked into the sleeping body of one of his Lykos. His big body cradled the small titian-haired female. Her skin was a pale pink, and the eyes that were closed to him now had been as unique as her power. A brilliant copper that had gone wide in shocked pain when he injected her. They'd grown even wider when he'd sent the wolf in hours later.

The spelled pheromones he used in the formula were meant to deceive an Immortal's system into thinking they'd found their mate. He inhaled deeply. The scent was doing exactly that. His cock stiffened further. He would enjoy fucking her, claiming her as his own. She would never be permitted to be around anyone else, forever hidden and chained for his use. He did not want to take the chance that others would attempt to claim her, take what powers melded with their joining. From this day forth she would be his and only his.

The scent was intoxicating. Looking back, he should have known the other formulas were useless by scent alone. There had only ever been a mild draw, not this potent craving he was feeling now.

He looked at the Lykos. Phelan had always been one of his weaker warriors, a fact that made him the perfect test subject. He would never have made this attempt on one of his stronger males. Partially because he would never give a strong warrior the potential to exceed his power, but he also didn't believe in wasting good resources. Phelan would be put down with no major loss to his ranks. Cyril cocked his head as he watched them. She was curled into the male's body as if she trusted him. He narrowed his eyes. Phelan was nowhere near strong enough to protect her. She would learn that soon enough.

He wanted to see how she responded once he claimed her. She'd already gone through the process of becoming an Immortal, cemented when she mated the wolf. With the Lykos' claim, she would not only have her ability but his as well. Telekinetic abilities were strong with the race, so it would be interesting to see how that manifested. She should be able to change form. He did not yet know if, after mating her, he would be able to take the wolf form. The Immortal races didn't blend. His father had learned that early on in his experiments on the original Immortals. They were only able to mate and reproduce with one of their own species or a mortal Mageia of any ability. It looked like his formula voided that since he felt a definite mating frenzy boiling under his skin. It didn't matter that she might get the Lykos form.

The potentials were innumerable, but he wouldn't think about other testing, his cock would not allow it. He needed to claim her. First, he needed to dispose of the wolf. He did not like the way his female was curled into the bastard.

He would put down this warrior. Claiming her wasn't an option. His senses and cock were beating at him to do it. He hadn't truly anticipated the need he was feeling. She was his.

He couldn't wait to add Subject Nine to his collection. The

Guardians would eventually release her into the capable hands of the covens. Then he would find a way to get her. If he had power over metal, the potential could be monumental. He would never again concern himself with being cuffed. Metal would no longer dampen his abilities, and he could potentially go anywhere. There would be no holding him back. Teleporting through metal was a tantalizing possibility. A shiver ran through his body. Things were definitely looking up.

The two stirred as he clicked open the cell door. The wolf gained his feet instantly, looking at Cyril with the golden gaze of his animal. His instinct no doubt informed him he was in danger. Phelan quickly put the shaking female behind him, and he stood to his full height. His animal side needed to protect its mate. Cyril got close enough that he stopped the male's heart.

An ear-piercing scream rent the cell. It was coming from the female. Phelan was on the floor now, the redhead practically on top of him. She looked up with a positively feral glint in her eyes as she launched herself, claws extended. She got in a bit of a slice to Cyril's stomach before he backhanded her into the cell wall. She was fortunate he did not do more damage, but he was in a good mood. He would enjoy playing rough with her. He began securing her flushed body with cuffs he'd brought with him. Clicked one on her small wrist, then pulled the connection through the metal bar of the cell. He wanted her to see this. See that he was her master. She fought, even burned him with her flames before he got the second delicate wrist secured. Phelan writhed on the ground while his body worked to even out his heartbeat.

The wolf finally gained his feet just as Cyril clicked the other cuff shut. Cyril used his power to shut down the male's heart again. Once the Lykos was back down, he was forced to listen to the damn female scream as she fought the cuffs. His cock twitched in response to her spirit, but the noise was grating on his nerves.

"I would not irritate me further. It could make for a highly unpleasant mating, Delia." The menace he infused into his words was enough to make her cry out in pain. He rarely used the ability he had with his voice. It was not one of his more efficient abilities. It tended to burn energies too rapidly for his liking, but it was always good to show his full range of power. It generally made them wary from the start. He sighed and shook his head when he still heard the clicking of the cuffs as she fought them.

He grabbed his blade from outside of the cell and brought it inside. He lifted it, and as she screamed, he took the wolf's head. Messy business, but necessary, he felt a grin lift his lips. If the damn female kept crying, he would have to gag her for the part of the mating that did not require the use of her mouth. His cock perked up as he pulled her titian locks close enough to smell. Yes, exquisitely his. The tides had turned drastically to his favor.

Chapter 35

New York, Earth Realm

"Damn it, Havoc, come here," Gregoire's voice boomed in the dank alleyway. He'd spent the last several hours in different cities, patrolling for possessed, and it was the dead of night. It wasn't ideal allowing the hound to hunt without Uri since Gregoire wasn't able to alter the memories of any humans that saw the beast, but his brother had needed to refuel and rest with his mate, and the pup needed fed.

Havoc bounded his way after wandering the alley and sniffing a vagrant's foot. Judging by the scent, the filthy human was drunk and passed out. Good thing or he would have gotten quite a scare. He shook his head at the beast. He needed to take him home. They'd taken down seven possessed in three cities. The most time-consuming part being the disposing of the bodies. It had been a long patrol. It took effort to rein in the beast, especially the more he fed. Uri said it was good to let him run it off. He was still shaking his head when he felt Dorian arrive.

"Hey, man," Dorian said and took a deep breath. "I feel like shit for what happened with Alyssa."

"No one touches her," he said to his brother with a firm look. "Now, what the hell's up with you? Did you see Sirena?"

"Yeah, she checked me out. She couldn't find anything wrong. It's something off with my senses. She's doing tests. I just wanted to apologize. I'm going to get a drink and fuck it out of my system. We good?" the Nereid asked as he rolled his neck.

He hoped shit was okay with his brother. "Just don't fucking touch her and we're good."

Dorian nodded and was gone.

It appeared the demon-possessed were down for the evening. They hadn't had a bite in about an hour. It was finally time to get back to his mate.

She was in the courtyard. He felt her and ported to her with the pup in tow.

Havoc immediately barreled in the direction of Sirena, who was sitting with Rain and Alyssa. His sister smiled wide and cooed at the pup. The healer loved that damn animal, and judging by all the wiggling he was doing around her chair, the feeling was mutual.

Alyssa beamed a smile in his direction.

Rain just looked at him, assessing. She had done the same the night before. The female issued a warning with her eyes, and he respected her for it. She was loyal to Alyssa and didn't give a shit that he was a Guardian.

"How was the patrol?" Alyssa asked as he sat next to her. Without a word he lifted her into his lap and kissed her. It had been a long fucking day, and he just wanted to take her home and bury himself inside all that heat, but he knew she'd feel guilty leaving Rain so soon. He would give it an hour; then he was fucking her, and he didn't care if it was on the patio table or in their home. She settled under his chin, and he knew she felt his cock under her firm little ass.

"Has there been any news about the females?" he asked Sirena.

The healer shook her head.

Vane walked up and informed them, "Alex just told me that she and Uri are going to try to get back to the female shortly. They've refueled and rested. We're all just waiting to see if they can get to her again."

The blond male headed over to the patio bar, still talking. "I saw Drake a minute ago. He just got back from doing aerial patrols with the Geraki clans. He ported a few to the other continents, but said that Cyril would be a needle in a damned haystack and that the Aletheia reported that they haven't found any other traitors in the cities." Cyril wouldn't be found easily. He'd hidden before. He knew how to do it, and he wasn't stupid. Gregoire didn't like it, but they might never find those females. They'd only found them the last time because of Erik connecting to his mate.

Havoc moved to Rain, who shook her head, laughing as she petted the demanding animal. "I still can't believe Uri has a hellhound as a pet. I almost threw a glass at him when I first saw the little monster."

"Yeah, we need to do something about him. I'm worried about what someone might do as a knee-jerk reaction," Sirena said as she looked at Havoc.

"I can make him something to wear." Gregoire couldn't help the burst of laughter that came at Alyssa's comment. She shot him a glare and he grinned down at her. His cock twitched, and he knew that she felt it against her ass when he saw her lids lower.

Sirena was cracking up too. "Oh, I'd pay big to see the look on Uri's face if you made Havoc one of those dog jackets that humans put on their pets," Sirena said, and the table erupted into more chuckles. "He just about has a fit every time the animal wiggles at me, hates that his manly animal is so cute and cuddly." Sirena's violet eyes were shining as she added the last.

"I could make something manly," Alyssa said, and she put her hand down to greet the animal. She glared at Gregoire and shook her head when he tensed at the thought of her touching anyone or anything but him.

What the fuck was wrong with him? It was just an animal.

She turned and scrutinized the pup, assessing the animal's size while Gregoire got his shit together.

"A collar wouldn't be a bad idea," Sirena suggested.

"Yeah, I could make a harness in a bright color."

"Erik and Sam will be here in a minute. Anyone want a drink?" Vane said, still rummaging through the cabinets in the patio bar.

"Good, I wanted to check on Sam again," Sirena said.

"Can you just bring the bottle of wine I left out?" Rain asked.

Gregoire loved feeling Alyssa snuggled into his chest. He smelled her hair and settled a hand on her waist. The frenzy was already pushing him to have her and he could feel her fighting the need as well. The patrol had been short, but it had still been too many fucking hours away from her.

He felt the tension coming from Rain. They still weren't sure which female Cyril had taken and injected, she had been in too much pain for Uri and Alex to get her name, but it could very well be the female Rain and Alyssa knew.

He heard footsteps and saw that Erik and Sam were walking up. Sam was taller than his mate by a few inches and had shoulder-length straight blond hair and tanned skin. She smiled at Sirena and was introduced officially to the rest of them. The two took seats at the table, Erik pulling his mate's chair in close to his and wrapping his arm over the back.

"Congratulations," Alyssa said to Sam and Erik.

Sam beamed a smile back. "Thank you."

Sirena asked how she was feeling while Vane brought drinks over. Havoc made the rounds and then went to sniff around the trees. Gregoire needed to get the animal to his brother's suite, and he was itching to get his mate home and under him.

Cyril has mated the female. Uri's words in his mind stilled him. He knew by Alyssa's tensing muscles that she'd heard it and his arms tightened around her.

Drake's fury was powerful within their link. *Do we know where they are?*

No, and it wasn't good. We were with the female after it happened and stayed with her as long as we could. She's in bad shape. We finally got her name. It's Delia, and she's fucking young. Her mind is barely holding on. We've given her as much information as we were able and helped set a shield in her mind when we went in, so Cyril isn't aware of our interference.

"What's going on?" Vane asked. He and his brother were not on the Guardian link, so Gregoire and Sirena explained what had happened.

Rain's gaze got dark and she said some expletives when he'd confirmed that it was the female she knew. After her outburst, she stared off, a hard glint in her aqua eyes.

Sam tensed, fury radiating from her, but when Erik tried to get her to leave, she refused, needing to know everything. Sirena gave them what little information they had.

It was beyond fucked. If the formula Cyril had worked, then the bastard could mate his warriors to the other females they'd taken.

"I think you two should complete the mating ceremony right away." Sirena's words were directed at him and Alyssa.

Gregoire's jaw tightened, knowing where Sirena was going, and she wasn't wrong.

"Wouldn't that be completely disrespectful while Delia's going through hell and who knows what the other females are suffering?" Alyssa said. Her voice sounded shocked that the healer would suggest it now.

"Cyril just gained mated power and has stolen several females that could be at this very moment being mated to his males. There were twelve females taken. This is not about being disrespectful. I would think she'd want for you to be strong enough to protect yourself. The added power might be needed sooner than later." Sirena's voice was dead serious as she looked at Alyssa. Vane and Erik also nodded their heads in agreement.

Rain's hard gaze met Alyssa's. "I agree with them. If I could get some power to take Cyril's ass out, I would," Rain said, fury radiating from her as she clenched her teeth.

Angel, I agree. I don't want your ceremony to be marred by necessity, but I need our connection as strong as possible.

Chapter 36

Guardian Compound, Tetartos Realm

Alyssa relaxed into the stone bath across from Rain. They were quiet. It hadn't felt right to be cheerful, so they'd gone about preparations fairly subdued. They had the relaxation room in the manor courtyard all to themselves. French doors opened on all four walls, looking out on the beautiful green lawn. There was a fountain trickling to one side and the sound itself was soothing while the warm waters relaxed her tight muscles. They had spent the last couple of hours getting waxed and preparing her gown. The traditional design was simple and made to take off with a single pull of fabric. Rain supervised while she made a simple adjustment to hers. That was code meaning that Rain drank while pointing out things Alyssa could do with it.

She grinned to herself.

She was surprised that with everything potentially going to hell around them, she was still excited to complete their ceremony. Not for power, but to claim her male. Her beast loved that he would be marked as hers. Swirling her hands in the warm water, she realized just how much things had changed in such a short time.

She laid her head back on the stone ledge behind her.

"This feels so good, but I feel crappy for enjoying it," Rain said with disgust as she sank lower into the steamy water. Her friend looked exhausted. She knew Rain was worried for Delia. They both were. Alyssa was just happy her friend had been on lockdown there when everything happened. She had a bad feeling that if Rain had been home, she might have been one of the victims.

Alyssa knew the others had arrived even before Rain sounded off greetings. She turned around to see a smiling Sirena, Brianne, Sam and Sacha walking in through one of the open doors. It had been nice enough outside to let the breeze flow through. When she'd had Gregoire relay an invitation to Alex, through Uri, he'd raised his brows. She heard Uri decline, explaining to Gregoire that Alex needed to try to keep tabs on Delia until the ceremony, but that they appreciated the invitation.

"Okay, I'm popping this shit open," Brianne said, holding up two bottles of wine, one in each hand. "You're going to need it." The Guardian smirked. She and Rain got out of the pool and dried off. The females looked beautiful, already dressed in short white flirty gowns. They were all ready for the ceremony. Sacha had a gold band around each arm. She was exotically striking and obviously powerful to allow metal to circle her flesh.

She wrapped her towel around her swimsuit-clad body and relaxed in the company of both new and old friends.

"Okay, drink up, Brianne wasn't kidding," Sirena said, laughing.

Alyssa looked over to where Brianne was busily pouring the wine and caught sight of her back. The Guardian's dress was completely backless, the front clasped by a thin strap around her slender neck. Her long, curly, titian hair was pulled back in a ponytail, showing a beautiful tattoo of wings that tipped down to the dips at the tops of her buttocks. The artwork was stunning.

"Your tattoo is gorgeous," Alyssa said, a little awed.

A grinning Brianne turned with filled glasses for them both.

Someone had planned in advance because stemware had been in the room from the start. "Thanks. I'll probably have more done soon."

She took a drink of the rich wine and let it warm her thoroughly. Rain actually moaned in delight when she drank some of hers. Alyssa smiled. It felt nice to have a group of female friends. It was good for Rain, too. Her friend was in a crappy situation, still trying to figure out what to do with her days. With the city on lockdown, she couldn't check on her store or really get any bearing on her new life, especially when no one knew what Cyril was planning next.

"Are you ready to do this? It's probably going to hurt for a second," Sirena said, shaking her head, then grinned wickedly. "He's going to go crazy when he sees this. We'll help you get ready after I've finished."

She nodded and then took a long fortifying drink in order to prepare herself for what she planned.

"I'm ready. Let's do it."

Chapter 37

Mountain Temple, Tetartos Realm

Gregoire impatiently awaited Alyssa's arrival at the temple. His brother Guardians along with Vane and Erik were waiting with him. All were dressed in the traditional black silk and standing in the opulent golden temple set high in a mountain cave.

The muscles of his bare chest twitched as his life force whirled in the anticipation of being marked forever as a mated male.

He watched as Uri and Alex walked in. Both their features seemed tense as they came up to him to wish him well. The experience with Delia was taking its toll on both of them. It was the worst of situations, and he felt for them. To have the power to go into the female's mind only to share her suffering had to be pure hell.

"I would have understood if you needed to stay with Delia," he told them. The others were behind him, no doubt hoping for news.

"It wouldn't do any good. She pushed us from her mind not long ago. We're going to refuel and rest before trying again. I hope to fuck he gives her some damn clue where they are." Uri's voice was filled with frustrated irritation and Gregoire noticed Alex squeezing his hand.

He was close to leaving and collecting his damned female himself when his sister Guardians along with Rain and Sam walked in to the room. As they parted, he got his first glimpse of Alyssa, and his fucking breath caught at how gorgeous she was. She wore a gown of pale green and there were jewels shimmering in her hair, holding the wild waves off her beautiful face. The diamond chandelier above moved and sent sparkling light over her flushed skin and bare shoulders. The gown cinched tight at her small waist. A tie to one side held it in place and the deep cutout in front gave him a view of her cleavage.

He growled low, wanting to rip away the thin material and suck the hard nipples peaking the thin material.

Her glossy lips parted on a gasp of desire as she moved toward him, and everyone seemed to fade away as he took her hand.

Drake began speaking, but Gregoire had no idea what he was saying. His essence was swirling with the need to be marked as hers. The intensity of it was compelling.

At a pause, words in the old language spilled from his lips. He vowed to honor and care for her, body, soul and in blood for all eternity. He hadn't even needed to think them; his lips moved as if on their own. The vow itself was filled with power that sank deeply into them.

When her small hand lifted to the muscle of his chest, his eyes nearly closed with the pleasure of it. His soul was surging under his skin, fighting to meet with hers. Sirena's hand came up and covered Alyssa's, and he clenched his teeth against his beast's reaction.

Power funneled through his mate's hand straight into his body. It was a biting pleasure-pain that held him immobile and completely in its thrall. There was an all-encompassing rightness to it. A sense of reverence that couldn't be described in words. He didn't want the sensation to end. He held his breath, snared in her pale green gaze, as he opened his mind to hers.

He wanted her to feel how perfect it was, and that was the only way for her to understand.

She moaned lightly as her hand moved the width of his chest, marking him, claiming him as hers.

The moment her hand left his skin, he leaned down and lifted her up so that she would be flush against his still-twitching flesh. Claiming her lips, he twined his tongue with hers, demanding she accept him. He tasted the depths of her soft mouth as he tilted his head for a better angle. Her fingers dug into his hair, and she moaned deep; her desire filled the air and he growled his approval against her lips. She was fucking his and he couldn't wait to bare her skin to him. He turned to take them out of the room.

Not yet, love. Her voice in his mind stilled his movements. He was caught off guard by the endearment.

She pulled at his hair, and he growled, his eyes narrowing. Her cheeks were flushed a pretty rose, and her eyes were glazed, but she shook her head at him.

He frowned at her.

She laughed softly and said, "We're not done yet. You need to set me down."

He set her on her feet with great reluctance, interested to see just what she had planned.

She took a step back and slowly brought her fingers to the clasp of the dress. He held his breath as she released it, allowing her breasts to spill free. He groaned as the material floated to her waist, leaving her exposed in full sight of everyone in the cavern. It was if the world stopped when he realized what she'd done.

An animalistic noise came from his lips as his pulse pounded in his chest. Her gorgeous breasts were pierced with a clear plastic, and each taut nipple sat nestled between two diamonds. His hands lifted to caress the beautiful mounds, and she moaned, arching into his palms. His eyes shot to hers, and his dick pulsed.

He was dying to get inside her while he loved her swollen flesh with his mouth. Her eyes grew heavy and he knew she heard his every thought. She'd done this for him. Bared her magnificent flesh, allowing his brethren to see just how blessed he was. How fucking perfect she was.

His.

His thumbs reverently caressed the jeweled tips, and she groaned. He felt gooseflesh rise on her swells. He could take her to the floor and make her his. His shoulders flexed, readying to do just that when she licked her lips and shook her head at him.

Her tiny palms came up to cover his hands. A second later he registered whispers in the space. Sirena's fingers were lightly touching his, and then her power flowed as he marked his mate. Alyssa groaned aloud as she opened her mind fully, and her pleasure in the act nearly dropped him to his knees. His chest swelled, and he groaned deep. He could feel the markings rise and surround first one rose-colored areola and then the other.

The second Sirena's power stopped flowing, he lifted Alyssa into his arms and carried her out of the room. Cheers exploded behind them. He couldn't wait to see just how gorgeous the markings were. If he'd stopped to look at them while they were in the cavern, he would have taken her. He was aching to get inside her, but they weren't fucking finished yet.

As they reached the one exit for the mountain, he saw Dorian porting away. He frowned, thinking that something was definitely wrong with his brother, but he couldn't think past his need for Alyssa. Finding out what was going on with Dorian would have to wait.

Chapter 38

Island Temple of Consummation, Tetartos Realm

Their life forces mingled and whirled, and Alyssa thought she'd lose her mind. It was even more intense after the ceremony. How was that even possible?

She smelled the salt air and heard the waves washing over the beach. The moon was bright as he carried her over sand and up the marble steps into the temple. His breathing was ragged, his eyes narrowed on her breasts. She felt just as needy as they entered a big room that had been lit with candles, giving it a seductive glow.

He lifted her higher to take her lips in a searing kiss that left her breathless and her skin tingling.

"I want to see my cock slide between your breasts. I didn't think it was possible to make them more beautiful, but fuck. All I can see is my come coating your nipples, and I don't think it can wait until after we've blood-bonded."

She moaned at the feral look on his face and his blatant need.

She was tossed on the bed a second later. He ripped off the silk pants he'd been wearing, and his body heaved in need as he crawled over her. He licked and suckled at her breasts, one at a time, as he groaned.

Through lowered lids, she saw his cock fisted in his hand as he toyed with the jewelry and devoured every inch of her marked breasts. She knew that each nipple bore a much tinier version of the mark that covered his chest. Twin serpents entwined in infinity circled around the dusky flesh. She moaned and writhed beneath him, so close to coming from his tongue against the mating symbol and her piercings. He pulled the tie at her side and released the rest of her dress. *Spread your thighs wide for me. I need your come all over my face and mine covering your beautiful breasts.*

She groaned deep and spread her thighs as he buried his face between them, thrusting his tongue deep and rubbing his lips all over her. Out of the corner of her eye, she saw Conn standing at the door. *He's here to stand sentry for the blood-bonding, but he gets to watch me eat your hot little pussy first.*

She fisted her hands in his hair and came hard. She felt him lap it up, and then he was over her. His big hand pumped his cock until heated spurts were all over her chest and stomach. His lids were lowered as he watched his seed cover the markings that declared her his. They stared at each other for long moments as their chests heaved.

We need to blood-bond, love, so that I can have all of you. I should probably have warned you about the ugliness you'll see, but remember any of the horrors from my past are centuries old. I'm not thrilled you have to go through this, but there's no other way to complete the bond.

She nodded slowly. She'd had enough history lessons to know what she'd see, but that didn't make any of it easier.

Let's just get through it, she said with more confidence than she felt. He gave her a sharp nod, and then seconds later Conn was standing next to the bed, a warm smile on his face. He handed her mate a beautiful blade adorned with intricate carvings as Gregoire lay down on his side and turned her to face his chest.

He quickly cut a small line on his torso and brought her lips to it. It was done before she had time to fully grasp what was happening. She barely felt the cut to her arm as her tongue instinctively lashed out at the sweet taste of him. She moaned when she felt the sensation of his suckling at the inside of her arm.

The flashes hit hard and fast, submerging her into a different time.

She felt Gregoire's pure, blinding hatred for the Gods. For all that Apollo and Hermes had done to him.

He was an animal. Rutting with females who hated it every bit as much as he. He despised it but knew the consequences of not completing the job. The females were to be used until they conceived. They were all nothing more than beasts to create an army. He banged his head against the metal walls of his cell, knowing that they would come for him again soon.

Years passed.

He'd infiltrated the Gods' warrior camp. The place where all their children had been taken. He faced a young boy with soulless forest eyes and a scent that told Gregoire that he was looking at his son. Furious. His heart nearly wrenched from his chest.

Suddenly the child was holding a blade, attempting to kill him. The boy's vacant eyes were completely devoid of anything but aggression.

Gregoire was forced to bat away the child's attempts, sickened by the thought of hurting him.

Later she was with him as the scent of blood and dirt under his knees filled his lungs. He was chained, roaring against the hold as he was forced to watch them beat the child for failing to kill his own father.

Gregoire's fear that the child was too far damaged by what was done to him to ever function if Gregoire was able to free him.

Months pass.

A bloody, battered female, limp and barely alive lay before him.

He and Uri unchaining her and vowing to find her a safe place where she could live in peace. The female's swollen and unseeing eyes gazed at nothing as he and Uri released her and carried her to freedom. It was Charybdis. The Immortal who'd sacrificed a part of her life force to create the mating spell that restricted all Immortals from bearing young with one who wasn't their destined mate.

Not long after saving her he was surrounded by stone and fire. It burned his feet and legs. He and the other Guardians searched the rubble for any young that might have survived Ares and Artemis' attack on Apollo and Hermes' warrior camps.

She felt his dark need to kill each and every one of the Gods. It burned inside him.

A day passes in the memories.

Standing on a cold mountaintop with only a swath of fabric wrapped around his waist.

Bitter, angry disappointment at the Creators' chosen punishment for the Gods. The Deities were to sleep off the dark energies of death and destruction until they would one day be needed in Earth again.

She felt the touch of the Creators' light and purity, their understanding and love.

A surge of power rushed through his veins as he accepted his role as a Guardian of the Realms.

Centuries pass and battles and time spent at the other Guardians' sides. She felt their connection. They'd all become more a family than true brothers and sisters.

Flickers of images passed rapidly until he was seeing his friend's joy and being escorted up to a room. She was seeing her father through Gregoire's eyes.

The sight of a babe with unique pale green eyes. Her. She'd looked up at him.

The jarring soul-deep knowledge that the tiny babe was to be his nearly forced him to his knees.

Utter fear and joy rolled into one and he didn't want to let her go. Vowed to himself that the tiny child would be happy and safe for all eternity.

Decades pass.

He stood atop a hill.

His first glimpse of beauty like nothing he'd ever imagined. He was taking in the sight of her at twenty. Searching out the eyes he knew would be the same unique shade as when she was a babe. He imagined wrapping his fist in her long hair to guide her lips to his.

Utter peace, so strong it was nearly his undoing.

Anger and pain as he battled his need, knowing she was still too young. Conceding with her father that she wasn't ready even though it felt like a knife to his gut.

More images of her running in the meadow, out to the lake.

Uri and Alex's mating and the sheer happiness for his brother that mixed with the sharp knowledge he would finally be able to claim Alyssa, because even the thought of another female's touch made him ill.

Then she felt their first touch. His sheer need when he finally felt her skin at Paradeisos and she was immediately swamped with a barrage of every single moment they'd spent together since. His watching her sleep. Blinding love. Exquisite peace. The need to protect and possess her for all eternity.

It was beautiful.

Her chest heaved as she woke and gasped for breath. Tears were streaming down her face as she sought his eyes.

Gregoire was gazing at her as he instructed Conn to leave. He held her tight against his chest as he reassured her. "It's done, love. Please don't cry. I hate seeing how much pain I caused you. I won't hurt you again, angel," he vowed as he rocked her softly. After a deep breath he spoke again. "I'm sorry you had to see any of my old life, love. It was a very long time ago." She felt how tense his muscles were as he held her and she'd never felt more loved in her entire life. After seeing that each moment he'd spent with her had been his most cherished, she was overwhelmed. Only the most important memories were shared during a blood-bonding... She'd been the good, the light in his life.

She looked up at him with watery eyes and so much love it was bursting inside her chest. He'd suffered so much and then found peace in *her*.

She lifted her lips to his and kissed him with all the love in her heart. She opened her mind and let him feel how overwhelmed and out of control she was. Her hands slid along his short beard, and she

SETTA JAY

held him to her as she crawled over him, slipping her tongue in to duel with his, reveling in the sound of their mingled moans of pleasure.

She wanted all of him. He massaged his come all over her breasts. How was it possible that she hadn't been under long enough for it to dry on her flesh? She didn't know or care as she shifted her head from side to side, exploring with her tongue as she straddled his stomach. Her hands tunneled into his hair and over his shoulders as her lips met his neck and then moved to nip his ear.

His fingers were busy playing over her heated flesh, pulling her tight to him. "Your pussy is coating me with all your sweet desire."

She was lost in him, pushing back. "I need you inside me while I use my lips to love every bit of the mark that says you're mine." Her voice was sultry even to her. She circled her wet opening over his tip until he took her hips and slammed his cock deep. Her back bowed with the blinding beauty of impact, and she set to work with her mouth. She began licking every line of the two serpents twining. Those dark lines told the world he was hers.

"Fuck, I love how you suck me in. Love that you're fighting and slamming your pussy on me." She licked around and over the marks before sitting up to ride him harder. His eyes were focused on hers as she slammed down on him, letting him fill her so perfectly full. "I love having your mind open, feeling every throbbing pulse of your pussy in my head. Play with those beautiful nipples and come on my cock."

His mind opened, and she was flooded with his heat and the sight of her impaled and stretched over him. She looked like a goddess. She was his vision of perfection. Seeing herself through his eyes as her body moved on him, her breasts bouncing. His knuckles went to her clit, and she groaned. Her nipples ached against her

268

fingers; it was so damn good she came in a rush, shouting and tensing as his warm seed finally filled her full.

He kissed her head as she collapsed against his warm chest. "We're not done, love."

She groaned and felt his cock pulsing inside her. No, he would never be sated. Neither of them would be. There were things that needed to be done for the consummation to be official, and her stomach fluttered with anticipation. She rubbed her cheek against his mark and practically purred. "How exactly do you want me to suck you?"

"I want it hard and fast, your cheeks hollowed and my dick all the way down your throat until your sweet little nose is on my balls. And I want to see your pussy and ass as you're doing it." He smacked her bottom and flipped her so that her legs straddled his chest. She smiled before licking and twirling her tongue over his crown while he spanked and caressed her ass. She took him deep, sucking and swallowing him as far as he would go.

After growling a warning for her not to bite down, he slapped lower. He was all the way down her throat, throbbing as she suckled his cock, and she wanted more.

"Fuck, don't move, and don't clamp down," he demanded, and her pussy clenched at his tone alone. She felt everything he did, every delicious sensation that rocked them both. She knew what he planned, and she couldn't wait. A series of slaps heated her bottom, and then with two sharp whacks lit against her pussy until she was crying out around his cock. It took everything in her not to clamp down as he came down her throat.

He gently pulled her lips from his cock and lay her down next to him, her back to his chest. His voice was a whisper in her hair. "I love knowing what you're thinking and feeling. Love how much you get off sucking my cock." He lifted her thigh over his so that she was wide open and he could play all he wanted in her liquid. He pushed it back to her ass, and she moaned.

"And I'm so glad you love me in your ass because I can't get enough of it. Taking you like that makes my beast roar. It's the ultimate submission it craves." He continued to take her fluid and push it inside, and she pushed back to meet every thrust of his fingers. He rolled his big body over hers, trapping her against the bedding, tossing the pillows aside. "Use both hands and hold on to the end of the bed. I'm going to give you all my weight as I fuck your ass deep and pin you down hard. You won't be able to move or fight my dominance, Alyssa. I know that's how you like me."

He rolled her to her stomach and spread her legs. Anticipation lit her nerve endings as she heard him opening a jar and felt cream sliding into her a split second before his massive cock started to tunnel into her ass. She stretched, and it ached with the bite of pain that added to her arousal. It was so damn hot she didn't know if she could take it.

"You can take it, love. You need it like I do. Now hold on tight." She gripped the bed and did as he said as the cream worked its magic. His weight settled on her, and he thrust, his hips pumping hard and deep inside her tight ass, and she loved it. Couldn't get enough. Was needy and panting as his hands covered hers, and the bed moved as he pounded into her over and over until she was screaming and coming. Spots filled her vision as he filled her. The pulsing of her life force slammed beneath her skin until she felt a resounding snap that was so perfect she gasped, dizzy, and then darkness took her under.

Chapter 39

Cyril's Compound, Tetartos Realm

Cyril was having trouble concentrating on Kane. Memories of his delicious mate were assailing him. He remembered the last few hours he'd spent with her before leaving for the damn meeting.

He had scratches all over his arms and face that he was quickly healing. He rolled his neck at the pure pleasure and power running through his veins. He had chained her but allowed her some freedom of movement. Just enough to give her the illusion that she might have a chance to get free, then taken it all away. The female had been pleasingly fierce in her ineffective fight against his nearly constant claiming. He still smelled her delectable pheromones, but it seemed she was not equally affected by him.

She lay beneath him, naked and bleeding from the wounds he inflicted as well as those that had come from her fight against the chains at her wrists. Her chest was expanding and contracting in her fury. He did not break her spirit this time, but he felt his need for her rising once again. There would be time.

Cyril was dying to get back to his beautiful Delia. He would still be buried deep inside her if Kane had not called him back. He clenched his teeth at the interruption, but he couldn't let anyone know that he'd mated her. He needed more power before they ever found out. He hid the grin he felt. His body thrummed with the melding.

He still remembered her screams after he forced his blood down her mouth. She must not have enjoyed seeing his memories. Her own were odd and disjointed and really pitiful. Her life had not had much of anything memorable. You only got big memories. Hers had centered on her time there. Her experience with the Aletheia and then Phelan. He'd been surprised to learn that Kane and Angus had given her venom. That seemed entirely too compassionate and suspicious. He eyed his second in command, wondering just what else the male was hiding.

Soon, his body would be used to the power of his lovely mate, and he would find out if his second was betraying him. The male would easily be dealt with, but for the moment he was useful.

His thoughts went back to the stunning copper eyes of his mate. She was his, never to be exposed to others. He remembered hearing her desire to kill him during the claiming and almost grinned. She had managed to quickly close her thoughts from him after that. He did not like that her abilities were coming so fast, but it didn't really matter. She would be locked away for eternity. She would live forever at his pleasure, which he'd been sure to tell her.

Kane's voice brought him back to the moment. "The lockdowns have finally been lifted, and my Mageia contact in Lofodes has heard of a female with a rare water ability. He is going to get me an image of her."

"Good, take Reve and bring her to me. Also, I still want the female the Guardian was interested in, since you said she is also from Lofodes; make sure to collect her as well. Call me immediately when you have them."

Pain radiated through his bond with Delia. It was so harsh it nearly took him to his knees. Instant panic filled him. *What is it?* he asked her.

Something's wrong, she whimpered back.

"I have to leave. Contact me when you've located both females and put them in a cell. Get the drugs you need from my lab."

He exited through the halls as fast as he could. What was happening? Was it the drug? If she died, what would happen to him? Fuck, he hadn't thought of the possibilities. He'd been too enamored with her power and cunt.

He ported in and flung the cell door wide. She was slumped and seizing with her arms still chained to a metal bar. He rushed in, livid and panicked. What had he fucking done? He went to her and was instantly caught by surprise. Cool cuffs slammed onto his wrists with lightning-quick speed, and fire filled his chest. His eyes went wide as agony hit him hard.

He looked down at her. She was covered in blood from his last frenzied attentions, but she wasn't broken, she was full of strength. Triumph invaded their mating link, and he saw burning hatred and vengeance in her eyes as he tried to fight the assault. The metal was dampening his power, and she was too strong. Stronger than she should be.

He roared in fury and panic as his creation killed him.

Chapter 40

Gregoire's Home, Tetartos Realm

Alyssa felt delectably loose limbed as she stretched and took her coffee with a grin. He'd taken her home after the consummation, and they'd spent the last few days immersed in crazed loving because they wanted to, not because their life forces were beating at them to complete their bond.

She'd even shown him her other form, and they'd spent hours running around the lake. He'd been stunning, and just as enormous as she'd imagined. She knew how ridiculous they must have looked, and she hadn't cared. Her head hadn't even come to his shoulder. His warhorse was a spectacular black, something that surprised her; his muscled flank was incredible.

Her beast matched her chestnut-colored hair, so she'd thought his would be the same. She shook off the memory.

"Now that the cities are out of lockdown, I promised to take Rain to see her family and the store. I also need to say hello to my parents," she informed him while sipping and moaning her appreciation of the brew.

"I can take you both when I get home from patrol," he said, leaning naked against the counter.

"That won't be for hours, and I'd rather have you to myself then." She wanted him anytime she could have him; not like when they were frenzied, it felt different.

He stiffened and growled, "No."

"It'll be broad daylight, and according to Alex and Uri, Cyril didn't mate his males to the other females. He bragged to Delia about hording the powers to himself, right? So we are not in danger of other uber-powerful mated males coming to the cities to attack."

"I'll take you when I get back." His eyes were hard.

"I'm not weak and will be watchful. I wouldn't risk my life or Rain's." She understood his worry, but she was also confident in her ability to keep them safe. Besides that, she needed to talk to her father without Gregoire there. It was time.

Alex and Uri had been communicating with Delia daily, and the reports just kept getting bleaker. The monster was obviously not worried about abducting Alyssa. Sadly, Cyril was too obsessed with Delia, tormenting and torturing her. It made her sick, thinking about what the female was suffering, but they were at a standstill. The aerial patrols continued their daily rotations and still nothing. Alex and Uri couldn't find anything useful in Delia's mind to indicate where he was holding her, so they were stuck on that front as well.

"According to Drake, the shields have been reinforced, and my father's warriors are constantly patrolling the area, right?"

He nodded, but did not look happy, which made her grin. "I can teleport now. There is nothing to worry about." She refrained from telling him she didn't need his permission. He was protective and she understood that.

He growled. "One hint of danger and you get your asses home."

"Agreed. My parents will likely be with us the entire time."

She'd spoken to her mother while Gregoire and Dorian had secured the breach, but she'd yet to have her "Come to Creators" moment with her father, and she knew that was where most of her problem had originated. That was something she needed to do alone. Her mother had explained their reasons for keeping Alyssa's mating to Gregoire a secret, but that hadn't made her feel any better. She understood her parents' worry, but it sucked to have been underestimated and suffocatingly sheltered by those she cared about.

Two hours later she and Rain teleported outside Alyssa's parents' home.

"Well, after two days of being your teleport experiment, I think I'm starting to feel less like throwing up all over our shoes when we reform," Rain said dryly as she took deep panting breaths.

"It's fortunate for us both that we've only tested it hours after you've eaten."

"I smell banana bread," Rain announced, perking up. So did Alyssa, and she grinned at the look of hunger on Rain's face. She'd informed her mother and father they would be coming. Her mother must have gotten to work right away.

They walked up and into the big cozy manor home set in the trees not too far from the city. It had been the home she'd grown up in, and the scent of baked goods was nothing new. They found her mother busy in the kitchen. Her long brown hair was pulled back in a ponytail, and when she turned around, Alyssa saw the features that were similar to hers. Her mother was taller by a good few inches, and her eyes were a darker green, but being Immortal, they looked nearly the same age.

"I'm so glad you're here. Rain, I could use some help with

wrapping these up, and I can see by the look on your face that my little tester is ready for sampling." Her mother's eyes warmed while looking at them. It instantly brought her back to her childhood.

"Alyssa, your father's out back if you want to talk to him." She heard the tension and guilt in her mother's words.

She nodded and exited out the back door, finding her father chopping wood. He did it for her mother, who always liked having a fire in the hearth. She'd always said it made the house cozier and Alyssa had to agree.

"So ya found me, sweeting." His eyes shone down at her. He was in his human form, wearing the old traditional breeches he favored. She shook her head. He wasn't one for modernization. "Are you okay? You're always welcome to come home if you're not." His concerned gaze galled her.

She set her hands on her hips and stared at him. "I'm perfectly happy with my mate, Father. What I'm not happy with is being treated like a child at twenty-five years old." She took a deep breath before continuing, "I'm angry that you kept the fact that I had a mate a secret from me, and I'm disappointed that you would disrespect your *old friend* by suggesting I leave him." She was furious and barely holding it together.

Her father's face got hard. "You're my child, my blood. He is a strong male and an old friend, but where is he now? His duty makes it dangerous for you. Yet he's let you come here alone when there are enemies about?" Her sweet bear of a father was out of line and had the nerve to be livid, which riled her up to an entirely different level.

"You think I'm not strong enough to take care of myself? That hurts. Gregoire may be possessive and protective, but he also sees me as a strong female. Your warriors have always thought me weak because *you* felt that way." She shook her head in sadness.

He scoffed, "I did not say that you are weak. I love you more than anything; you are my babe." His eyes were still hard.

"That's just it, Father. I'm not a babe. I'm a grown female with power and strength of my own and a mate that respects me. Unfortunately, I have a father that only sees me as a child to be coddled. Until you figure out that's not who I am, we can't move on. I know you love me and I love you, but I'm not going to be cast into this role, and I'll not have Gregoire disrespected by you or anyone." The stubborn look on his face said he didn't get it. She shook her head. "I have things to do. Think about what I've said."

Her father looked at her in disbelief; then his gaze shot over her head. She turned around and saw Rain and her mother on the back steps. Her mother was gazing furiously at her father. Her green eyes were flashing, and air was whistling in the trees. Rain held a basket of goodies, and her eyes were a bit wide.

"We'll drop off the stuff from Rain's shop later," she informed her mother. There were too many feelings circling inside her, and she could see her mother was about to lose her mind. Maybe she'd have luck where Alyssa had failed in making him understand. She walked up to Rain and grabbed her hand, teleporting them next to a few trees close to the city walls.

"Oh, God. I get that we needed to make an exit, but I really think I'm going to throw up this time." Rain was hunched over, the basket at her side. Alyssa cringed for her friend.

She rubbed Rain's back, wishing she had some water to give her. "I'm so sorry. I didn't think, well, other than the childish act of trying to get one up on my father." She shook her head, thoroughly disgusted with herself at how ridiculous she'd behaved. Nothing like proving his point. She hadn't even considered that Rain had likely been gorging on banana bread with her mother. She was too caught up on wanting to prove her father wrong, with her "watch how I teleport my friend out of here and you don't have the power to come after me" crap.

They stayed like that for a good few minutes. A couple of her father's warriors patrolled past, and she wondered if they'd seen her teleport with Rain. The announcement that she was Gregoire's mate hadn't gone out. Considering that they moved on with nothing but a nod, she doubted it.

"Any better?" she asked Rain, wincing at her friend's misery. Misery she'd caused.

"I deserve a medal for not getting sick everywhere. Just give me another second," her friend said through steady breaths.

Alyssa grabbed the basket, and they walked up to the city and made the rounds. They first went to Delia's and dropped off the baked goods. A note on the door said her family wasn't up for visitors but appreciated all the offers of support. She and Rain exchanged a sad look and left the basket outside the door of the townhome. Rain's parents were next and that visit went quickly, as they'd needed to get back to work packing for their move to a cottage outside the Guardian manor.

"Are you okay? You haven't been quite yourself all day," Alyssa asked. They were in Rain's shop, getting things to take back with them. They'd let Mrs. Lewis leave a few moments ago to run and make her husband lunch. She only lived a few doors down, so she'd likely be back soon. Rain threw a few more clothes in a bag and got out the lotions they were supposed to take back to Alyssa's mother before they left for home.

"I don't know." Her voice was strained; her friend hadn't looked quite like herself for days. At first she'd imagined it was the stress and worry for Delia was getting to her.

"Really, you need to spill it. I know you're going through a lot, but it's not just the business or Delia, is it? Did something happen at the manor?"

"It's a lot of things, I guess. I was telling the truth; I'm ready for a change with my shop. It's tough because it was my baby for years, but now I just feel like it's too much. I'm still in limbo on what to do." She rummaged around, straightening and checking shelves while she'd said the words.

"And..." she prodded, knowing there was more to it.

"I feel terrible for Delia. She's so young, and the bastard's fucking torturing her. It makes me want to throw up, rage, and kill him. What makes the whole thing worse is I feel guilty for being safe. I'm thankful *I* wasn't taken. I just feel very mortal and powerless right now." She huffed.

"I get that. It's okay to feel powerless; I do too. I feel like I should be doing something too, but we're stuck until someone finds a way to get to her." Alyssa imagined her feelings were nothing compared to Rain's. Rain knew Delia, whereas she had only met the young girl a few times.

"Keep going. I know there's more." She felt like her friend was holding back.

She ripped into a box and started unpacking candles, and Alyssa helped her shelve them. "I've gotten no sleep for days, and I'm feeling crazy horny, if you must know. Maybe I need to check up on Conn when I get back," she grumbled.

Alyssa burst out laughing and quickly cut it off at Rain's narrowed gaze. "I'm sorry for laughing. Why haven't you taken the wolf up on his offer?"

"You can tell, can't you?" Rain looked at her with accusation in her eyes.

"I'm sorry." She cringed. She didn't want to embarrass her friend, so she hadn't mentioned knowing Rain was in the mood.

Rain turned pink and blew out a breath. "Damn Immortal senses. I'm going to take care of it when I get back. I don't know what's wrong with me. I've been dreaming and lusting over a male that looked at me as if I were ophiotaurus dung at your mating ceremony."

The bell chimed, and Mrs. Lewis walked in. "I'm back," she said cheerily as she entered, her rosy cheeks flushed.

"I see you've gotten to the stock Astrid dropped off earlier. She asked about you two. I told her you were popping in and out while you were still on vacation. She said she'd come find out about your adventures when she could. The lockdown on the cities put her behind." Her eyes turned sad. The circumstances behind the lockdown were tragic. Everyone knew Delia was gone, but they didn't know what was happening to her. That knowledge was being kept under wraps. Drake had made it clear to them all, including Rain, that they were not to tell anyone about Alex's power and that they knew what was happening.

Rain hadn't even shared that she was living at the Guardian compound with anyone but her parents, who were told to keep it under wraps.

"Are you still okay watching the place for another week?" Rain asked the older Mageia.

"It's fine. It gives me something to do. As long as you don't mind my closing up at lunchtime?"

"Of course, just leave a note," Rain said with a smile. "I'll be back next week and you can let my parents know if you need anything." She and Alyssa both lifted bags and walked out the door.

"Please don't port me back to your parents'. It's broad daylight and less than a kilometer away. Besides, your father's warriors are everywhere right now." Rain groaned.

"Yeah, fine. Sorry about that." She was dreading going back there, but so be it.

They walked through the gates and passed some of the warriors in question, who were headed in the other direction. "Now, what were you talking about earlier? What Guardian looked at you badly?" Alyssa was irritated; she bet it was Sander. He stood off from the others and looked like he could be a dick. He'd been respectful when meeting her, but there was something about him.

Rain just shook her head. "It doesn't matter. I just feel stupid for still being attracted to someone who has absolutely zero interest in me. It's not pleasant and is starting to make me feel a little crazy."

Rain stumbled on a loose rock, which made her curse in frustration. Alyssa helped her right herself as they walked around the first bend, when, out of nowhere, the same Kairos who'd been in Paradeisos appeared behind her friend and grabbed her. Alyssa lunged for Rain only to be caught around the waist. She felt a sting in her neck and grabbed for whatever it was. She yanked the needle away, already feeling light-headed. As she fought the hold, she heard something break and another growl from the male holding her. Through blurry eyes, she saw that Rain was slumped in the Kairos' arms.

She knew it had to be the same Aletheia from Paradeisos holding her. She could have fought him off, could have probably teleported him away to the manor to get help, but the Kairos had her friend and she wouldn't leave Rain. Her heart pounded as she realized her only option was to let them take her too. Damn it, she would never allow her friend to be lost, like Delia. Fuck that. She made sure her mental shields were tight against the Aletheia's ability, the shields of Immortals were generally strong, and hers were locked tight. He wouldn't see into her mind. She slumped into his arms as if she were also unconscious.

What's happening? Gregoire's voice settled her nerves. He must have felt her panicking.

You need to track me. As much as it went against the grain to let herself be taken, she had no other choice, and it might be the only opportunity they had to find Delia and the others.

The Aletheia growled at the Kairos, "Get us the hell out of here. I don't know how much she got. She pulled the fucking needle free and broke the other."

They were porting before she could explain to Gregoire what was happening. He was going to go insane.

Chapter 41

London, Earth Realm

*A*lyssa!

Drake, I think Cyril's bastards have Alyssa and Rain. I'm tracking her now. His message went out to the link with all his brothers before he teleported. He felt her moving and his mind was splintering with rage. He ported from Earth to the manor, waiting to see where she stopped, leaving Conn to bring Havoc back. She seemed to be moving slowly. She was being ported by a fucking Kairos, and they likely had Rain too. They fucking had his mate!

Son of a bitch. Everyone but Uri and Alex get to Gregoire, Drake demanded.

Drake continued in the link, *Uri, see if Cyril is still with Delia. I want the bastard's location.* Gregoire paced the balcony of the manor, not wanting the piece of shit anywhere near his female. His jaw was as tight as his fists. His vision had gone hazy red knowing they'd touched her. The bastards were trying to take his mate. He would mutilate those motherfuckers. He tried to breathe through the panic as her link continued to move slowly. It was coming over the sea separating the continents.

We're going to Delia now. Alex said to wait one more minute before going to Alyssa. Uri's voice was livid. Fuck that. He wouldn't wait a second. He didn't give a shit about Alex's *knowings.* Everything in him screamed to go to her.

Drake and the others started porting onto the balcony behind him. Vane and Erik were with them. "We'll get her," Drake said, and his voice was dangerously low.

He felt when her movements stopped; they had to be rematerializing. Drake put a hand on his arm, and he tried to shake it off. Drake was a strong fucker and so were his other brothers. P took one side, and Drake the other. He fought their hold, knowing they were trying to delay as Alex instructed. He didn't care if he did damage as he fought them. "One fucking minute. Alex would not risk your mate. What if that one minute means her life?" Drake's green dragon eyes were dead serious, smoke billowing from his lips. His other brothers were right at his back as he waited, his jaw clenched tight, and his muscles felt like they would tear from his body.

It felt more like an hour when he heard her voice. *Gregoire?* Her voice was soft in his head. *I'm unharmed. I just feel like I had one too many shots.* She was mentally sending him the images from around her. He saw through her blurry eyes the sight of a tree with a distinctive knot. Rocks and mountains in the distance. He sent the images to the others through the Guardian link.

Then he was gone.

*****

Alyssa kept still as they carried her into the mountain. She felt sluggish and woozy and knew it was from the injection. She was just lucky it didn't knock her out. She must have removed the needle in time, or her new powers were combatting it. Thankfully, Cyril's male hadn't seemed to realize that she was awake. She'd had to keep her eyes a mere slit when checking their surroundings. Her neck was starting to ache from being tilted back.

The Aletheia holding her spoke as they carried her and Rain

down a tunnel. "I don't like having the Hippeus here, but Cyril insisted. This could end badly. Nothing's been said that proves she means anything to the Guardian, but she is Adras' daughter. They will search harder for her than the others, and who knows how much of the sedative she got. I need to get the other serum into her system before she wakes up." He growled before continuing, "I can't reach Cyril now, and he said to notify him immediately when we had them. Fuck, all we can do is put them in cells until he comes. I don't like it."

"Do you think he perfected the formula? Is he closing us out? I've heard rumors that he moved one of the females. No one knows where. Now he wants Mageias with special abilities?" The Kairos whispered the words. Dissention in the ranks?

I'm here. Explain what's happening, Gregoire growled in her mind.

She thought she heard chatter in the Guardian link and lifted a shield to it. All that mattered was the link she shared with her mate, and she didn't want to get distracted.

I'm okay, but the Kairos from Paradeisos grabbed Rain. I had no choice but to play unconscious or chance losing her to them. All they're doing is taking us to a cell. She relayed the conversation she'd heard to Gregoire. Special abilities? What did that mean?

I'll fucking kill them. Stay with me and tell me everything you see as we get the fuck in there.

She heard steps, and another guard came up to them.

The Aletheia was speaking again. "You might be right. I'm going to have a look at some things in the lab." She heard footsteps and the one holding her commanded, "Take her and put them in the cells." She was shifted into meaty arms, and it was really hard to lie limp and not cringe at the touch of yet another male.

286

Keep still, and don't do anything until I get there. They don't know we're here yet. It was hard to hear the words through the growling. She sucked in all the energy that she could, but the walls and ceilings were coated in metal, so she only got a trickle from the ground. She felt the drugs slowly leaving her body.

How many? Gregoire demanded.

The Aletheia just left. One holding each of us. We've gone through two doors with key pads. I couldn't see the numbers without getting caught.

I'm coming.

As the drugs wore off, she found it harder to play dead. It was difficult not to move her arms and legs... her neck. She wished they would talk more. But it seemed that the new guy and the Kairos were not as friendly. She saw metal bars sliding open. Shit. *We're being put in a cell now.*

Alarms started a low thrumming in the tunnel, and the male holding her tensed. "Damn it. We knew this was a mistake." She was dropped to the ground and heard a similar thump as Rain hit the floor next to her. She opened her eyes and assessed where they were. Alyssa opened her arms and used the air currents to slam both males into the metal doors they hadn't closed. She didn't want to get locked in now that the game was up and alarms were sounding.

The weak air currents in the tunnels didn't stop them for long. She wasn't a hundred percent yet, but she hoped to fend them off. The Kairos teleported beyond the cell door and was gone through the tunnel. He wouldn't be able to port through it, but he would get further down the halls that way. She was left with the other one, a damn Hippeus at least three times her size. His long black hair was trailing down over his massive shoulders, hazel eyes zeroed in on her.

The menacing glint she saw was not promising.

"You feel like playing? Maybe I'll take you somewhere private to play. I'll tell the others you escaped." His grin was full of dark sadistic intent. The look made her nauseated and settled like a stone in her stomach. The big mountain of a male was in her way. He didn't look right. He was like an experiment gone horribly wrong; his muscles were huge all along his arms down to his hands.

What the fuck is happening? Gregoire's voice was dangerously low. Damn it, she had this. She didn't want her emotions distracting him from finding her.

I'm completely fine. Give me a second, she sent back, relaxing her limbs and settling her emotions. She was powerful and would wipe the cell with the sick bastard. He was just inside the doorway and coming for her. She ported behind him just as he reached big meaty hands for her. With a push of air currents, she slammed him into the wall inside the cell and quickly lifted Rain into her arms and out of the room. He turned around fast, breaking her hold quickly. She used her power and pulled the air from his lungs. Soon he was gasping and flailing in the small space as she carried her friend out of the cell and into the hall. She had just settled Rain down and away from the door when a female with slick black hair rushed in. A damn Fire Mageia. Alyssa tried to trap the giant in the cell, using air currents to slam it shut, but his arm jammed it. She heard bone crunch, but there was no closing it.

What the hell is going on? Gregoire demanded. He was livid.

Stop distracting me. I need a minute.

A series of fireballs were launched and hit just inches from her. She pulled the air from one and then ported out of the way of the others. The Mageia had aimed at her arms and legs, not going for a kill shot. That was promising. Priority was getting the fire blasts away from her unconscious friend.

She teleported behind the dark-haired bitch. The female's abilities were incredibly enhanced for a Fire Mageia. The bitch's elbow slammed back and almost hit Alyssa in the face. She dodged and swept the female's legs out from under her. She heard a roar as she was preparing to suck air from the female's lungs to get her to pass the hell out. She was breathing heavy and slower with the small amount of drugs still left in her system, and the air currents were weak indoors. Looking over, she saw the giant move in her direction. The low sound of the alarms bleating in her ears and loss of energies from porting was wearing her out quicker than she would have liked.

She needed to make her next moves count. The female kicked up, landing a blow to Alyssa's stomach, knocking the wind from her. The heavy steps of the giant had gotten closer. He was waiting for his opportunity. Looking around, she saw that the metal doors at both ends were shut. She was trapped with them, so she just needed to take the two of them out and only the Hippeus was Immortal.

She bent at the waist, panting a little. Best for them to think she didn't have any power or fight left in her. She had successfully maneuvered between them, waiting as she watched the female's lips lift in apparent satisfaction.

"You need to get back into your cage, bitch." The Mageia thought she had her. Her tightfitting black fighting gear and her slicked-back hair made her appear brutish. Her oversized muscles flexed under the snug clothing, and her features were harsh even with the grin tilting her lips. Alyssa assessed her to be around Rain's mother's age and strong. That was likely the reason she was part of the guards and not a lab rat for Cyril. The female's brown eyes were full of evil delight as she glared at her.

"That's not going to happen. And you're not male enough to make me," Alyssa taunted. The Mageia's dark eyes lit with rage, exactly the response Alyssa had been hoping for. She felt the heat of the flames as she ported just in time. She heard a deep bellow, knowing the fireball must have hit its mark in the giant's body. Alyssa didn't have time to waste. She used air currents to knock the big mass of angry Hippeus onto the Mageia. His bulk kept her down and thankfully his body trapped her sideways so her damn hands and torso were beneath him. She wasted no time in pulling the air from the asshole's lungs. He flailed and turned a deep purple as he struggled for breath. The female pushed and tried to yell beneath him. She had to be getting crushed under all that weight.

As soon as the flailing subdued, she ventured in and grabbed the blade at his side. She didn't have a lot of time. She didn't dare squander more energies than needed in case she had to help fight their way out. She was getting a little wiped out. Thank the Creators the male felt the need to carry a large blade. It was a good two feet with a sharp edge to its deadly curve. One cut sliced through the air and hit its mark. Shit, that wasn't enough, and she was getting squeamish. The second hard cleave separated his head. She'd never had to kill anything but hell beasts and felt nauseated, but she refused to balk past the initial shock. He deserved to die for threatening to rape her.

She shook it off. Her khakis and white top were covered in blood splatter and so was the Mageia's face.

The bitch's dark eyes grew even more deadly as the head stopped at the wall. Blood flowed, and the smell of it was sweetly pungent. The Mageia didn't speak, just lay there trying to gain her breath. The sound of the alarms and her heavy breathing were all that Alyssa could hear.

Is everything okay out there? she sent to Gregoire, wanting to be out of there, away from the smell.

What happened? He was definitely getting more enraged as time passed.

Everything's fine. We're safe and locked in until you get us out. She didn't want him worrying. Now that her fight was over, she felt his emotions beating at her. Fury. Panic. It wasn't good, and she knew he was clearing a path straight to her.

She walked around to the female and slammed her head into the ground. She didn't think she could stomach another beheading, but she sure as hell wasn't going to leave the female conscious. Her creepy stare was starting to become unnerving; Alyssa was sure that was her intent.

Uri and Alex might be able to get some information from her if she lived through being crushed under the giant Hippeus. Alyssa wiped the blade on his clothes and tried to get some of the blood off her face, using her shirt, before checking on Rain. She was still unconscious, and Alyssa tried to lay her in a more comfortable position before moving to check the cells that lined the wall.

We're almost there. Are you hurt? he said, and she heard a blast that shook the ground. She was forced to brace herself against a cell for a second until it stopped. She hoped the ceiling wouldn't come down.

No, I'm okay. I promise.

She reopened the Guardian link, wanting to know what was happening out there.

She heard Gregoire demanding Jax to get his ass over to blow another door. She grinned at his bossiness and then cringed. Her ass was going to hurt for a week after this. She didn't think for a second

291

that he wouldn't snap at her for letting herself be taken.

She shook her head, knowing she'd do the same thing all over again. She peered into the first cell, two naked females lay asleep on cots and her heart soared.

Yes! She went to another cell and another and counted eleven unconscious females. Not including Rain. She blew out a relieved breath. It was bittersweet. She'd known from Alex's reports and what the males had said Delia wasn't here. At least these females would get home to their families. Hopefully, there were clues somewhere in this place about where Cyril was keeping Delia.

Move away from any doors. Gregoire's voice in her mind sounded like a deep growl. Her stomach fluttered. He was here.

We're away.

Another blast hit, and a cloud of dust filled in the hall as the door was slid aside with a harsh grind of metal on stone. The noise made her shiver.

She stood next to Rain's unconscious body as she watched her mate walk in, Dorian tight on his heels. She'd never seen a more gorgeous sight in her life. His muscles were flexed, and his eyes were like green jewels as they scanned the area and landed on her. She ran to him, and her breath caught when his strong hands lifted her into his arms and crushed her to him, his angry face right in hers. Her legs automatically circled his hips. His hands were in her hair, pulling her lips to his. *I'm going to beat your ass till next week for this shit.* His tongue plunged deep, devouring her. When he broke the kiss, his feral gaze met hers as he bit the words out that seemed so highly offensive to him. "You're covered in fucking blood."

"It's not mine," she assured him, settling her arms around his neck and savoring the feel of him. "There are eleven females in the cells."

I've got Alyssa and Rain. The females are here, he informed the others.

Conn replied, *I'm in the security room now. No self-destructs. Facility looks cleared. They didn't put up much of a fight. With Cyril dead, they scattered, but we caught a couple.*

Alyssa saw Dorian cradling Rain's small body against his chest. His jaw was tight as he walked past them and out the door.

Satisfied that her friend was safe, she snuggled into Gregoire's neck. She heard talk as more Guardians filtered in to get the women out. She looked up and saw Bastian and Sacha each carrying a sleeping female.

He walked her around the bodies, and she heard his teeth grinding again. She looked into his eyes. "You got Cyril?" Alyssa was both shocked and excited when she realized what Conn had said.

"Not us... Delia." His eyes shadowed as he said the word. Her stomach clenched, knowing what was coming would not be good. "She ended her life after she killed the bastard. Uri and Alex were with her, in her mind, through all of it." His jaw tensed even more as he shook his head.

"We need to get the hell out of here. There is going to be a lot to clean up. A lot has happened, and you're going to explain every damn minute of it." She relaxed into him. Safe.

Chapter 42

Guardian Compound, Tetartos Realm

She was taken to Sirena and checked out. The healer had taken a blood sample to be safe, but said the drugs she detected would have only caused sleep.

Gregoire had taken her straight home from Sirena's office and scrubbed every inch of her body, in record time, telling her all the things he wanted to do to her when he got back to her. Muttering about how fucking scared he'd been and how the sight of blood on her and the fucking dead body near was something he never wanted to see again. He ranted about how he didn't care that she'd done it for her friend and that he still planned to beat her ass blue for scaring the shit out of him. He tenderly checked her entire body with his jaw clamped down tight. All she'd wanted was to touch him, hold him, but knew he was needed to help with the others, so she settled for trying to soothe him.

After she grabbed some sewing stuff, he'd taken her to the manor.

Her heart clenched for him, knowing he'd been holding on by a thread, tempted to leave his brothers to do all the work while he stayed with her. His emotion was boiling through their link without his even knowing. Before he'd left, he lifted her in his arms and devoured her lips like a male on the verge of going to battle.

It'd only been a few hours, but it felt like he'd been gone now for years. She'd gotten bits of information through the link, but nothing solid.

Alyssa was strung tight as she nervously sewed while waiting in the Guardians' media room with Sam in a chair and a nearly passed out Alex lying on a couch with Havoc. Alex had barely spoken and Alyssa's heart went out to her. She couldn't imagine what the female had gone through in Delia's mind.

They stayed there, some DVD playing in the background so there wasn't dead silence. Sam had put something on about female friends going on a road trip to stalk a guy at a wedding, a funny movie meant to calm them.

"How's Rain?" Sam asked when Alyssa came back after checking on her friend again.

"She's still unconscious. Sirena said she'd be out for at least a few more hours."

Sirena had people monitoring her with instructions to inform Alyssa if her friend stirred at all. She planned to head back down in a couple of hours, just to make sure Rain didn't wake up alone.

After a while she asked, "Alex, would you mind waking Havoc? I want to see if this fits." The other female grinned and coaxed Havoc off the couch. Both Sam and Alex knew what she was making.

The pup stood on the floor, staring at Alex, looking dejected at having been ousted from the couch. Alyssa came up to him and gave him a little scratch before fitting him with the harness. She'd had to make it bright, there was no getting around that, but she thought the red with some black spikes in the thick material gave him a tough look. He stood there looking at her, still drowsy from the nap she'd disturbed. Her lips twitched at his expression. "He doesn't seem to be bothered by it."

"Oh, Havoc, you look so handsome," Alex chimed at him, grinning. He tilted his head and wiggled a little at her so that she would pet him.

"It's really a great idea," Sam said, nodding.

She felt his presence before she saw him. She turned around to see the others filing in through the balcony. Vane and Erik walked in with them, and Sirena came through another door. Gregoire went straight to her and lifted her into his arms, kissing her hard.

"I have to check on Rain again. I don't want her waking up alone," she said with regret because she knew he wanted to carry her away.

"We're having a meeting now anyway," he growled. He settled on one of the big chairs with her in his lap.

"Fuck, Havoc. Did you even put up a fight when they put this shit on you?" Uri sounded completely disgusted, and she heard giggles and a couple male barks of laughter.

"Where's Dorian?" Conn asked.

"He wanted to check one more mountain range. He asked that I give him the information later," Bastian said with a perplexed look on his exotic face.

The Guardians all took seats on couches or at the game table. She was tucked into Gregoire's chest and didn't care what the others were doing. She did catch an interesting interaction between Brianne and Vane, but it was there and gone in a second. Sirena came from the hall, and Drake stood to the side.

Alex began going over the horrifying experience of what Delia had been through and what the poor female had done. The Demi-

Goddess absently rubbed Havoc's ears as she relayed what had happened during their last "hop" to Delia. "We could tell something was bad the second we went in the last time. Delia seemed different; calm determination was woven with the hatred and insanity invading her mind. She'd gotten the cuffs off and had already called Cyril to her. Uri and I had been giving her tips on how to use the powers from the start, hoping she would be able to use them to defend herself at some point."

Uri finished as he, too, tucked his mate into his lap. "She tricked him into thinking she was having a horrible reaction to the mating. He came within seconds of feeling the distress she filtered into their bond. She acted as though she was still cuffed while her body seized. When he got close enough, she telekinetically cuffed him and used their combined powers to set flame to his heart. The element of surprise was her biggest advantage. His eyes were shocked as hell when she used his own power against him."

Alex nodded her head at Uri's words, and Alyssa saw the respect in her eyes. "It was brilliantly done. We stayed with her while she walked out of the cell and found another room that had a bed and some blades. She took one long sword into the cell and promptly severed the bastard's head. I was so excited until I saw in her mind what her intentions were."

The room was quietly somber as they waited.

Alex continued, "Cyril had been telling her from the start that he would keep her locked away so that no one would ever attempt to take her from him. Apparently the serum caused her to produce pheromones with the potential to attract any and all Immortals. The production didn't stop when she mated the wolf and then apparently was still there after mating with Cyril. At least that's what he'd told her. In her mind, she was convinced she would never be safe from those compelled to claim her. Her life would be a living nightmare. It already was. Her wolf mourned Phelan, and she hated herself. When we tried to assure her that we would find a way to help her, she told us, 'Even if you could, you would never be able to truly erase the memories.' She said that she just wanted peace, even after Uri tried to convince her he could take her memories."

Alyssa felt hollow. It was a nightmare.

Uri held his female tight as he told them the rest, "She brought in the bedding and lit it on fire and kicked us out of her mind as she took the blade to her own heart. She planned to burn to ash. She took her vengeance... She should be honored for it."

"I think we should do something in her memory," Sam said adamantly. "It should be big for getting rid of that son of a bitch."

Alyssa snuggled against her male's warmth as she listened to them ask about others in Cyril's ranks. The Aletheia and Kairos who'd taken her and Rain, and a female named Elizabeth.

"I checked all the bodies. They weren't there," Erik said, fury in his icy eyes.

Drake answered, "It looks like she got away, along with most of their people. I don't know what that means. Whether Elizabeth will take charge of his people or another? She's able to contact the other Realms and work with Cynthia or the Tria, so the threat is still there. The only good news is that we hope the mating formula died with Cyril. He hadn't wanted his people to know about it, according to Delia."

Conn interjected, "The labs were mostly cleaned out, but we collected what we could for Sirena to go through, just in case."

Drake said one more thing before sending them off. "No one is to know about that formula or what Alex and Uri are able to do. I will come up with something to tell the coven and her family so that they know she died with honor."

The others filed out, and Sam said she'd like to get together the next day to find something to do for Delia.

Gregoire walked up to Sirena. "Is Rain fine to go home with us?"

The healer smiled and nodded.

Within ten minutes Rain was snuggled on their couch, and he had Alyssa naked in his bed.

His mouth met hers, and he loved her with slow deliberation, his mouth on her neck and then caressing her marked breasts. He licked and savored her flesh like he'd never get enough of her. Then he moved down and lapped at her slick pussy. He forced her into a harsh climax before burying himself deep, moving inside her as he held her hands on the pillow next to her head. He stared into her eyes and let her inside his mind, claiming her body and mind. She opened for him too and lost herself in the sensation as he thrust inside her. She throbbed and clutched his hands as she crashed over the edge to searing ecstasy.

"I love you," she whispered.

He nuzzled her neck, growling, "Love's not a strong enough word, angel."

Chapter 43

Lofodes, Tetartos Realm

It was a beautiful sunny day. The trees were a lush green, and birds sang around them in the crisp air. Alyssa and the other females had all worked together to come up with a fitting memorial for Delia. Cyril had been all of the races' most vicious threat, and they all wanted to honor her for what she'd done.

So much had happened in that last couple of days. The Guardians had worked through the compound and found no clues as to where Cyril had taken Delia. It was horrible not to be able to provide her family with her remains. They told her parents that Uri saw Delia stab Cyril in the chest as a cave collapsed above and crushed them. That was the official story given to those of the Realm.

Delia was at peace now. No longer in the clutches of a monster. Secrets would be kept. Her family need never know the details and horrors of her captivity. The other females had not been mated, and it seemed that those captured were unaware that Cyril had perfected his formula. That disaster had thankfully been averted.

The chatter of visitors lightly filled the square in the center of Lofodes. It was a peaceful space. People were moving around Delia's family, offering gifts and paying respects. The Guardians had built a small stone temple, where a gorgeous bronze sculpture Sam created stood tall and proud. Sam's power to manipulate metal was incredible. The statue was shaped in an almost exact likeness of

Delia, with a small plaque situated at its feet. The words *"With honor and courage Delia selflessly gave her life. Her sacrifice for the Realms will never be forgotten"* were etched into the surface.

Gregoire stood at Alyssa's side as they watched the people amble around. Rain was to her left.

"At least her family has some closure." Rain's words were somber.

Alyssa's parents walked over. Her father's jaw was clenched tight as he nodded at Gregoire. Her mother smiled. "We'd like you to come to the house after," her father said, a clear edge to his tone, but she knew he planned to apologize; her mother's happy face said it all. Alyssa was relieved. She didn't want to fight with her father anymore.

*****

Rain was sitting in her room, frustrated as she wrote down lists of all potential vocations in the Guardian compound since she was a permanent resident. It didn't matter that Cyril was dead. His people were still out there, so she had to stay where she was for the foreseeable future.

She blew out an irritated breath. Alyssa said she could work with her and at least it would get her out of there. Everywhere she went she looked for the tall blond God of her dreams. He haunted her.

She'd had such intense dreams the night before that she'd woken feverishly sliding her fingers over her aching clit, rubbing and circling until she'd gotten herself off while imagining big aqua eyes and blue-tipped blond hair. He appeared so incredibly intense. Why did he keep invading her dreams? She hadn't even seen him since Alyssa's mating the week before.

A knock sounded at her door, and she uncurled herself from the chair. "Hey," she greeted Sirena and invited her inside before shutting the door.

The healer looked pensive. "How have you been feeling?"

Dread pitted her stomach, and her mouth dried up. Sirena had taken blood samples after her abduction. "What's wrong?"

"Your blood showed the signs of the mating frenzy."

Glossary of Terms and Characters for Reference:

Adras – Hippeus (half warhorse), Immortal warrior in charge of the city of Lofodes, mated to Ava, Alyssa's father

Ailouros – Immortal race of half felines, known as the warrior class, strong and fast

Akanthodis – Hell creature with spines all over its body and four eyes

Aletheia – Immortal race with enhanced mental abilities and power within their fluids, can take blood memories, strong telepathy

Alex – aka Alexandra, Demi-Goddess daughter of Athena, sister to Vane and Erik, mate to Uri

Alyssa – Hippeus (half warhorse), Daughter of Adras and Ava, mate to Gregoire

Angus – Aletheia, second in command to Kane

Aphrodite – Sleeping Goddess, one of the three good Deities, mother to Drake

Apollo – Sleeping God that experimented with the Immortal races, adding animal DNA to most in order to create the perfect army against his siblings

Ares – Sleeping God and father of the Tria

Artemis – Sleeping Goddess and mother of the Tria

Astrid – Kairos, business associate to Alyssa and Rain

Athena – Sleeping Goddess – One of only three Gods that were good and didn't feed off dark energies and become mad, mother of Alex, Vane and Erik, mate to Niall

Ava – Mageia/Hippeus, mated to Adras, mother to Alyssa

Bastian – Kairos (teleporter), Guardian of the Realms, diplomat for the Guardians within Tetartos Realm

Brianne – Geraki (half ancient bird of prey), Guardian of the Realms

Charybdis – Immortal abused by Poseidon and then sold and experimented on in Apollo's labs, she gave a portion of her life force to create the mating spell, aka mating curse, so that no Immortal could breed with any other than their destined mate.

Conn – Lykos (half wolf), Guardian of the Realms

Creators – The two almighty beings that birthed the Gods, created the Immortals and planted the seeds of humanity

Cynthia – Mageia on Earth Realm working with Cyril

Cyril – Demi-God son of Apollo, Siren/healer, bad guy

Delia – Mageia, power over fire, works for Rain

Demeter – Sleeping Goddess

Dorian – Nereid, Guardian of the Realms

Drake – aka Draken, Demi-God Dragon, leader of the Guardians of the Realms, son of Aphrodite and her Immortal Dragon mate Ladon

Efcharistisi – City in Tetartos Realm

Elizabeth – Aletheia – evil

Emfanisi – Yearly, week-long event where Immortals and Mageia of age go to find mates

Erik – Demi-God son of Athena, Ailouros (half-lion), Vane's twin, Alex's younger brother, mated to Sam

Geraki – Immortal race of half bird of prey, power with air

Gregoire – Hippeus (half warhorse), Guardian of the Realms, mate to Alyssa

Hades – Sleeping God – One of the three good Gods, father to P (Pothos)

Healers – aka Sirens Immortal race, power over the body, ability with their voices

Hellhounds – Black hounds blood-bonded to the Tria in Hell Realm

Hephaistos – Sleeping God

Hera – Sleeping Goddess

Hermes – Sleeping God and Apollo's partner in the experimentation and breeding of Immortals for their army

Hippeus – Immortal race of half warhorses, power over earth

Jax – aka Ajax, Ailouros (half tiger), Guardian of the Realms

Kairos – Immortal race whose primary power is teleportation

Kane – Aletheia, bad guy

Ladon – Immortal Dragon, mate to Aphrodite, father of Drake

Limni – City in Tetartos Realm

Lofodes – City in Tetartos Realm

Lykos – Immortal half wolf with power of telekinesis

Mageia – Evolved humans, mortals compatible to be an Immortal's mate, have abilities with one of the four elements; air, fire, water, or earth.

Mates – Each Immortal has a rare and destined mate, their powers meld and they become stronger pairs that are able to procreate, usually after a decade.

Mating Curse – A spell cast in Apollo's Immortal breeding labs that ensured the God wouldn't be able to use them to continue creating his army. Charybdis cast the spell using a portion of her life force and now Immortals can only procreate with their destined mates.

Mating Frenzy – Starts when an Immortal comes into contact with their destined mate, sexual frenzy that continues through to the bonding/mating ceremonies.

Nereid – Immortal race of mercreatures, power over water

Niall – Immortal mate to Athena, father of Alexandra, Vane and Erik, experimented on in Apollo's lab and turned into an Ailouros

Ofioeidis – Huge serpent hell beasts, hardest to kill out of all the hell creatures

Ophiotaurus – Hell beast with the head of a bull and tail of a snake

Ouranos – City in Tetartos Realm

P – aka Pothos, Guardian of the Realms, Son of Hades, second to Drake in power

Paradeisos – Island pleasure resort in Tetartos Realm, owned by Tynan

Phoenix – Immortal race with ability over fire

Poseidon – Sleeping God

Rain – Mageia, best friend of Alyssa

Realms – Four Realms of Earth: Earth – where humanity exists; Heaven – where good and neutral souls go to be reincarnated; Hell – where the Tria were banished and evil souls are sent; Tetartos – Realm of beasts – where the Immortals were exiled by the Creators

Sacha – Kairos (teleporter), Guardian of the Realms, diplomat for the Guardians within Tetartos Realm

Sam – aka Samantha Palmer, mated to Erik, power over metal, Mageia

Sander – Phoenix, Guardian of the Realms

Sirena – Siren (healer), Guardian of the Realms, primarily works to find mates for Immortals in Tetartos

Tetartos Realm – The Immortal exile Realm

Thalassa – City in Tetartos Realm

Tria – Evil Triplets spawned from incestuous coupling of Ares and Artemis and imprisoned in Hell Realm; Deimos, Phobos and Than

Tsouximo – Hell beast resembling a giant scorpion

Tynan – Aletheia, owner of Paradeisos Island

Uri – aka Urian, Aletheia, interrogator, Guardian of the Realms, mate to Alex

Vane – Demi-God son of Athena, Ailouros (half-lion), Erik's twin, Alex's younger brother

Zeus – Sleeping God

Up Next:

Denying Ecstasy

Subscribe to Setta Jay's newsletter for:

book release dates

exclusive excerpts

giveaways

http://www.settajay.com/

SETTA JAY

About The Author:

Setta Jay is the author of the popular Guardians of the Realms Series. She's garnered attention and rave reviews in the paranormal romance world for writing smart, slightly innocent heroines and intense alpha males. She loves creating stories that incorporate a strong plot accompanied by a heavy dose of heat.

An avid reader her entire life, her love of romance started at a far too early age with the bodice rippers she stole from her older sister. Along with reading, she loves animals, brunch dates, coffee that is really more French vanilla creamer, questionable reality television, English murder mysteries, and has dreams of traveling the world.

Born a California girl, she currently resides in Idaho with her incredibly supportive husband.

She loves to hear from readers so feel free to ask her questions on social media or send her an email, she will happily reply.

Subscribe to her newsletter for giveaways, exclusive excerpts and release information: http://www.settajay.com/

Where you can find her:

http://www.settajay.com/

https://www.facebook.com/settajayauthor

https://twitter.com/SETTAJAY_

https://www.goodreads.com/author/show/7778856.Setta_Jay

CPSIA information can be obtained
at www.ICGtesting.com
Printed in the USA
FSHW02n2017140818
51449FS

9 781544 269115